"Do you feel as strange as I do?"

Samantha saw a nervous smile break out on Jessica's face. "Yes."

Nick's hands were gripping their daughter's shoulders. "I told Jessica you two should spend this time together by yourselves." He tousled her curls in such an affectionate gesture, Samantha could have wept. "Call me when you're ready and I'll come for you, honey."

"Okay, Dad."

"Enjoy your meal." His eyes studied Samantha's face for a heart-stopping moment. Was he remembering the way it used to be with them? Did he still find her attractive after all this time?

"Thank you, Nick," Samantha whispered. But he moved away with such lightning speed, she ended up saying it to his back.

Her gaze returned to Jessica. It was hard to keep from staring at her. Samantha had missed out on examining her from head to toe when she was a baby. She'd missed the first thirteen years of her life. The realization tortured her all over again.

This lovely girl was her baby, her daughter, her flesh and blood.

Dear Reader,

One of my children had a friend who as a teenager gave up her baby for adoption. It was no doubt one of the most painful experiences of her life. Even though it seemed the only thing to do under the circumstances, I have often thought about that courageous girl. Whatever happened to her? Over the years, how did she deal with her decision? Did the baby find a wonderful home? Did everyone involved find peace?

Those are questions for which I have no answers, so I wrote a story about a teenager who made the similar choice to give up her baby. I followed the lives of the characters involved to see what kind of impact such a decision had on them down through the years. From the first paragraphs I began to cry, and I cried all the way through their story. Some tears sprang from anguish, others from joy. Perhaps you, the reader, will have a similar reaction as you read their story and experience that emotional journey with them.

Rebecca Winters

P.S. If you have access to the Internet, please check out my Web site at http://www.rebeccawinters-author.com.

To Be a Mother
Rebecca Winters

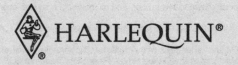

TORONTO • NEW YORK • LONDON
AMSTERDAM • PARIS • SYDNEY • HAMBURG
STOCKHOLM • ATHENS • TOKYO • MILAN • MADRID
PRAGUE • WARSAW • BUDAPEST • AUCKLAND

ISBN 0-373-71233-2

TO BE A MOTHER

This book is dedicated to all the courageous young women
who have given up their babies for adoption.

Books by Rebecca Winters

HARLEQUIN SUPERROMANCE

Don't miss any of our special offers. Write to us at the
following address for information on our newest releases.

Harlequin Reader Service
U.S.: 3010 Walden Ave., P.O. Box 1325, Buffalo, NY 14269
Canadian: P.O. Box 609, Fort Erie, Ont. L2A 5X3

CHAPTER ONE

Coeur D'Alene, Idaho
October 29

By some miracle I'm still here. It appears my cancer has gone into remission. I just heard the news this afternoon.

Maybe it's a coincidence, maybe it isn't, but tonight the pastor of my church came to see me. It was a comfort, rather than a shock, when he said that every person on this earth is dying, yet none of us knows the exact moment we'll be called home, not even me.

Instead of concentrating on the past, he suggested I think of my remission as permanent rather than temporary, and treat it as a rebirth.

Before he left my condo, he asked me if there was anything in my past that might be troubling me. He reminded me that matters of the heart have a strange and powerful effect on the body's ability to continue to fight disease.

The pastor's unexpected visit has left me haunted by thoughts of Nick and our baby to the exclusion of all else.

Memories are bombarding me. Memories, questions. Regrets.

Oh, the regrets…

Since the moment Nick walked out of my hospital room, not a day, not a minute, not a second has passed that I haven't yearned to be with both of them.

I could try to contact Jessica directly, but that would add cowardice to my list of sins. I have to do this the right way and approach Nick first.

My need to see my daughter is the height of human selfishness. Yet being given a second chance at life has caused me to search my soul, which has always hungered for both of them.

Nick will either tear up my letter or hang up on me. No matter. I have to try. Otherwise this life has made no sense at all….

SAMANTHA LET GO of the pen and buried her wet face in the pillow. "Nick—" she whispered in agony.

"NICK?"

Nick Kincaid glanced up from his field biology book. Everyone in the basement of the Lory Student Center at Colorado State was seated on couches or at tables studying for the last day of finals tomorrow. It was the place where Samantha had first met the rugged-looking twenty-year-old junior from Gillette, Wyoming. They'd been seeing each other since the beginning of fall semester in August.

"Hi," he said in a husky tone. Beneath dark-brown hair and brows, his gray eyes flickered with an awareness of the intimacy they shared. Hers probably did the same. "I thought maybe you weren't coming. Another ten minutes and I was going to phone you."

"I'm sorry I'm late."

"How did your last final go?"

"Fine."

"That's good. Have you eaten?"

They normally bought a hamburger in the center's Ramskeller Restaurant, but tonight food was the last thing on her mind.

"I'm not hungry. Could you leave now? I know you have your last final in the morning, but there's something important I have to tell you. It won't take long. I brought Mom's car."

Nick didn't own one. He worked as many hours as possible at his part-time job with campus security in order to support himself while he earned his undergraduate degree in biology. If he needed transportation, he got around on his bike.

He lived with a hundred other young men at the Hilan Apartments on Lake Street near the campus, and he had friends who helped him out and lent him their cars when he wanted to be alone with her.

His pride refused to let Samantha chauffeur them in one of her parents' cars, but tonight she wasn't giving him a choice.

He must have sensed her urgency. Without saying a word, he got up from the table and put everything away in his backpack. After shrugging into his sheepskin jacket he murmured, "Let's go."

She felt his hand slide to the nape of her neck beneath her parka to guide her to the stairs. He had a tall, powerful physique and was whipcord lean. Samantha was a curvy redhead who didn't stand much taller than his heart. She loved the way he made her feel feminine and protected.

In truth, everything about him appealed to her. It wasn't just the physical attraction, although the chemistry between them was explosive. What drew her to him on other levels was his innate maturity and intelligence.

She was counting on those particular character traits to help him cope with what she had to tell him. Though she hadn't really lied, there were some things she hadn't told Nick the truth about. For the last four months she'd managed to push those sins of omission to the back of her mind in the hope they would never have to come to light. What a foolish, foolish girl she was....

A cold winter wind buffeted them as they left the center and walked to the corner of the next block, where she'd parked her mother's Lincoln. It didn't take long to drive to the foothills near her home. Samantha parked the car at Horsetooth Reservoir overlooking Fort Collins.

By now the interior of the car was too warm. She started to turn off the fan, and Nick anticipated her movement, then pulled her into his arms. For the first time, she resisted him.

"We can't do this right now, Nick. I promised Mom and Dad I would be home by eleven. That gives us an hour."

She felt his reluctance before he relinquished his hold on her and sat back in his seat. "What's wrong?"

"Everything."

A grimace broke out on his face. "Why do I get the feeling this has something to do with your parents?"

"I—it's not just Mom and Dad."

"The hell it isn't," he said without raising his voice. "It's no secret I'm not from a wealthy, well-connected family like yours."

Samantha's hand tightened on the steering wheel. "You're jumping to conclusions about that, Nick."

"Then enlighten me!" he demanded. "If you've met someone else and want to break up, just be honest about it. Don't hide behind your parents' disapproval of me."

Nick's forthright personality fascinated and intimidated her at the same time.

"There's no one else. Surely you know that by now. As for them not considering you a suitable person for me to be dating, they'd feel the same way about any other guy. In all honesty it's *my* fault they've forbidden me to go on seeing you."

"Forbidden? How could they forbid you to do anything? You're in college and are able to make your own decisions."

She shivered. "You're going to hate me when I tell you."

A sound of exasperation escaped his throat. "That wouldn't be possible. Come on, Sam. Don't keep me in suspense any longer."

"I'm pregnant," she confessed. "I couldn't believe it when I found out, not when I know you took precautions."

To her shock, his eyes blazed with light. A smile lit up his handsome features. "We're going to have a baby?"

"Yes."

"What's the due date?" He sounded too happy.

"June twenty-fifth."

"That makes you almost three months along. Sweetheart—when did you find out?"

"Two days ago."

"Two days and you didn't say anything until now?"

"I've been too scared."

He reached for her and crushed her in his arms. "How could you be scared to tell me something so wonderful? You *know* how I feel about you."

"Do I?"

"How could you doubt it? I was going to surprise you with a ring on Valentine's Day so we could start planning a summer wedding. But with a baby coming, we'll get married over the Christmas holiday instead. I'll always take care of you and our children, Sam."

"Wait…" She pushed her hands against his chest to prevent him from kissing her. When he held her close and told her the things she'd been dying to hear before now, she couldn't think clearly. "There's more I have to tell you. I'm afraid it's going to change the way you feel about me."

"As long as we love each other, nothing else matters."

"I do love you, Nick, but—"

"But what?"

"I'm not old enough to get married."

"Of course you are!"

She shook her head. By now the tears had started. "No. I may be taking some college classes, but the truth is…I'm still in high school."

"High school?" he whispered, staring at her as if he'd never seen her before.

"Yes. Since I was in advanced placement and had

taken all the math and science classes my school offered, I started some college classes early on scholarship. But I—I won't turn eighteen until March.''

"Sam!"

"I knew you'd be angry," she blurted in panic. "I
should have told you the first day we met, but I was
afraid you wouldn't ask me out, so I didn't say anything. After you started dating me, I never seemed to
be able to find the right time to tell you the truth because…'' She hesitated. "Because I wanted you to
love me.''

He shook his head. "Didn't it once occur to you I
could be accused of statutory rape for making love to
you? You're only seventeen!''

"The thought never entered my head until the doctor told me I was pregnant.'' She wiped her eyes but
the tears kept coming. "When he glanced at my chart,
he said I wasn't of age yet and warned me he would
have to tell my parents.''

Nick pursed his lips. "How soon can I expect to be
hauled into court?''

"At first Mom and Dad threatened to do just that,
but I told them *I* was the one who talked you into
making love to *me*. I also admitted that you didn't
have any idea I wasn't eighteen. Dad said he wouldn't
press charges if I agreed to break up with you and
never see you again.''

"That's archaic,'' Nick retorted. "You're younger
than I thought, but it doesn't change the fact that we
love each other. We'll get married now. It's as simple
as that.''

"No, it's not,'' she cried. "They won't give me

their permission. In their shoes, I wouldn't, either," she added in a quiet voice.

"What do you mean?"

"Let's be honest here, Nick. You never mentioned marriage. I'm not at all sure you would have if you didn't know I was expecting."

"It was always in my mind, Sam, but I wanted to give you a little more time. In two months I would have put a ring on your finger."

"That's easy enough for you to say now that you've been told the news."

"Because it's true!"

"Maybe, but I'll never know for sure, will I? You've sacrificed so much to get this far in college. With only a year and a half to go before you receive your degree, you don't need to be saddled with an unwanted wife and baby."

"Those are your parents' words, not yours."

"Does it really matter? I don't want to hold you back. After talking it over with them, I've decided to give up the baby for adoption when it's born."

"No you're not!"

"Please hear me out. To avoid talk, they're going to buy a home in Denver. We'll be moving there, where no one knows me, over Christmas. I only have two more high school classes to take to get my diploma. I can go to a local school there as well as attend Denver University."

He clasped her upper arms. "We're going to be parents. There's no need to uproot you when I'll be marrying you and taking care of you."

She shook her head. "No, Nick. Some other couple has been praying for a baby because they couldn't have one of their own. They'll raise ours. Years from now when we're both settled in our careers and have met someone we love, then it will be the right time to marry and have children.''

"What career could be more important than being a mother and father to *our* child?''

"I'm planning to be an attorney, like Dad. It's been a dream of mine for a long time.''

His brows furrowed. "You never told me that.''

"You never mentioned marriage.''

"Sam—''

"You might as well know everything. I was accepted at Harvard undergraduate school. It has been arranged since July, when Mom and Dad flew me back to Boston. I'll be attending there in the fall of next year.''

His hands slid down her arms. He kissed the tips of her fingers. "I knew you had an exceptional mind. I just didn't realize how exceptional. Why don't we get married now and keep attending Colorado State? Next summer, after the baby's born, we'll move to Boston. I'll get a night job and help take care of our child during the day while you go to school. We'll make it work, Sam.''

As much as she wanted to believe him, she couldn't be sure he wasn't saying that just because he knew it was what she wanted to hear. "What about your degree?''

"I'll get it. The important thing is that we'll be together raising our son or daughter.''

"I wouldn't know how to be a mother.''

"No one knows what to do until the time comes. We'll learn as we go.''

"It won't work."

"Because your parents told you it wouldn't. Come on. I want to talk to them. Let's go."

Her heart raced. "They don't want to see you, Nick."

"That's too bad. I'm the father of our unborn baby and have an equal say in its future."

Ten minutes later they'd arrived at the house and he'd echoed those same sentiments to her parents, but her father remained intractable.

"I'm sorry, young man, but neither of you is in any position to be a parent. Can't you see that giving up the baby for adoption is the only sensible thing to do, not only for yourselves, but for the child?

"You're still three semesters away from getting your undergraduate degree. Samantha isn't even out of high school yet. Given the chance, she has a brilliant future ahead of her. But you can both kiss your planned careers goodbye if you have to sacrifice everything because of a mistake."

"My husband's right, Nick," Samantha's mother chimed in. "Why not turn this into a blessing and give the baby to a well-deserving married couple who've been preparing to become parents for a long time? They'll have the financial and emotional means to give it everything it needs and shower it with love."

Nick turned toward Samantha. "I already love our baby. I'm prepared to shower it with all the love I have in me. How about you, Sam?"

"I don't know, Nick. This wasn't something we planned. You might grow to resent me and the baby later."

"There's no 'might' about it," her father declared.

"You don't have the right to speak for me, Mr. Bretton." Emotion caused the cords in Nick's neck to stand out. "All I can see is that Sam and I will have a brilliant future with our child. I intend to take care of the two of them forever. The day she turns eighteen we'll get married."

Her dad shook his head. "You're deluding yourself if you think our daughter will be ready for such a step."

"Maybe neither of us is ready, but I'm going to at least try," Nick said, still staring at her. "I'll be the one taking care of our baby, Sam. I'm the father. God gave me that divine right, and no court will take it away from me."

His head swerved toward her parents once more. "If in the end your daughter is swayed by your arguments and opts to forgo marriage and motherhood, then let me give you fair warning. I'll hire the best attorney around and sue for full custody of our baby, because there's no way under heaven I'll let it be put up for adoption."

"Nick!" Samantha cried, running after him because he'd wheeled around and disappeared out the front door. "Wait!" she called into the wintry darkness. "I'll drive you back to the center!"

But he'd broken into a run and was gone.

"Let him be, honey. It's better this way," her father murmured as he shut the door. "He needs his space to think about everything. By the time you deliver the baby, the two of you will have spent six months apart. He'll have finished another semester. It'll give him the perspective to understand that your mother and I were right about this."

Samantha stood there with her wet face buried in her hands. "No, Daddy. He's not going to change. You don't know him the way I do. Nick's a man of deep convictions. That's why I love him."

"He's still a boy. Not even twenty-one. One day when you're both all grown up, you'll fall in love with other people and it'll be right."

Her mom put her arm around her shoulders. "Listen to your father, honey. Concentrate on giving the baby to a wonderful couple who want a child more than anything in the world and can't wait to have a family."

"Mom," Samantha blurted, "you heard Nick. He said he was going to keep it!"

"I agree he gave a very impassioned speech. I'm sure he meant it at the moment. But that was the impetuosity of youth talking."

"Your mother took the words right out of my mouth, honey. In a few months, another girl will catch Nick's eye. He'll be thankful for his freedom, and relieved that the baby will be going to a perfect home with loving parents waiting to dote on it." Sam's father put a protective arm around her.

"Come on. It's time for bed. Tomorrow I have a surprise for you. The old Tudor mansion you've always loved on Sixth Avenue in the country club area is for sale. A Denver Realtor is going to show us through it at eleven."

Once upon a time nothing could have excited Samantha more. Now nothing mattered. Not friends or school, or where she lived. Not even Nick, who'd said all the right things tonight. Did he really mean them? If she hadn't gotten pregnant, would he have asked her to marry him? Or was her mother right and he'd only said those things in the heat of the moment because he'd felt obliged and guilty? To marry him without knowing how he truly felt would be horrible.

They would be another one of the many couples in the world who'd made a mistake.

As Samantha's mother was quick to point out, Samantha's best friend, Brenda, had an older sister who'd gotten pregnant in high school and had married the boyfriend she thought she couldn't live without. But six months after the baby came, he took off and never returned.

With the inevitable divorce she turned bitter and started dating other guys, while her parents took over the responsibility of raising their grandchild along with their other children.

Brenda's sister never went to college and eventually left home. She rarely saw her child, leaving their whole family in upheaval. If she had done the sensible thing and given up her child for adoption, all their lives would have been different. Better.

"Nick has his dreams, too, Samantha," her father reasoned with her. "But if you marry, he'll have to put them on hold for years while you're in school at Harvard. Do you really think he'll stay the course? Don't you know he'll come to resent you?"

OVER THE NEXT few months her parents' arguments dominated her fears. Once her family had moved to Denver, Samantha went through the motions of living, of visiting the doctor, of being a part-time student. Yet because of her doubts she refused to see Nick, who called her every day without fail.

Each time she heard his voice, she grew more confused and heartsick. On her birthday he sent her an engagement ring by courier. In the letter that accompanied it, he asked her to marry him. Though it wrenched her heart, she sent everything back, convinced he felt trapped.

Nick still kept calling. When the day finally came and she started having contractions, she phoned him because she'd promised she would let him know the baby was on the way. Throughout her long labor she knew Nick was out in the hall waiting.

The doctor understood she was giving the baby up for adoption. As soon as it was delivered, he took it away before she could get a look at it.

Her parents were there to comfort her. They said it was for the best that she didn't see the baby. That way she wouldn't form an attachment.

Both sets of her grandparents came to the hospital. They sided with her parents. All agreed that giving up the baby was the right thing for her to do.

But Nick came to her room in the middle of the night. He kissed her lips gently and begged her to let him bring in their beautiful little daughter, who had red-gold hair like her mother. She could tell by the way he spoke that he was enamored of the baby, but that didn't mean he was enamored of Samantha.

She shut her eyes against him, too vulnerable and afraid to believe his avowal of love. They quarreled.

He gave her one last chance to tell him she would marry him. When she remained silent, he told her she wouldn't be seeing him again, and he left the room.

Contrary to what Samantha's parents had assumed would happen, Nick did sue for and obtain full and sole custodial rights of Jessica Kincaid, infant daughter of Nicholas Pratt Kincaid and Samantha Frost Bretton, born June 25 at Stapleton Regional Hospital, Denver, Colorado.

"DR. LOFSKY? Thank you for returning my call. As I told you in my message two days ago, my name is Samantha Bretton. I'm an attorney in Coeur D'Alene, Idaho, working for the Idaho National Wildlife Federation. At the moment I'm trying to reach a field biologist named Nicholas Kincaid.

"The placement office at Colorado State in Fort Collins indicated he went to work for the Rocky Mountain Biological Research Lab after graduating with his master's degree nine years ago. Is there any way you could tell me if he's still on the staff there?"

"The name's familiar. Just a minute while I transfer you to Dr. Crapo's office. He'll be able to help you."

"Thank you." *Could it be this easy to track him?* Samantha squeezed the pen in her hand while she waited.

"Ms. Bretton? This is Dr. Crapo. I understand you're asking about Nick Kincaid."

"Yes. Because of a case I'm working on, I'm very anxious to locate him." It wasn't a lie. She *was* working on a case. Her own.

"I remember him well. He did excellent work for us on the High Elk Conservation Corridor Project. That was before he turned traitor after a year and accepted a position at Grand Teton National Park." The doctor chuckled.

The Tetons! "Is he a ranger then?"

"That I don't know, but we sure hated losing him."

It was all she could do not to ask a lot of personal questions about Nick, but she didn't dare. "Thank you for the information, Dr. Crapo. I'm very grateful."

"You're welcome. Good luck finding him. When you do, tell him to give me a call."

"I will. Goodbye."

She glanced at her watch. Her Friday afternoon meeting with the conservation board wouldn't begin until two o'clock. That gave her twenty minutes to make the call.

Without hesitation she dialed the Wyoming operator to get a phone number for Teton Park. After listening to the recorded messages she finally made contact with a live female voice.

"You've reached Moose Headquarters Rangers Station. Mindy Carlson speaking."

"Hello. I'm sorry to bother you, but I've been trying to get in touch with a biologist who was hired by the park service about eight years ago. I have no idea if he's still working there or not."

"What's the name?"

"Nicholas Kincaid."

"You've found him. He's the resident chief ranger in charge of biological wildlife research for Teton Park."

Nick...

Tears welled in Sam's eyes. Despite the enormous responsibility of raising their daughter, he *had* realized his dream. Thank God for that.

"I—is he there?"

"He has an office here at headquarters, but he's rarely in it. I can take a message. When he checks with me later, I'll give him the information."

Think fast, Samantha. You don't want to tip your hand yet.

"Will you ask him to phone Lori Watts?"

"You bet. What's the number?"

After she gave it to the woman Samantha said, "Tell him to call collect."

"Will do."

"Thank you very much."

After she hung up the receiver, she rushed out of her office to talk to the receptionist in the other room. She was breathing hard, but knew it wasn't because of her physical health.

"Lori? Before the day is over, you might receive a collect call from a man named Nick Kincaid. If so, the operator will ask if you'll accept the charges. Say yes. When he identifies himself, tell him to wait a moment, then poke your head around my door so I'll know he's on the line."

"Okay."

Samantha didn't know what to expect. By now Nick was thirty-three years old and undoubtedly married with a family. Jessica would be the oldest child. But maybe not. He could have met a woman with one or more children and they'd combined their families.

Anything could have happened in the intervening years. Samantha was going to go crazy imagining the various scenarios while she waited for the call that might or might not ever come.

If Nick were happily married, then he had a lot of things to consider once he found out who was trying to reach him on the phone.

Besides his own violent reaction, there would be his wife's when he told her Jessica's birth mother was trying to make contact with the daughter she had given up.

As for Jessica herself, she might not want anything to do with the woman who'd refused to look at her after the delivery. The heartless woman who'd resisted Nick's pleadings to let him bring Jessica to her hospital room in the middle of the night for one tiny peek.

CHAPTER TWO

IT WAS HALLOWEEN. Knowing Jessica was waiting for him, Nick bypassed the park headquarters located in Moose, Wyoming, and drove the truck straight to the complex of ranch-style houses a couple of blocks away.

He'd just come from the tailwaters below Jackson Lake Dam. The investigation to find out why there were so many young, dead, fine-spot cutthroat showing up was going to take time. The ones he'd just examined had gaping jaws, misshapen heads, trunks and spinal curvature denoting *Myxosoma cerebralis.*

Tomorrow he would have to spend the day gathering samples from the soil and water to look for spores.

"Hi, Dad!" his daughter called to him as he entered the kitchen from the garage. Her hair was in tiny rollers all over her head. "You're only a half hour late! That's pretty good for you."

Nick chuckled. "I timed it so I could test out your cupcakes." He reached for a couple she'd iced with orange frosting and candy corn, and popped them in his mouth. "Umm, they're good. I could eat a ton of them."

"No more!" She put out a hand to restrain him, but he managed to snatch another one. "You're impossible!'' But he detected a smile as she said it. ''These are our contribution to the Halloween party.''

''How soon do we have to be there?'' The monthly get-together for the park employees at the teepee in Moose Village was something they always looked forward to.

''As soon as you shower and change into your costume. They're getting things going a lot earlier than usual so the little kids will have time to trick-or-treat.''

He'd already started down the hall for his bedroom, but paused midstride. ''What costume?''

''I told you about it yesterday.''

''You did?''

''Yes…! As usual, your mind was on salmonid whirling disease or some such thing.''

He burst into laughter. ''If I'm not mistaken, that's exactly what those cutthroats have. I'm going to make a biologist out of you yet.''

''Maybe! Anyway, I put the outfit on your bed. Don't touch anything until you've washed. You smell like dead trout. Yuck.''

Besides possessing a razor-sharp brain, she was turning into quite the little homemaker. Fussy, fussy, fussy.

A few minutes later he emerged from the shower and opened the garment bag from Brough's Costume Rentals in Jackson. She'd draped it over the end of the bed. Inside was a man's black suit with a black vest and white shirt. She'd gotten the sizes right.

At first he assumed he would be escorting his daughter to the party as Count Dracula. That was until he saw the outrageous brown-and-white polka-dotted bow tie.

"Are you dressed yet?" Jessica called.

"Almost! Who am I supposed to be?"

"Just a minute and you'll find out!"

As he was fastening the tie in place, a perfect facsimile of Little Orphan Annie appeared in the doorway. She'd taken out the rollers and had backcombed her red curls in a style that looked so much like the famous cartoon character, he was stunned.

She wore a little red top and a skirt with white trim. To complete the outfit she'd donned knee-high white stockings and oxford shoes.

"Figured it out yet?" Her heart-shaped mouth broke into an artless smile. For a moment it reminded him of another heart-shaped mouth. He'd loved everything about Jessica's mother, especially that mouth he could never get enough of. No kiss was long enough, deep enough.

The memory coming from out of the blue filled him with intense longing. If he'd received an actual physical wound, it couldn't have been more painful.

"There's no doubt who *you* are," he managed to murmur.

"Here." From behind her back she produced a full head mask. "Put it on."

He did her bidding. When he looked in the mirror he discovered bald-headed Daddy Warbucks staring back at him.

"Don't forget your cigar."

She handed it to him. His daughter had thought of everything.

Too full of emotions—some that didn't bear close scrutiny—he grabbed Jessica and swung her around. "We're going to knock 'em dead tonight!"

Her face broke out in a happy smile. "I think so, too. After Leslie drove me to the rental shop, she showed me how to do my hair."

"It's perfect, honey."

His daughter was crazy about Leslie Gallagher, the new wife of Nick's best friend, Pierce, the chief ranger of the park. Nick was pretty crazy about Leslie, too. Talk about the perfect woman.

Six-year-old Cory Gallagher already called her Mom. As for Pierce, being deeply in love again after having lost his first wife in a plane crash had made a new man of him.

Some men were lucky. Pierce was twice lucky to have married the two women he'd fallen in love with.

"Dad?"

Nick blinked. "Yes?"

"Are you all right?"

"Of course. Why?"

"Because I've been talking to you and you're miles away."

Already the mask had made him claustrophobic. He pulled it off. "Sorry. I guess I couldn't hear very well with this thing on."

"Do you mind wearing it?"

"No," he lied. "Do you know what? The only thing missing is Annie's big yellow dog named Sandy."

"Cory offered to let us take Lucy on her leash."

Nick laughed. "Cute as she is, I'm afraid a basset hound would spoil the effect." He remembered the day he and Pierce had brought the puppy home to Cory. What a happy moment that had been for Pierce's boy.

"I thought the same thing," she said as they left the bedroom and started down the hall for the kitchen. "Leslie told him it wouldn't have worked, anyway, because Lucy would have been too frightened by all the costumes."

"She's right. Animals should be kept home and safe on a night like this. What's Cory going to be?"

"Sponge Bob."

"I should have known."

"Leslie glued a whole bunch of sponges to a box he's wearing over his head. She's so clever I can't believe it!"

Pierce's wife had made a huge impact on his little teenager. Her advent into their world underlined Nick's daughter's need for a woman in her life. He had been able to provide Jessica everything but that.

"Dare I ask if I'll recognize her and Pierce?"

"Nope. You'll have to die of curiosity while you wait." She rolled her big blue eyes, and he immediately thought of a similar pair of dancing blue eyes.

Nick took a moment to ponder the reason for tonight's painful recollection of past memories, then he realized it was because his daughter was growing up faster than he could imagine.

Soon he would turn around and discover she'd become a woman. That day wasn't far off. He suddenly felt old and wished to God he could stop the march of time.

After his daughter picked up the covered tin of cupcakes, they went out to the garage and he started the motor of their silver Xtera. En route to the teepee over by the visitors' center, he phoned headquarters to find out if he had any messages.

There were five of them, four names he recognized. There were no emergencies, and he could wait until Monday when he was back in his office to return the calls.

The message from a woman named Lori Watts was something else again. He'd never dated a Lori or had dealings with one on a professional basis. Her name rang no bells. He glanced at his watch. It was twenty to six, probably too late for anyone to answer. But the fact that he'd been asked to call collect gave him pause.

"Hold on a minute, Mindy."

He pulled into the parking lot, which was filling fast, and drew a notebook and pen from the glove compartment. "Okay. Go ahead and give me the Watts number."

More curious than ever because it was an Idaho area code, he wrote it down. Maybe some of the trout in Idaho waters had whirling disease, too. After thanking the receptionist, he clicked off, then punched in the digits.

His daughter's protesting sigh resounded in the vehicle's interior.

"Honey, give me thirty seconds to find out if this is urgent, then Daddy Warbucks is all yours for the rest of the night."

"Promise?"

He nodded.

She opened her door. "I'll take in the cupcakes and be right back so we can make our grand entrance."

"It's a deal."

Distracted by everyone in their costumes, Nick was ready to hang up on the fifth ring when a female voice said hello. Unless he had the wrong number, he found it odd she didn't say something to identify herself.

"This is Nick Kincaid returning Lori Watts' call."

After a silence she said, "You were supposed to phone collect."

Her voice sounded vaguely familiar but he couldn't place it. "Is this Ms. Watts?"

"No."

He frowned. "Is she there?"

"No. She's gone home, but it doesn't matter because I'm the one who wanted to talk to you."

Nick had reached the end of his patience. He could do without Halloween pranksters. "Who is this?" he demanded, ready to click off.

"If I tell you, you'll hang up on me, which is your right. But if I don't tell you, I'll never find the courage to do this again."

What in the hell?

"Forgive me, Nick. I—I'm not trying to be deliberately provocative."

The slight catch in her voice, the way she said his name, hurled him back through time. His heart slammed into his ribs so hard it hurt to breathe.

"Sam…" he whispered.

"Yes. I'll make this fast. I've been battling cancer for a year and a half. At first I thought the transplant and chemo hadn't done me any good, but two days ago some tests proved my cancer has gone into remission. For how long, only God knows.

"I'm doing everything possible to fight it so it won't come back. The other night my pastor asked me if my life was in order. Was there anything I needed to resolve that might help me keep the disease at bay?''

Lord.

''*Resolve* isn't the right word. He should have asked me, 'Is there anything I want?' Then I could have told him I want to go back thirteen years to that hospital room and beg you to bring our daughter to me so we could be a family.''

Soul-destroying pain and anger ripped through Nick's body. ''It's too late to ask to see her.''

''I know, but I had to take the risk. Nick? W-would it be possible for me to look at her from a distance?'' she stammered. ''Just so I had an idea of what she's like? She would never have to know. If you were at a mall or something, and I was hiding so she couldn't see me, I swear I wouldn't reveal myself.''

The desperation in her voice was killing him. ''I don't think it's a good idea, Sam.''

A palpable silence ensued, followed by such a tortured sob, he knew he couldn't handle this conversation much longer.

''You're right,'' she replied at last. ''Thank you for not cutting me off.'' He could hear her voice shaking. ''You always did have more nobility in one little finger than anyone else I've ever met had in their whole body. I'm sure the woman you ended up marrying considers it your greatest character trait.

''Tonight when you're kissing your children, give Jessica an extra squeeze. She won't know it's from me, but *I* will. Through you I'll be able to feel her in my arms, because I know what your arms feel like. I've forgotten nothing. Goodbye, Nick.''

His low groan coincided with a rap on the window. He jerked his head around to discover a tall man in a Herman Munster costume peering at him through the glass. In the next instant Pierce had flung off the mask and opened the door.

"Nick—you look like you're going to pass out!"

That was one way to describe his condition.

"How can I help?"

"Dear God, Pierce—I don't believe what just happened."

His friend's compassionate blue eyes studied him with alarm. "Jess said you were on the phone and asked me to come and get you. Who were you talking to? What the hell's going on?"

Another groan escaped Nick's throat.

"Can you still drive?"

He nodded.

Without saying a word, Pierce shut the door. He walked around the car and got in the passenger side. "Drive to the back of headquarters, where we can talk in private."

As Nick pulled out of the parking lot, Pierce called his wife. He told her a small emergency had arisen, and asked her to keep an eye on Jessica until they returned.

"Okay," he said, putting the cell phone in his pocket. "Everything's taken care of."

The skeletal night staff had parked in front of headquarters. Nick braked at the rear of the building and shut off the headlights.

Pierce turned toward him. "In all the years I've known you, I haven't ever seen you in this kind of pain. It must have something to do with your past."

"Your instincts are never wrong," Nick muttered. "When Mindy gave me my messages a little while ago, one of them was from a person named Lori Watts. I was asked to call her collect." He took a breath.

"The name meant nothing, but I sensed it might be important so I asked Jessica to give me a minute to call the woman back before I went inside the teepee."

"And this Lori turned out to be Jess's mother?"

"Yes." Nick's eyes closed tightly. "For the last year and a half she's been battling cancer. Evidently it has gone into remission. Now she wants to see our daughter."

"Good Lord."

"I told her it was too late."

"How did she handle that?" his friend asked in a quiet voice.

Tears prickled beneath Nick's lids. "With amazing grace before she bade me a final goodbye." He pounded the steering wheel with his fist. "What am I going to do, Pierce?"

"What do you *want* to do?"

Nick couldn't articulate his thoughts, not when Sam's words still filled his head, blotting out his ability to reason.

"You've known a call like this would come one day."

Pierce read him like a book. He nodded. "I expected her to get in touch with me years ago. You'll never know how I ached to hear her voice telling me she'd made a mistake and wanted to be with me and Jessica forever.

"But in those dreams she'd been young and eager.

I'm afraid the threat of death didn't play a part in any of the scenarios created by my imagination.''

"No. It's the one finality none of us is prepared for."

Nick glanced at his friend. "If anyone understands, you do. When Linda was killed, I honestly don't know how you handled it."

"As I look back, I'm convinced the only reason I did is because we didn't have any issues left unresolved. But Jessica's mother has been given a second chance at life. I have to presume the soul searching she has been through led her to make that phone call."

A cry of grief escaped Nick's lips. "I can't believe I just told a woman who thought she'd be dead by now that she couldn't see the daughter she gave birth to, not even from a distance. What kind of a monster does that make me?"

"You were speaking as Jess's loving father, a great man who has done everything to make her life happy and shield her from pain."

"But do I have the right to go on shielding her, knowing what I know now?" he cried.

"Give it time and the answer will come, Nick."

"Except that Sam doesn't know how much time she has been given."

"Does anyone after they've gone into remission?"

Nick bowed his head. "No. Some people stay there for the rest of their lives. Some have recurring bouts...." He let his voice trail off.

"Maybe she's one of the lucky ones. Is she well enough to travel?"

Nick stared blindly out the windshield. "I don't know. I shut her down too fast."

"Then you didn't find out if she has a husband or family?"

"No. She assumes I'm married and have other children besides Jessica. The call ended before I could disabuse her of those facts."

"I'm sure the thought has occurred to you that a less honorable woman, one centered only on herself, might have shown up at your door without warning and caused real trouble."

This was agony. "Where was that honor when she wouldn't let me bring her own flesh and blood to her in that hospital bed?"

"Perhaps if you saw her again, she could explain so you would understand."

"I'll never understand, Pierce. But this situation isn't about me."

"Does Jess have a driving need to find her mother?"

"Not that I'm aware of. All I've told her is that Sam was underage when we found out she was pregnant, and that her parents prevailed on her to give up the baby. Jessica has never questioned that explanation. But since I haven't encouraged her to talk about her mother, for all I know my daughter has been harboring feelings she has been afraid to share for fear of hurting me."

"It would only be natural. If ever a daughter loved her dad…"

"How in heaven am I going to keep a secret like this from her?"

"Some people I know could manage it. You're not one of them, because you have too much integrity.

Whatever you choose to do, I have no doubt it will be the right thing for everyone.''

"Then you have a lot more faith in me than I do.'' After expelling the breath he'd been holding, Nick pulled on his mask and started the car. "Tell Leslie I'm indebted to her for helping Jessica with my costume. Little did I know I was going to be thankful for this camouflage.''

"Amen,'' Pierce muttered as he put on his own mask.

"THIS IS SUCH A GREAT condo, Samantha. I love it more every time I come over.''

She eyed Marilyn May, who'd become more than a best friend and confidante. "You always say that.''

The two women, still dressed in their sweats, sat curled up on opposite couches facing each other with mugs of herbal tea in hand. After their Saturday morning sessions of qigong, they looked forward to this time of sharing.

"The view of Coeur D'Alene Lake is beautiful, even if it's raining. When you've lived in the desert all your life, this is paradise.''

"I like it, too, especially because the balcony overlooks McEuen Park and I can see the downtown area as well. When another condo in the building goes up for sale, I'll let you know right away.''

Marilyn set her mug on the teakwood coaster. "I'm afraid I'll be going home to Phoenix before that, but thank you for thinking of me.''

The revelation brought more pain to Samantha, who would never recover from last evening's experience of hearing Nick's voice. She'd taken the greatest risk of her life. As it turned out, her chances for licking cancer, at least for now, were greater than those for being allowed to see her daughter.

"So you've decided to let your parents take care of you when you go through your series of chemo next month?"

Marilyn nodded. "I've fought burdening them for so long that I think they're worse off than I am."

"I can't bear to see you go, but I know all about not wanting to be a burden. For the last thirteen years I've suffered the consequences because of that decision, and I can tell you now it's not worth it. You're much wiser than I ever was."

"Stop crucifying yourself. You didn't want Nick to feel he had to marry you."

"I should have believed in him, in us."

"You were afraid to trust in Nick's love. It's perfectly understandable, when you were so young and influenced by your parents and grandparents. They only wanted the best for you and your baby."

"I know. In the end, my baby got the best. Nick's the best there is. That's my consolation."

"Samantha? Now that you're in remission, would you be willing to visit me in Phoenix next month? There's plenty of room, a swimming pool in the backyard."

The invitation hadn't been extended lightly. Over the last year their friendship had come to mean everything to both of them due to their common enemy. They'd been through so much together.

Samantha had been an only child, and Marilyn represented the sister she'd never had. The friends she'd made at law school and at the wildlife federation were great. But she felt a spiritual closeness to Marilyn, who reciprocated those feelings although she had two other sisters.

"Tell you what. I'll talk to Reed about the possibility of my doing work for the federation long distance for a couple of weeks. He's been a very understanding boss so far."

"That would be wonderful."

"I agree." Samantha swallowed hard. "Though my parents have been saints and have done everything possible for me, I don't know how I would have made it this far without you."

"I feel the same. No one else understands the way you do. To be honest, I don't want to go through the chemo without you to talk to," Marilyn admitted.

Samantha stared at her dear friend and smiled. "Depending on what Reed says, you won't have to."

BY THREE IN THE AFTERNOON Nick had gutted the last dead trout from below the dam and had prepared some slides for examination. Jessica had spent the day helping him gather the rest of the water and soil samples, which she was now putting in his carrying case.

A recent snowstorm over the park had made the work more difficult, but she hadn't once complained. After they'd won first place in the costume contest last night, his daughter's mood was euphoric.

All day he'd tried to find the courage to talk to her about a subject that was going to change her life, but the moment never seemed to present itself.

So far she hadn't seemed to pick up on his private agony. Maybe that was because she was looking forward to their plans for the evening.

The organizers of the Halloween party had given them the grand prize—two free movie passes and two gift certificates for an Italian dinner in Jackson. As soon as they got back to Moose and showered, he planned to drive them into town to return their rental costumes and celebrate their winnings.

"Dad? How come you've been so quiet since last night?" she asked after they'd been driving for a few minutes.

Nick stifled a groan. He hadn't fooled his daughter, after all.

"I'm always concerned when I find unexplained problems in natural habitats."

"I noticed Pierce was really quiet."

"You know he always has a lot on his mind."

"I think you do, too. Do you want to talk about it?"

His daughter had turned the tables on him. When had she grown so wise?

The moment he'd been waiting for had come. He couldn't avoid it any longer.

"Yes. I do."

Her eyes rounded in surprise as he brought the truck to a halt on the slushy shoulder of the road. "What's wrong, Dad?" She looked and sounded anxious.

"Let me ask you a question first." Inside his chest, his heart was pounding like a sledgehammer. "If you had a chance to meet your mother, how would you feel about that?"

He'd already made up his mind he wouldn't tell her about Sam's battle with cancer or the fact that she was in remission. Any decision on his daughter's part needed to come from a gut reaction, not sympathy or pity.

"Was she the person who asked you to call her back last night?"

Nick could barely breathe. "Yes."

"Was it hard to talk to her?"

He jerked his head toward her. "Hard?"

She nodded. Her capacity to feel empathy endeared her to him in ways he couldn't explain.

"I have to admit it was."

"If you don't want me to meet her, I won't."

"Jessica..." He fought not to give way to the dichotomy of emotions exploding inside him. "This doesn't have anything to do with me. She gave you birth. Now she's asking to see you."

His daughter stared at him for the longest time. "Would you do it if you were my age and the same thing was happening to you?" Her purity and earnestness utterly defeated him.

Jessica might not know a lot about the past, but he'd never been dishonest with the things he'd been forced to tell her. If he lied to her now, it would be a betrayal of everything he believed in.

"I'm sure I would."

"Where does she live?"

"She phoned from Idaho, but that's all I know."

"Does she want me to call her?"

"Is that what you would like to do?"

It was a foolish question. He didn't need to hear the answer because he could already see her heart in those hopeful, thirteen-year-old eyes.

The deed had been done. Heaven help them all.

CHAPTER THREE

"SAMANTHA? Line two for you."

She glanced at her watch. Four-thirty already. Monday was almost over. "Do you know who it is? Unless it's important, I'm finishing up a brief for court in the morning."

"Her name is Jessica Kincaid. She said she was returning your call. Sounds like a teenager to me."

The room started to spin. Samantha clung to the edge of her oak desk.

Nick had changed his mind!

Perspiration soaked her body. She stood up, then felt so weak she had to sit down again. For thirteen years she'd been waiting for this moment. Now that it was here, she didn't know what to say, let alone how to say it.

"I—I'll take the call, Lori. Thank you."

As if it had a will of its own, her hand crept to the receiver. She lifted it to her ear, then pressed line two to connect them.

"Hello, Jessica?"

"Hi." The female voice sounded young and tentative.

"Hi, yourself." Emotion had practically closed off Samantha's windpipe. "After all these years, I can't believe I'm talking to my own daughter."

"I can't believe it, either."

Samantha's body started to shake and couldn't stop. "When you were born, your father told me you had red hair."

"Yup. And blue eyes. A long time ago Dad gave me a picture of you. We look a lot alike."

My darling girl. Tears rolled down her cheeks. "I would give anything in the world to meet you in person."

"Me, too."

"Honestly?"

"Yes."

Maybe she'd given birth to Jessica, but there was no doubt the girl was Nick's child. Samantha could hear it in the mature, forthright manner she had of expressing herself.

He had probably told Jessica about the cancer. It was possible her daughter had only made this phone call out of a mixture of obligation and pity. If that was true, so be it—Samantha was through second-guessing feelings or motives. His unselfish goodness had brought about this miraculous exchange. She would consider whatever happened from here on out a blessing she didn't deserve.

"I understand you live in Grand Teton National Park. I could come there if you'd like."

"How soon?"

The rapid-fire question thrilled her. "As soon as your parents say it's all right."

After a slight pause Jessica said, "There's only Dad and me."

"Oh." Once again Samantha's world reeled.

"Do I have any half brothers or sisters?" her daughter asked in a quiet voice.

"No. Only you. I never married."

After a silence, she asked. "Are my grandparents still alive?"

Tears stung Samantha's eyes. "Yes. And a great-grandma and great-grandpa who are both in their early nineties."

"Dad's parents died when he was a little boy." With that comment her daughter had just discreetly steered the conversation back to her life and Nick's.

"I know." Samantha had to clear her throat. "How is your great-uncle Willard?" The older brother of Nick's father had been a widower by the time Samantha met him. He'd raised Nick along with his own children after Nick's parents had been killed in a fatal car accident.

"He died of cancer when I was eight."

Samantha's body shuddered at the news. The fact that her daughter hadn't hesitated to give her that information led Samantha to believe Nick hadn't told his daughter about her illness. But she couldn't be positive about that.

"I'm so sorry. He was a terrific man." No doubt he'd helped Nick to hire an attorney to make certain he retained full custody of Jessica.

"I loved him! Dad and I go to Gillette on the holidays to visit his cousins and their kids." Another silence ensued before she asked, "Have you ever been to the Tetons?"

"No, but I've always wanted to see them. I bet you think you live in the greatest place on earth."

"We do!" Her enthusiasm fairly leaped through the phone line. "Where do you live?"

"In Coeur D'Alene. That's in northern Idaho. It's French for Alene's heart."

"That's pretty. Do you have a house?"

"No. A condo."

"What kind of job do you do?"

"I'm an attorney."

"Whoa." Her daughter made a sound of surprise, provoking a chuckle from Samantha.

"Are you in eighth or ninth grade?"

"Ninth."

"Do they have a high school in the park?"

"No, we're bused to Jackson. It's about a half hour from Moose."

"I see. Do you like school?" Samantha wanted to know anything and everything about this fabulous child of hers. She couldn't get the questions out fast enough.

"I love it."

"I did, too. What's your favorite subject?"

"Science and math. What was yours?"

"Science and math."

They laughed at the same time before Samantha said, "Your father was brilliant in both."

"I know. He's so smart he makes me sick."

There was a wealth of personal information she could tell her daughter about Nick, but she didn't dare. Not yet. Depending on a variety of factors, maybe not ever.

"Your dad's views on the preservation of nature in the wilds had such a great influence on me, it's the

reason I work for the Idaho National Wildlife Federation today.''

''That's so cool!''

It killed Samantha to think of bringing this conversation to a close, but she had an idea Nick was close
by, waiting for her to get off the phone. He wouldn't
appreciate it if she took advantage of the situation.

''Jessica? Why don't you have a talk with your father and decide when would be the best time for me
to visit.''

''Okay,'' she said in a wistful tone, as if she didn't
want the call to end, either.

The problem was, Samantha was flying blind here.
This was the first contact she'd had with her daughter,
and she didn't want to push too hard at this precarious
stage.

''I could come to Jackson and stay overnight at one
of the lodges. Maybe you would meet me for dinner.
How does that sound?''

''I'll check with Dad, then call you later. Oh—you
probably won't be at work then. Do you have a cell
phone?''

''Yes. If you've got a pen, I'll give you the number.''

''Just a sec and I'll get one.'' By the time her
daughter came back on the line, Samantha's face was
bathed in moisture. ''Okay. What is it?''

Once she'd given her the information Sam said,
''I'll be waiting to hear from you.''

''Don't turn off your phone.''

No, darling, I won't. ''I'll leave it on.''

''Good. Sometimes Dad forgets. Bye for now.''

''Bye.''

Before Samantha broke down completely, she punched in Marilyn's cell phone number. To her chagrin she got her voice mail.

"Marilyn? It's Samantha. I spoke to my daughter for the first time a few minutes ago! She's so wonderful I don't know where to begin. Call me back as soon as you can. I'm going to die if I can't talk to you."

WHEN NICK DROVE IN the garage at six, Jessica was waiting for him in the doorway leading to the kitchen. The fact that she came running around to the driver's side of the truck meant she had made contact with Sam. The excitement in her eyes blinded him.

She opened his door before he could. "I just got off the phone with my mother."

Nick drew in a sharp breath. He'd hoped she would have waited until he arrived home, but it was too much to expect.

Sam had only left a work phone number with Mindy. Nick's daughter had been forced to suffer through the whole weekend, then put in a full school day before making the most important phone call of her life.

"That must have been an amazing experience."

Her nod caused the red-gold curls to bounce. "At first I was really nervous."

"And now?"

"She was easy to talk to, like Leslie."

His body quaked. Putting Sam on a par with Leslie Gallagher was high praise for someone his daughter hadn't even met yet.

"When I told her I wanted to meet her, she said she

would fly to Jackson and stay at one of the lodges so we could have dinner together. Would that be okay with you?"

Nick felt relief Sam had suggested a meeting on neutral ground. "I think that's a good idea."

"When should she come?"

"Not on a school night." Though he was aware both mother and daughter were anxious, Jessica had to be his first priority. The emotions already building would drain her in ways she couldn't possibly anticipate.

"How about this Friday? I'm supposed to baby-sit Logan, but I'll call his mom and tell her I can't come."

Friday—that was only four days away. He broke out in a cold sweat. "If she can come that soon, it's fine with me." Better to get this over with right away.

"She's never been here before. Which lodge should she stay at?"

Trust his little nurturer to be worried about her mother's accommodations.

"I'm sure she'll be coming with her husband. Let's let them take care of those details."

"She doesn't have a husband, Dad. She said she never got married."

Not married?

"Dad?"

He took a steadying breath. "In that case the Elk Inn is comfortable and has a good restaurant," he muttered.

It sat on the outskirts of town, where they'd be less likely to run into people Nick knew. For thirteen years he'd kept his past private. That was the way he intended things to stay. Two redheads at one table would be a dead giveaway.

The uncomfortable thought that Sam might have lost her glorious flame-colored locks tugged at him. He had no idea what physical shape she was in, after her fight with cancer.

Obviously she wasn't too weak from the chemo or she wouldn't be able to fly here. Nevertheless, that didn't preclude the possibility of her arriving in a wheelchair, wearing a hat or a wig.

Though she'd told him the cancer was in remission, the fact that her voluptuous body had come close to death at the age of thirty-one was still anathema to him. His thoughts flicked to her parents.

Though he'd never had any reason to like them, there was no question they adored their daughter. Being a parent himself, he realized they had to have been grief-stricken when they'd first learned about her illness. The joy they must be feeling now to learn it was in remission would be indescribable.

"Dad?"

Once again his daughter's voice brought him back from his torturous thoughts. "Yes, honey?"

"I was asking if we could pay for her room. I'll give you my baby-sitting money."

Bewildered by her question, he said, "Why would you be concerned about that?"

"Since she's never been married, I thought it would be a nice thing to do. She lives alone in a condo."

To hide the shocks his daughter kept giving him, Nick levered himself from the truck.

While he was reaching for his carrying case in the back he said, "Since she's the one who phoned you and made plans to come, I think it best to let her handle her own arrangements.'' His daughter's protective instincts were working overtime, the very thing he'd hoped to prevent.

"Okay."

Jessica followed him through the modest ranch-style house to the third bedroom, which he'd turned into a lab a long time ago. He set his case on the floor.

"Guess what? Math and science were her favorite subjects in high school, too."

"Your mother had a brilliant mind. So brilliant, in fact, she took college classes while she was still in high school."

"She said you were brilliant, too."

Nick grimaced, not wanting to hear any more. Talking about Sam made it feel like yesterday, but in reality thirteen years had gone by. She still wasn't married?

"Will it be all right if I phone her now and tell her to come on Friday? Dad?" she prodded.

He jerked his head around and nodded. "Go ahead while I shower, then we'll fix dinner."

His daughter remained in place. She gazed at him with soulful eyes. "Do you really feel okay about my seeing her?"

"Of course."

"Even if you didn't, you wouldn't tell me. Leslie was right. You and Pierce always act tough no matter what."

He reached for her and wrapped her in his arms. "It's not an act, honey. You have every right in the world to see your mother now that she has decided she wants to meet you.

"I lost my parents when I was very young, but I have memories of them. Now you'll have a memory, too. It's important, so stop worrying about my feelings."

She raised up on tiptoe and kissed his cheek. "Thanks, Dad. I love you."

"I love you."

"Oh…" She paused in the doorway. "Guess what? I found out she's an attorney."

"That doesn't surprise me," Nick acknowledged. "Her father's a very well-known, wealthy corporate lawyer in Denver. After she graduated from Harvard, I'm sure she went to work in his firm."

After his daughter's eyes widened at that unexpected piece of information, she said, "No, she didn't. She works for the Idaho National Wildlife Federation in Coeur D'Alene. And guess what else? She says *you're* the reason why."

SAMANTHA TIPPED THE LIMO driver, who'd carried her suitcase to the front desk of the lodge.

"Hi!" said the friendly female receptionist. "Welcome to the Elk Inn."

"Thank you. I made a reservation for Samantha Bretton."

"Let me look it up on the computer. Have you ever been to Jackson Hole before?"

"No, but I've heard about it all my life. The area is more breathtaking than I had imagined."

"I know what you mean. We've had bad weather all week, but today it cleared. You flew in at the right time. There's no sight like the snow-capped Tetons from the air just before the sun goes down."

"The mountains are incredible."

More than ever she could understand her daughter's excited outburst about living in the greatest place on earth. Nick had been working here eight years. They'd already experienced so much of life in this beautiful part of the world without Samantha being a part of it. Pain pierced her heart.

"Found it. If you'll sign the register, I'll get your key."

Samantha filled it out and gave her a credit card. The receptionist handed her some brochures, then directed her to the hall on the right. "Enjoy your stay."

If only the receptionist knew what this visit was all about.

Since Samantha only intended to be here for one night, she'd packed everything she would need in a small, easy-to-carry suitcase. Halfway down the corridor she found her room and let herself inside.

Once she'd hung up the clothes she planned to wear to dinner, she lay down on the queen-size bed, which had called to her the minute she'd locked the door behind her.

Physically, her stamina was pretty good. She owed it to the strict routine of exercises and meditation she followed when she was away from her qigong class. Obviously the fatigue she was experiencing right now had everything to do with her emotional state.

She was scared. In fact, terrified was more like it.

Though a person's voice might not change over the years, Samantha was certain there'd been plenty of changes in Nick's life—and in her own. Like the fact that she was no longer the barely eighteen-year-old mother Nick remembered from his visit to her hospital room.

That girl was gone.

What he would think of her now, she couldn't imagine. When Samantha looked at herself in the mirror, all objectivity left her.

Marilyn insisted Nick would see a beautiful redhead who looked to be in her late twenties. If he were really observant, he would detect her suffering in the fine lines around her eyes and her weight loss in the faint hollows of her cheeks. Ah, the lies of a good friend...Samantha loved Marilyn for it.

Her gaze drifted to the black suit she'd bought. From junior high to the advent of cancer, she'd stayed five feet four and had always worn a size ten. Though still the same height, she now fit into a size four and could buy the styles she liked at Ann Taylor.

The blouse she'd purchased to go with the suit was an oyster-pink with white trim on the lapels and wrist cuffs. She hadn't thought the color would go well with her hair until she'd tried it on. Even before all three salesgirls raved that the outfit was made for her, she'd felt it suited her.

Never in her life had she cared so much about the way she looked. Not just for Nick, but for her daughter. If this was the only night they would have together, she was desperate to appear at her best despite the illness that had ravaged her body for more than a year.

Samantha had told Jessica she would meet them in the lobby of the inn at six-thirty. That gave her an hour to rest before she had to shower and get ready.

Succumbing to a sudden lack of energy, she closed her eyes with two prayers on her lips.

Let Jessica like me a little bit.

Don't let Nick completely despise me for what I've done.

NICK LEFT HIS OFFICE to find Pierce. He didn't have to go far. His friend was walking down the hall toward him at a fast clip.

It was after five and the receptionist had already gone home. On Friday nights headquarters emptied fast before the skeletal night crew arrived.

"How about a beer before you and Jessica have to leave for Jackson?"

"Do I look like I need one?"

Pierce flashed him a penetrating gaze. "The truth?"

"Always."

"I'd say you're a candidate for a bottle of Jack Daniels."

"Don't think I haven't thought about it."

"No matter how late it is when you get back, Leslie and I will be up if you want to talk. Don't bother to phone. Just pull in the driveway and I'll hear you. Jess can sleep on the other twin bed in Cory's room."

"Thanks, Pierce. I just might take you up on your offer."

His friend nodded. "What's the verdict on the cut-throat?"

"Swirling disease. The good news is there's no outbreak above the dam. If the men at the spillway will do a series of flushing flows, that ought to wash out the spores. They could have been lurking there for thirty years. It's anyone's guess why the mud brought

them back to life. I'll have a full report on your desk
Monday morning.''

"Great work as usual. I'll call Ralph at the dam and
get things moving.'' They both walked out to the parking lot.

Pierce clapped him on the shoulder. "Agonizing as
this is, you're doing the right thing for your daughter,
Nick.''

"I realize that. Just knowing her mother wants to
see her has done something for her I could never do.''

"That's true. All you can do is go on being the
terrific father you already are.''

"I hope it'll be enough, Pierce, because Jessica's
riding for a fall.''

"Unfortunately, our children aren't exempt from
pain.''

Their eyes locked. "In Cory's case, he overcame
his pain when he gained a new mother. My little girl's
pain is going to start as soon as she meets her mother
for the first time and Sam does something to disappoint her. Then there won't be a thing in hell I can do
about it,'' Nick said in a quiet voice.

"You already have done something by making tonight possible. Meeting her mother is going to answer
many questions for Jess. No matter what the future
holds, she'll be a stronger, more confident woman for
it.''

Nick grimaced. "I'll try to keep that in mind when
everything hits the fan. Thanks for being there.''

"You mean the way you were there for me when I
was shattered?''

They didn't come any better than Pierce.

"I'll talk to you tomorrow, if not before.'' With

that, Nick climbed in his truck and took off. Already he was anticipating a lecture from Jessica about getting home later than he'd promised.

She didn't disappoint him. The second he walked into the kitchen from the garage she said, "We're going to be late, Dad! You'll have to take a quick shower. I put out the charcoal suit and blue shirt you wore to Pierce's wedding."

"I appreciate your thoughtfulness, honey, but I'm not getting dressed up."

She followed him down the hall to his bedroom. "How come? We're going out to dinner!"

Up to this point he'd tried to fall in with her wishes, but this was one time where he had to draw the line.

"Your mother invited *you* for dinner. Once we've all said hello, I'm not going to stay."

Her face fell. "Why?"

He started unbuttoning the shirt of his uniform. "I've had you to myself for thirteen years. She's only asking for one evening. With me there, you won't be able to talk freely."

She didn't have an immediate comeback, which meant she couldn't refute his reasoning. Finally she said, "Where will you be?"

"I'll grab a steak at the Cowboy Grub."

He'd been thinking of asking out the new manager of the restaurant, an attractive brunette named Amber Sharp. The last few times he'd been in, she'd done everything except stand on her head to get him to make a date with her. Now would be a good time to follow up on her interest.

"When you're ready for me to pick you up, call me

on my cell phone.'' He chucked her chin. ''I like that sweater and skirt you're wearing. You look beautiful.''

''Thanks,'' she whispered in a tremulous voice. ''Leslie took me shopping.''

''Pierce's wife has good dress sense.''

He disappeared into the bathroom, making further conversation impossible. His daughter might feel as if he was abandoning her, but he couldn't see another way of dealing with the situation. The fact that Sam was a recovering cancer patient only exacerbated the violent emotions churning inside him. The less contact between them, the better.

A half hour later he backed the car out of the garage and they were on their way to Jackson.

''Dad?''

He heard a lot of angst in that one word. His hands tightened on the steering wheel. ''Yes?''

''The ninth grade girls' association has planned a mother-and-daughter party for next Friday night. We're going to have a talent show and a sleepover in the gym.''

Here it comes.

''I was going to ask Leslie if she would go with me, but now that my moth—''

''Hold on, honey.'' Nick broke in before she could say another word. They hadn't even left the park boundary so she could meet her mother for the first time, yet already his daughter was anticipating a future that included the woman who'd given her up at birth.

Only now did Nick realize how long he'd been deluding himself that his daughter hadn't missed having a mother. All these years he'd tried to be both mother and father to her, but that wasn't possible. He understood that now.

A woman was required for the mother's role. And if that woman was Jessica's biological mother?

Through some mystical bond that defied logic, his daughter had already accepted and embraced Sam into her life, sight unseen.

For thirteen years it had been just he and Jessica. His daughter hadn't wanted anyone else.

Only recently had she reached out to Leslie, who was safe. Because she was another man's wife, she couldn't come between Nick and Jessica to ruin their father-daughter relationship.

Yet all Jessica had to do was hear that the woman who'd signed away all rights to her child, the woman who hadn't once held her baby or looked at her in that hospital, the woman who hadn't come near her in all these years, suddenly wanted to see her. In an instant, this stranger had full access to his daughter's mind and heart. No password needed.

Nick's lips twisted in bitter pain at the irony.

His daughter had even been willing to give up her baby-sitting money to get her mother a room because she lived alone and didn't have anyone to look after her.

His poor, innocent Jessica. If Sam hadn't married, it wasn't because she'd lacked opportunity. She'd been a raving beauty. That, combined with a great mind, assured that any man would have been attracted to her. She wouldn't have gone without a lover all these years. Probably a fellow attorney on her same wavelength.

"Dad? I'm sorry if I said something that made you mad."

He swallowed hard. "I'm not mad, honey. I just want you to slow down. It's taken thirteen years for her to even attempt to make contact with you. She may not be married or have other children, but that doesn't mean she isn't involved with a man who has other claims on her time."

"*You're* not. Involved with another woman, I mean. Maybe it's the same with her. Maybe she's a workaholic like you."

He darted her a stunned glance. "Is that what you think I am?"

"Yes," she answered with gut-wrenching honesty. "Whenever I go over to Logan's to baby-sit, his dad always says 'doesn't that workaholic father of yours ever knock off early?'"

Nick had to stop the rebuttal he could have made in defense of his actions. Like the fact that in the last five years, every relationship he'd had with a woman had been sabotaged.

No one could do it better than his pint-size daughter, who managed to get stomachaches and hysterical crying spells the moment she sensed her daddy's interest strayed from her, however temporarily.

It was another strange irony that for the first time in their lives his daughter was showing an interest in someone besides him. Now Nick seemed to be the one who suddenly had a stomachache and was feeling hysterical.

"Dad?"

He knew what was coming. No force on earth could stop it.

"If my mother wanted to go to the party with me and could find the time, would it be all right with you?"

CHAPTER FOUR

AT SIX-TWENTY, Samantha left her room and walked down the corridor to the lobby. She planted herself on a bench at the side of the entry so she'd be able to see Nick and their daughter before they spotted her.

She could hear the music of a live country-and-western band coming from the bar. Judging by the number of people filing into the lodge, bringing the cold air with them, the restaurant located down the hallway near the bar was a popular place to dine.

Her heart fluttered faster than it had the first time she was given her prechemo medication to control anxiety and nausea. That was a black period, when she didn't know if she would survive her disease.

At twenty-five to seven she stood up unable to sit still any longer. That's when she spied a tall, powerfully built male with dark-brown hair appear at the entrance. While he held the door open for their redheaded daughter, Samantha's hungry eyes fastened on him first.

The promise of the man in the boy had come to fruition.

Like the rugged Tetons thrusting majestically in the rarified air, the father of Samantha's baby was every bit as spectacular. Beneath a sheepskin jacket similar to the one he used to wear, she glimpsed a black turtleneck. Faded denims molded his rock-hard thighs.

Lines of experience added character to his strong, handsome features—the same attractive features bequeathed to their daughter. No amount of imagining what Jessica might look like would ever measure up to the reality of her vital, living presence.

In a word, she was adorable.

The closest description that came to Samantha's mind was the shining star on top of a Christmas tree. The wonder of the moment left her breathless.

An instant later she became aware that she was the target of a pair of dark-fringed eyes the color of gunmetal. Like someone battling a riptide, she tried to stay upright and survive their merciless scrutiny.

"Hello, Nick," she murmured.

"Sam." He gave an almost imperceptible nod of his head.

She'd asked the impossible of him. She knew that now.

The only thing that saved her was another pair of eyes, blue like her own, staring at her in total fascination.

"Jessica—"

"Hi," she said, just the way she had done over the phone.

"Do you feel as strange as I do?"

A nervous smile broke out on her precious face. "Yes."

Nick's hands were gripping their daughter's shoulders. "I told Jessica you two should spend this time together by yourselves." He tousled her curls in such an affectionate gesture, Samantha could have wept.

"Call me when you're ready and I'll come for you, honey."

"Okay, Dad."

"Enjoy your meal." His eyes studied Samantha's upturned features for a heart-stopping moment. Was he remembering the way it used to be with them? Did he still find her attractive after all this time?

"Thank you, Nick," she whispered. But he moved away with such lightning speed, she ended up saying it to his retreating back.

Her gaze returned to Jessica. It was hard to keep from staring at her. Samantha had missed out on examining her from head to toe when she was a baby. She'd missed the first thirteen years of her life. The realization crucified her all over again.

This lovely girl was her baby, her daughter, her flesh and blood.

"Jessica? I'd planned for us to eat dinner in the dining room, but I was wondering if you'd like to go to my room instead. We could have dinner delivered."

"I'd like that a lot better."

"I hope you're not saying that to please me. It's just that there's so much I have to say to you, and so much I want to learn about you, I don't want to be around a lot of other people. But if you don't think your father would approve, or if you're uncomfortable with the idea, we—"

"I'd rather be alone, too," the teen declared with the maturity of someone twice her age.

"Then let's go. My room's down this hall."

It was an incredible experience to be walking alongside her daughter. Jessica was probably an inch shorter than Samantha and about the same weight. She radiated an energy and vibrancy that was almost tangible.

"I love your suit. You look beautiful."

"So do you. I'm crazy about that sheepskin jacket. I wish I had one just like it."

"Dad and I went to Western Outfitters to get ours. I could show you where it is tomorrow."

Much as Samantha wanted to take her up on her offer, she couldn't. Nick had made it clear she'd only been given this one night.

"If I had more time, that would be wonderful."

"You mean you have to go back to Idaho tomorrow?"

The disappointment in her daughter's voice was a balm to Samantha's soul. She knew the answer she should give so she wouldn't undermine Nick's wishes.

"Tomorrow evening I have plans with a friend I can't break, but we've got all of tonight to get acquainted. Come on in."

She used the card key to let them into the room. After turning on the lights she said, "Make yourself comfortable while I find the menu."

Jessica removed her coat. "I just want a hamburger and fries."

"Me, too. What about a drink?"

"Root beer."

"I think I'll have the same."

Samantha called room service and placed their order. Once that was accomplished, she reached in the dresser drawer and pulled out one of the scrapbooks she'd brought in her suitcase.

"Jessica? If you'll come over to the table, I have something to show you. I would have come back to the room after dinner to get it for you, but since we're already here, now seems the appropriate time.''

Her daughter did as she asked, eyeing her with avid curiosity as she sat down opposite her. ''What is it?''

''Hopefully the answers to questions only I can give you. Go ahead and look through it to your heart's content.''

Maybe it was a trick of the light, but she thought her daughter's fingers were trembling as she opened the cover.

''Oh my gosh! It's Dad! He looks so young I can't believe it!''

''You look just like him. You're his daughter, all right.''

''No one ever says that, because of my red hair.''

''All they have to do is picture you with brown hair and you're the exact replica of your handsome father.''

''My girlfriends think he's gorgeous.''

Samantha winked. ''He is. Take it from me. We met the week he turned twenty. I'd seen him several times in the campus student center studying at one of the tables.

''Nick Kincaid was so attractive, I never looked at another guy after that. You could say I fell in love with him on the spot. The kind of love that hurt, it went so deep.

''One night in desperation I dropped all my books next to his chair to get his attention.''

Jessica's face lit up in a huge smile. ''Did he pick them up?''

''Yes. But it was the most horrible moment of my life. When I thanked him, he didn't say one word. He just gave me one of those scary silvery looks only he can give, and went back to his studies.''

Jessica laughed. "He still does that when he's really mad about something."

"Well, I was so hurt, I left the building and ran to my mom's car in tears. Before I could unlock the door, he caught hold of me."

"Then what happened?" Jessica cried, totally caught up in the story.

"He said he thought I was really cute, but he didn't date cute little freshman girls. I told him he was crazy if he thought I wanted a date with him. He said he didn't believe me and could prove it. The next thing I knew, he kissed me."

"Oh my gosh!"

"You can say that again. It lasted kind of a long time."

Her daughter giggled in pure delight.

"When we had to stop because everyone was honking at us, he asked me if I wanted to celebrate his birthday with him that weekend. The cake in this first picture is the one I made for him. I used my grandmother's recipe. It was a real hit with your father."

Jessica lifted her head. Her blue eyes were blazing. "Is it chocolate mint cake?"

Samantha's heart turned over. "Yes. How did you know?"

"'Cause Dad always tells me to put peppermint extract in the chocolate icing when I make us a cake. I've always wondered why."

Even a simple thing like finding out Nick still enjoyed the type of cake she had first baked for him was almost more than she could stand.

"Will you give me the recipe?"

"Yes. Of course."

Her daughter turned to the next page, then squealed. "That's you and Dad on a motorcycle! Every time a motorcycle gang comes roaring into the park, he tells me motorbikes should be abolished."

Sam smiled at her. "You know how parents are. Do as I say, not as I do."

A grin broke out on Jessica's young, enchanting face. "I can't wait to show this to him!"

"It'll bring back memories, that's for sure. He had a close friend, a roommate named Joey, who let us ride around Fort Collins on it. In fact, we couldn't have gone on all the dates we did without it.

"You could go a long way on a tank of gas, and it was cheap. Back in those days your dad didn't have a lot of money. He had to work hard just to pay for his tuition and housing."

"He put himself through school, huh?"

"Absolutely. Unlike some students, he took a full load of classes and held a job, yet he still got straight As. I lived in awe of him."

"I still do," Jessica admitted.

So do I, darling. So do I.

"Joey took this snap of us on his cycle with my camera. Your dad hated having his picture taken, but I forced him to endure it."

Jessica chuckled. "He still hates it."

Every photo had a story. Picnics, football games. Samantha had recorded every precious moment of their lives together. At seventeen, she had imagined this scrapbook would be the first of many she would fill throughout the rest of their lives.

As it turned out, they'd only had ten months, the last six being long distance.

Dinner arrived. Samantha and Jessica ate their hamburgers between anecdotes. Her daughter begged to hear every detail. Samantha was so excited to share with her, they completely lost track of time. After dinner, they returned to the scrapbooks.

"That's you on water skis!" the girl cried.

"Yes. In this picture you can see your dad in the back of the boat, spotting me."

"You're fabulous!"

"Hardly."

"Dad's still a good water-skier. That is, when he quits working long enough in the summer to go for a couple of runs on Jackson Lake."

"Your dad was good at everything. Turn the page and you'll see some more photos of him. One of his friends took these pictures from another boat."

"Oh my gosh! Dad's on a slalom ski! I can't believe it. My girlfriends have got to see these pictures! Would you let me borrow this scrapbook sometime?"

"It's yours. That's why I brought it. I want you to take it home so you'll have it forever."

Her daughter's blue eyes filled with tears. "Thank you," she said in a tremulous whisper.

"You're so welcome. No one else in the world could ever appreciate this scrapbook the way you do. Someday when you're married and have children, they'll love to pore over these pictures. You can say, 'See? There's your grandpa and grandma when they were young.'"

Jessica's eyes held a faraway look before she finally

lowered her head to finish reading the explanations below the snaps. "Horsetooth Dam. Where is that?"

"Right by my old house in Fort Collins. You could always water-ski there until Halloween. Then the weather turned cold."

When her cell phone rang, they both looked at each other in consternation.

"I'm sure that's your father."

"I am, too."

Samantha let out a quiet gasp when she checked her watch and saw that it was close to midnight. Where had the time gone? Five and a half hours had passed in a blink. "I'll get it."

If Nick was angry, let it be at her, not Jessica.

"Hello?"

"I'm in the foyer," said the deep, familiar voice. "Will you please tell Jessica I'm waiting?"

"Of course. Thank you for this, Nick. You'll never know how grateful I am. She'll be right out."

He clicked off before she could say anything more.

Hardly able to breathe, she turned to Jessica. "As you heard, that was your father. He's in the lobby."

Forcing her legs to move, she walked over to the bed and picked up Jessica's jacket. After helping her on with it, she handed her the scrapbook lying on the table.

Her daughter's eyes never left Samantha's face. "When does your plane leave tomorrow?"

"At noon."

"Do you want to have breakfast together?"

"I'd love it, but that's up to your father."

Jessica nodded. "Can I call you in the morning?"

Only if Nick lets you....

"Of course. I'm always up early. Before you leave, I have one more gift for you."

She hurried over to the dresser and pulled another scrapbook from the drawer. With trembling hands, she handed it to her daughter. "This is the baby book I started when I found out I was pregnant with you.

"I'm sure your father told you why I gave you up, but I'm equally certain you've still never understood how I could have done what I did. I wouldn't be able to understand it if I were in your shoes."

At this point Samantha was shaking so hard, she couldn't stop. "Though we can't go back and do it over again, I'm hoping this book will help you realize I loved you with all my heart from the second you were conceived.

"My parents didn't know I kept a baby book. No one did. It was something I made for myself and for you, hoping the day would come when I would have the opportunity to give it to you. That day is here.

"Just know that there's never been a moment when you haven't been a part of me, Jessica. You'll always be a part of me. I love you."

She opened the door for her, then clung to it so she wouldn't reach out and crush her daughter in her arms. If she ever did that, she wouldn't be able to let her go.

"Now you'd better hurry. Your dad's anxious to take you home."

"Okay," she replied in a quiet little voice. "I'll talk to you in the morning. Good night."

"Good night."

Your father isn't going to let you have breakfast with me in the morning. Goodbye, my darling, darling girl.

NICK WAS ABOUT TO PHONE Sam once more when he saw his daughter come running around the corner of the lobby with her head down. She was carrying what looked like a couple of albums.

Without saying anything, she rushed past him and hurried through the double doors to the parking lot. By the time he'd helped her into the car, she was sobbing her heart out. He'd never felt so helpless in his life.

Right now she was too upset to talk. The scrapbooks seemed welded to her body. All he could do was start driving and wait until this first paroxysm of tears had passed.

To his chagrin she was still broken up by the time they drove into the garage twenty-five minutes later. The second he shut off the motor, she slid out of the car and ran into the house.

After he locked everything up and turned off lights, he entered her bedroom and found her under the covers poring over the smaller of the two albums.

He sat down next to her. "Do you mind if I look at this?"

She shook her head.

He reached for the larger one propped against her knees and opened the cover. For the next ten minutes he was treated to a painful trip down memory lane. It was all there.

Sam had preserved every conceivable memory of their love affair. She'd saved literally everything....

The effort she'd put into its photographic presentation, not to mention the tiny mementos she'd placed under clear plastic, astounded him. Nick remembered she'd like to take pictures, but he'd had no idea she had this sentimental side.

His incredulous gaze took in the halves of a pair of Denver Broncos football game tickets, his old student ID picture, a postcard they'd bought in Gillette, a program from a concert they'd attended, a napkin from a friend's wedding reception, every card or note he'd ever written her.

Each item had a history, one that worked his heart over until he had to close the scrapbook because he couldn't take any more.

"Jessica?" he whispered.

She lifted tear-drenched eyes to his. "My mother loves me, Dad. This is the baby book she made for me."

Baby book?

"Look—"

Now *he* was the one who had trouble functioning as she put the photo album in his hands.

When he opened the cover he saw the title Sam had printed there: "The Family Tree of Jessica Bretton Kincaid."

He blinked to see photographs of Sam, her parents and grandparents glued to one side of the tree. Photos of Nick, his parents and grandparents, his uncle Willard, had been glued to the other. She must have gotten the pictures of his family from his uncle when they'd gone to Gillette.

Nick had had no idea....

At the bottom of the page she'd put in a lock of her red-gold hair with the following note: "When you look at the pictures on your family tree, you'll see you inherited your red hair from your great-grandmother O'Roark on my mother's side.''

There were photos of Sam posing sideways in front of her house in Fort Collins. One had a caption: ''Today the doctor told me I was pregnant. I'm eleven weeks along.'' Everything had been given a date and a time.

The next pictures showed her at each stage of her pregnancy, with notations about what the doctor said at each medical checkup.

Another picture showed a side view of her standing in front of the Bretton's Tudor mansion in Denver. ''Today I'm six months along.'' Her flat stomach was now a tiny mound. More pictures showed her at seven and eight months. She'd even managed to get in a photo of herself two days before the delivery, when she'd blossomed.

Stunned, he turned to the next page and saw a photograph of the hospital where Jessica had been born. Sam had even put in a picture of the doctor, which she must have taken at one of her office visits.

She included a chart of her weight and blood pressure, the first time the doctor detected the baby's heartbeat. Everything to do with the baby and its progress had been noted, including her feelings.

On the inside back cover she'd put in a one-page letter under clear plastic. It had been signed and dated one day before she'd gone into labor.

To my beloved baby—
I don't know if you're a boy or a girl yet, but I've lived with you for nine months and you're a

part of me and your father forever. When the doctor told me I was going to have you, I couldn't believe such a fantastic miracle had happened to me.

I've barely graduated from high school, and my parents believe you'll have a better life if you go to a home where there's a loving couple waiting to adopt you.

Your daddy has said he won't let you go to anyone else, that he'll take care of you by himself.

I believe him and know he will honor that commitment because he loves you and he's a wonderful man. I can promise you he's going to make you the best father in the world.

If the time should ever come when you read this letter, then know that I made this baby book just for you. All you have to do is put a picture of yourself in the center of the family tree and it will finally be complete.

Since I can't be there to put my arms around you and hold you close, I've asked God to help your daddy raise you. I'll pray for both of you every night for the rest of my life.

I love you, my dear innocent angel child.

Your loving mother.

Nick's eyes swam until everything went blurry.

He closed the baby book and got to his feet, too torn apart by conflicting feelings and emotions to articulate his thoughts.

Sam had given their daughter two priceless gifts, gifts he hadn't known existed. The baby book was the one thing he would never have credited her with making.

Over the years he'd gradually come to accept the fact that Sam really had been too young psychologically and emotionally to be a mother, that her parents had understood their daughter's immaturity better than he had.

At the time, the knowledge that she hadn't known what she was doing had helped him to forgive her for giving up their baby. But it had taken him many years to forgive her for not marrying him, for smashing all his dreams.

The baby book, which she must have hidden from her parents, changed his perception of the situation, of Sam. Her moving, heart-wrenching letter to their unborn child contained the words and emotions of a woman, not a girl. The letter confused him in new ways he didn't want to analyze, and filled him with fresh pain.

"Dad? I asked her if I could have breakfast with her in the morning before she flies back to Coeur D'Alene. She said yes, but only if it was all right with you."

No.

It wasn't all right with him.

Nothing was ever going to be all right with him again. But he couldn't say that to his daughter, who'd been starving thirteen years for a moment such as this.

Now that she'd feasted on every jot and tittle of these memory books—guaranteed to fill her hungry heart with joy—Nick would no longer be the wonderful, honorable father if he thwarted her wishes.

"Wake me in the morning when you want me to

drive you," he muttered. His legs felt leaden as he headed for the door.

"You're upset, aren't you."

He turned slowly toward her. "This situation isn't about me, honey. I only want what's best for you."

"Do you know what?"

His eyes closed tightly. "What?"

"I was afraid I wouldn't like her."

Nick had been afraid she *would*. Now his worst fear had come true. Sam had become a breathtaking woman, exhibiting a depth of character he'd only this moment discovered. What daughter wouldn't be thrilled, overjoyed to know this beautiful, intelligent woman was her mother? A mother, furthermore, who'd always loved and wanted her.

"Dad?"

"Yes?"

"Besides you, I like her better than anyone I ever met."

Jessica, Jessica. My poor, transparent daughter.

"I can see why you loved her, Dad."

Don't say any more. "That was a long time ago. We were kids."

"She *really* loved you." Jessica spoke as if he hadn't responded to her comment.

Apparently not enough.

Yet there was no doubt in his mind that giving up their daughter had affected Sam's life as profoundly as it had affected his own.

That was news he hadn't suspected or expected, in spite of the role her cancer had played in the scheme of things. In spite of everything else she'd told Jessica.

"Let's drop the subject and say good-night. Morning will be here before we know it."

"I'm not going to sleep yet." Jessica had survived her baptism of fire. The tears were gone. In their place a new light shone in her eyes, a tangible radiance only Jessica's mother could have put there.

"I've got to find a picture of me to put on the family tree in my baby book. If you want to talk, you can come back in after you get on your pj's."

Reverse psychology from his thirteen-year-old? He watched her sort through the pictures in her wallet, trying to choose the right one, and was unable to process the fact that they were actually having this conversation.

In truth, he couldn't comprehend that the woman he'd consigned to the far reaches of the universe was back. Tonight Nick had learned a lot more about Sam than he wanted to know.

Lord—she was staying in a hotel room only twenty-five minutes away from the house. All he had to do was drive over there and show up at her door.

And then what, Kincaid? Take up where you left off before she told you she was pregnant?

"Dad?" Jessica had found her scissors in her top dresser drawer. Now she was cutting the picture she'd chosen into an oval. "Before you go to bed, I need to talk to you about that school party next week."

He knew what was on her mind. No force on earth could stop it.

"Tomorrow morning I'm going to ask my mother if she'd like to go with me. I know she might be too busy, but maybe she'll say yes. The thing is, she told me she had a date tomorrow night and that's why she has to get back to Coeur D'Alene. So you're probably right that she has a boyfriend.''

Nick felt the impact of that word like a blow to his gut.

''I thought Leslie was beautiful, and she is, but my mother is even more beautiful. No wonder you kissed her after she dropped all her books to get your attention.''

Good grief. Sam had told Jessica all that?

''She said you were so handsome she fell in love with you on the spot, that it was the kind of love that went so deep it hurt. You must have felt the same way because I can't picture you running out of the library after her and then kissing her in front of all those people. Whoa, Dad!

''Wait till I tell Pierce and show him these pictures of you and Mom on your friend Joey's motorcycle! He won't believe it!''

She taped the picture of herself to the root of the family tree. ''How come you've never mentioned Joey to me?''

''A week before our college graduation he died going around a mountain curve on his motorcycle.''

Jessica lifted soulful eyes to him. ''That's awful.''

''It was.''

''So that's why you hate motorcycles so much.''

''Yes.''

''I bet my mother doesn't know he died.''

''No. She was in Boston by then.''

''She had to be superintelligent to go to Harvard, huh.''

Nick nodded.

''Is my grandfather Bretton superintelligent, too?''

"Both your grandparents have fine minds. They met at Stanford, where he received his law degree. Your great-grandfather Bretton was a brilliant federal circuit court judge before his death. As for your grandmother Bretton, she has a masters in nineteenth-century English literature."

"They're sure different from your side of the family."

Before the phone call from Sam on Halloween night, Jessica would have said, "They're sure different from *our* side of the family."

"That they are, honey."

The Kincaids were ranchers from Gillette, Wyoming. None of them had gone to college except Nick. But that didn't count to the Brettons, who were much more ambitious for their daughter.

What a devastating blow to have found out Sam had been diagnosed with cancer, the one thing in life no amount of schooling could prepare her for.

Her parents, along with Sam herself, had to be thanking God she was in remission. *For how long would she be given this miraculous stay of execution?*

That was the question worrying Nick. His daughter's newfound happiness could be destroyed if Sam's immune system suddenly shut down again.

CHAPTER FIVE

SAMANTHA CHOSE THE TABLE next to the window of the Elk Inn's restaurant so she could look at the magnificent snow-swept Tetons while she waited for Jessica.

Her daughter had phoned at seven-thirty and said she'd be there by eight-thirty. Again there'd been no mention of Nick. Samantha knew he had to be impatiently counting the seconds until she boarded the plane and flew out of their lives.

That gave her two more hours to cram in a whole lifetime with her precious daughter before she had to bid her farewell.

The scrapbooks had been delivered. Since it was out of the question to live with Jessica and help finish raising her, the albums were the only tangible proof of love Samantha could offer.

When she'd signed those custody papers giving up all her rights to Jessica thirteen years ago, they'd been final. She had no legal recourse to her daughter. None.

Only out of the goodness of Nick's heart had she been given this sliver of time to let Jessica know she'd always been, and always would be, loved and cherished.

Most of last night Samantha had kept Marilyn on the phone talking about her darling offspring. Tonight there would be more talk with her friend once Sam returned to Coeur D'Alene.

More talk, more tears. Oh yes. There were going to be more tears. Days, weeks, months and years of them flowing over the what-ifs.

Marilyn would tell her it was a torturous gesture in futility. Samantha would agree with her friend before she again wallowed in fresh layers of remorse over what might have been, what could have been.

Seeing Nick—the man he'd become—had fueled her desire for him all over again, with a burning new intensity.

"Hi!"

"Hi yourself!" Samantha's hungry eyes took in the vision of her delightful daughter wearing jeans and a kelly-green sweater beneath her sheepskin jacket. Her coloring might be Samantha's, but her classic bone structure and demeanor shouted Nick.

She didn't dare ask where he was or she would give herself away. There had to be a woman in his life. Samantha would find out soon enough, and dreaded the moment.

"Are you hungry?"

"Kind of."

"What do you say we order some juice and rolls, then call for a taxi and go shopping?"

Jessica's eyes sparkled at the idea.

A half hour later they climbed out of a taxi onto sidewalks store owners had shoveled since the blizzard a few days earlier. Samantha glanced at the sky. No new snowstorms threatened, although it was cold and overcast.

Western Outfitters carried everything. Jessica led

the way to the department where, after some consideration, Samantha bought a jacket similar to hers. Then they walked around the store eyeing the latest sportswear.

Both of them stopped to admire some new brushed-suede cotton suits in a rich chocolate. Paired with silk blouses in a café au lait color, they made a striking outfit.

"With your red hair, you two would look terrific in those," the female clerk commented from a nearby counter.

Samantha glanced at Jessica. "Shall we?"

"Yes!"

Because the clothes had just been put out, they both found a size four before hurrying into the same fitting room. Jessica beamed when the two of them faced the mirror. "This is so cool. Mom and daughter look-alikes."

It *was* cool. In fact, it was the kind of experience Samantha had dreamed about having with her daughter. Growing up with her own mom doting on her, her younger self had taken for granted that she would share this kind of experience with her child. She took nothing for granted now.

She stared at Jessica in the glass. "We need the right shoes to go with our outfits. What do you think?"

The second Jessica nodded, they left the changing room and walked across the store to the footwear department. Soon they'd both been fitted with brown leather flats.

Conscious of the time, Samantha paid for everything, then they left in the outfits they'd just bought.

The clerk put the clothes they'd worn before into shopping bags for them.

After a stop at a photography studio, where you could get passport photos on the spot, Samantha asked the taxi driver to take them to a local jewelry store.

"We'd like to see some lockets, please."

Her daughter bubbled with excitement as they picked out matching round gold ones hanging from gold chains. With the clerk's help, they were able to insert the new pictures. Samantha took turns with her daughter fastening them around each other's necks.

With her hands still on Jessica's shoulders she said, "There. Now we've preserved a memory we can both share."

Jessica's eyes glistened with unshed tears. "Could I ask you something important?"

Samantha's heart swelled with emotion. "Anything."

"Do you think you could come to the mother-and-daughter's ninth grade party at school next Friday night? There's going to be a sleepover in the gym."

Her breath caught in her throat. *Nick let you have this time with her, Samantha. He didn't have to do it. He's expecting you to play fair, so you have to prove to him you can be as noble as he is, even if it kills you.*

"Thank you for asking me, darling. I can't think of anything I'd rather do, but I'm going to be out of town on federation business for the next while," she lied.

"Oh." That was all her daughter said before turning away.

As they left the store and got in the taxi to head

back to the Elk Inn, the pain and disappointment in Jessica's expression almost incapacitated Samantha.

This was the downside of a once-in-a-lifetime reunion. It was what Nick had dreaded, she was sure.

Samantha had been afraid of it, too, but she'd believed her daughter would grow up to be a happier, healthier woman if she knew how much her mother loved her.

Now Samantha knew better.

You didn't sweep into your long-lost daughter's life one night, then disappear into the blue the next day without creating chaos.

Nick had every reason to view Samantha as the most selfish creature who ever existed. No one had a greater right to despise her.

Yet *he* had allowed this visit.

Because he's the personification of unselfishness. Dear God, what have I done to my daughter? To Nick?

In the next little while Samantha would be leaving, and once again he'd be left to pick up the pieces. It was utterly cruel to Jessica, and totally unfair to him.

If the ride back to the Elk Inn had lasted longer than a couple of minutes, Jessica's silence would have been excruciating.

"There's Dad."

Samantha could see his distinctive profile at the wheel of an Xtera parked in front of the lobby entrance. The taxi pulled up behind him. She found the sack containing Jessica's clothes and handed it to her.

"I'm sure he's impatient to get you home. What are your plans for today?"

"He usually works on Saturdays so I go with him."

"You lucky girl. My father didn't have the kind of job that allowed me to tag along. You'll probably end up being a biologist, too. A brainy one, just like your dad."

"Maybe." She opened the door. "Thank you for the clothes and the locket. Every time I wear them, I'll think of you."

"I'll do the same," Samantha whispered with her heart in her throat. "Now you'd better go."

"Okay." She climbed out her side of the taxi. "T-thank you for everything," she stammered in a tear-filled voice before closing the door.

Goodbye, Jessica.

Samantha purposely took her time getting money from her wallet to pay the driver. She didn't want Nick to see she was wearing the same outfit as Jessica. It would have been like plunging in the knife that much deeper. Enough blood had already been spilled.

NICK HAD NEVER THOUGHT of his daughter as stunning. She was too young. But the shopping spree with her mother caused him to reassess his thinking. Seeing her in such a grown-up outfit, he could imagine Jessica the way she would look three years from now. The way Sam had looked....

Smothering a groan, he drove away without glancing in the rearview mirror.

"Do you want to see my new locket?"

No. He knew what would be inside. Sam had thought of everything. No stone had been left unturned. The takeover was complete.

Jessica removed it from her neck and opened it for him.

There they were. Mother and daughter, both wearing the same blouse and suit, from what he could see.

"She bought me new shoes, too."

"I noticed." He handed the locket back to her before accelerating. "Your mother always did have great taste in clothes. I hardly recognize you, looking this sophisticated. You're very lovely."

"Thanks. So's Mom."

Nick had noticed that, as well. If Sam hadn't told him about her battle with cancer, he would never have been able to tell. Her glistening, chin-length red hair, worn shorter than he remembered, flattered her features. In that black suit and pink blouse she'd worn last night, she'd stolen his breath.

Sam had always been a knockout. She always would be. He'd be lying to himself if he insisted that his reaction to her was based solely on the fact that she'd surprised him by not looking ill.

If anything, her slight weight loss enhanced the beauty of her bone structure. More than ever her eyes reminded him of the brilliant blue alpine forget-me-nots growing at the highest elevations.

The old Sam was unforgettable. The new one had an allure that had caught him off guard. She brought his senses alive just being near.

"Is she coming to your school party next week?"

"No. She's busy with a court case she's working on."

Nick's hands tightened on the steering wheel. He had a gut feeling Sam was rushing back to a man. How long had they been lovers? Had he seen her through the stages of her illness? Had he held her and comforted her, done the things that should have been Nick's privilege?

Forcing down the gall rising in his throat, he said, "Did she suggest coming another time?"

"No. She doesn't want to see me again, Dad."

His head jerked around in anger. "She *told* you that?"

Jessica blinked in surprise. "No. She didn't say anything at all. That's how I know." She bit her lip exactly the way Sam used to do. The unsolicited memory devastated him.

"I should never have asked to eat breakfast with her. I—I'm sure she didn't want to," Jessica's voice faltered. "She only took me shopping for something to do until it was time to catch her plane. That's what divorced parents do."

He couldn't bear the resignation and pain in her tone. "What do you mean, honey?"

"I've told you about Marsha Gardiner's parents." He nodded, wondering what was coming next. "Her dad only sees her once a year. As soon as he arrives, he takes her shopping."

"That's probably because he wants to do something nice for her." Nick defended the other man when there was no defense for a father who'd virtually abandoned his children.

"Marsha wishes he wouldn't come at all if that's the only thing he can think of to do."

"What would she like him to do?"

"Anything! Invite her to visit him in California. See where he lives. Go to his work. Stuff like that."

And you wish your mother had asked you to come to Coeur D'Alene and stay with her, Nick thought.

Damn you to hell, Sam. You set up our daughter with those scrapbooks, then fly out of her life as easily as you flew in. But then you're the pro at dangling the carrot before snatching it away.

"How would you like to drive to Gillette and wow your cousins with your new outfit?"

"You mean today?"

He'd never heard less enthusiasm. "Why not? I can afford to take the time off."

"No you can't. I heard you talking to Pierce about needing to meet with the men at the dam this afternoon."

"That can wait until next week." Trying to help his daughter recover from this nightmare was the real emergency here.

"I don't want to go anywhere."

"Then why don't we invite the Gallaghers for an early dinner and a video." Leslie was good for his daughter. So was Cory. Nick would tell him to bring his little basset hound along. Jessica was crazy about Lucy.

"Can't we just be by ourselves? I'd rather go to work with you, anyway. Do you mind?"

"What do you think?"

Nick wrapped his arm around her shoulders and gave her a squeeze. Inside he could feel his rage building. He hadn't experienced that destructive emotion for thirteen years. But it was back, it was alive and it was doing well.

"Let's get you home first so we can both change clothes."

She nodded. "Mom asked me what I was going to do today."

Don't, honey.

"I told her I'd probably go to work with you. She said I was lucky because when she was young, she couldn't hang around with my grandpa."

"Robert Bretton was too high-powered and driven to give his daughter the time she craved."

It was probably the reason she'd sought a serious relationship with Nick so early in her life. But he could never forget she had a lot of her father in her to opt for a law career instead of early motherhood.

"I'm so glad you're not like that, Dad."

"I thought you called me a workaholic," he teased to cover his emotions, which were spilling all over the place.

"But you always let me be with you. That's the difference. Mom said I'd probably turn out to be a brilliant biologist like you."

Mom this, Mom that.

Nick wondered how often that emotive three-letter word would come up in their conversations from now on.

"I've decided I'm going to be a biologist. Then I can live in the park and work with you until you're old. You'll never have to worry about anything because I'll always take care of you."

Oh Jessica.

He shook his head. "A lot of water's got to shoot through the spillway before you're all grown up. Life will be very different by then."

"No it won't. Mom said there was no mistaking me for your daughter. I'm going to get straight As like she said you did. And then I'll graduate with a degree in biology, too."

They'd already entered Moose. A couple of rangers on patrol honked in greeting, but Nick was so immersed in what Sam had told his daughter, he forgot to honk back.

"Even so, honey, there'll come a day when you'll meet a man and want to get married."

"I'm not going to get married. I plan to be like you. We don't need anybody else."

Oh hell.

He roared into the driveway, afraid he was going to lose it right there. Fortunately, Jessica shot out of the car ahead of him with her shopping bag.

By the time he'd changed into work clothes and went to collect his daughter from her room, he'd pulled himself together enough to realize it had been her pain talking.

Time would heal her wounds. He had to believe that.

As for their conversation, it had jarred Nick out of the deep sleep he'd been in. He was going to act on the advice Pierce had given him at the wedding two weeks ago.

Pierce had been right about him letting Jessica's insecurities manipulate him for too long. But after seeing Sam again, Nick realized there was an underlying reason why he'd never been able to commit to another woman and settle down.

There was only one Samantha Bretton. No other woman in his past had ever compared to his memory of her. After seeing her again, he feared no other woman would ever come close. But for the sake of his future happiness, he had to try to make it work with someone else. ASAP!

On Monday Nick had business over in Yellowstone Park. While he was there, he would stop by the Mammoth ranger station to see Gilly King.

He'd always toyed with the idea of asking her out, but had held back because she was a ranger and colleague who until three months ago had worked in Teton Park. Nick hadn't acted on his inclination because of the gossip it would create.

But her transfer to Yellowstone Park due to harassment by another ranger, now out of the picture, had changed the dynamics of the situation. If Gilly was still interested in going out with him—and she'd given out certain signals that said she was—the distance between the two parks was far enough to squelch a lot of the usual talk.

Better still, Jessica wouldn't be intimidated by seeing Gilly around all the time. Depending on how things progressed—*if* they progressed to a stage where Gilly came to mean something important to him—then his daughter would have to deal with it.

The brunette ranger from Billings, Montana, was smart, cute and nice. All the traits that would threaten his daughter. But after what Jessica had said about taking care of him in his old age, Nick needed to dispel that myth in a hurry.

He was about to knock on Jessica's door to let her know he was ready to go, but stopped when he heard her sobs. The kind that poured from her soul.

His head reared back in agony. He knew in his heart of hearts that time wasn't going to heal this wound.

Filled with fresh alarm, he entered her bedroom and sat down on the bed next to her prostrate body. She was still dressed in the suit Sam had bought her.

"Honey...." He put a hand on her back in an attempt to calm her.

She rolled over, presenting a tear-ravaged face. "I thought she loved me, Dad. She said she did, so why couldn't she come to one little party with me next week?"

Nick bowed his head. He needed all the strength he could muster right about now. "If she's caught up in a legal dispute with set court dates, then it might not be possible for her to get away."

"At night? On a weekend?"

Sam wasn't the only one with a razor-sharp brain. Their daughter had inherited more than her fair share. Sam's excuse didn't ring true with him, either.

Yet he couldn't reconcile Sam's rejection with the agony he'd heard in her voice when he'd told her outright it was too late to see Jessica.

He supposed there could be another explanation. Though her cancer was in remission, maybe she still didn't feel well yet. Perhaps the effort of coming last night had drained her. If that was the case, then she wouldn't be able to make future travel plans knowing she might have to cancel them.

No matter what, he didn't think Sam would intentionally hurt their daughter. If she thought she couldn't follow through with arrangements, then it was possible she'd decided it was better not to make any.

But he said something quite different to Jessica. "Maybe she's involved with a man who's possessive of her time. Naturally she wouldn't want to tell you that, so she used her work as the excuse why she couldn't say yes."

"I don't think she's in love with another man, Dad."

He struggled for breath. "You don't have to be in love to enjoy a relationship with someone, honey."

"My mom's not like that."

He blinked. "Like what?"

"You know." She sniffed. "She said she lives alone. I believe her."

"Jessica—she could be seeing someone on a regular basis and still live by herself."

"I don't think so. You once told me that before Mom went to the hospital, the two of you agreed that if you'd waited to get married first, and then had sex, you would still be together. Was that a lie?"

Good grief. "No, honey."

"Well then, I don't think Mom would do the same thing again *now*. Unless you're just making everything up like a lot of parents do."

"I've always told you the truth," he declared. "It's important you understand what happened so you won't repeat our mistake."

Tears gushed from her eyes. "That's what I was, huh."

"Jessica…" He raised her up and cradled her in his arms. "No, No. That's not what I meant."

"I know you love me, Dad, but I *was* a mistake. So was Amanda."

Amanda Tanner was Jessica's best friend, yet this was the first time he'd heard that surprising bit of news.

It was true what they said about parents being the last to learn what their children were up to. Nick had thought himself privy to Jessica's secrets. With that small revelation, he realized it was probably the tip of the iceberg of the things he *didn't* know.

With all animation wiped from his daughter's face, she looked older to him. Before he knew it, she'd eased out of his arms and stood up.

"Why do you think Mom bothered to get in touch with me after all these years? What was the point? If she wanted me to have these scrapbooks so badly, why didn't she tell someone to mail them to me after she was dead?"

Jessica, Jessica.

His daughter needed help. He got to his feet. "Why don't you call her and ask her those questions yourself?"

"I think I will," she said without hesitation. She glanced at her watch. "There's still forty-five minutes before she boards her plane."

He hadn't meant right this minute, but it was too late to recall his words.

With his heart knocking against his ribs, he watched his frantic daughter look for Sam's number in her purse and reach for the phone next to her bed.

She punched in the digits and waited. Her body was shaking. He wanted to go over and hold her, kiss her forehead. Tell her it was going to be all better. But he couldn't do that. She was no longer a little girl he could heal with a hug and a cookie.

After two more attempts to reach her mother, she hung up. "She must have turned off her phone. I'll call her later."

"That might be better," he murmured. "Honey? Why don't you change? We'll grab some lunch on the way to the dam."

"I've decided I don't want to go. Will you drive me to Amanda's instead? She wanted me to come over."

Nick didn't know if that was a good idea or not, but his daughter was in too much pain to hear any arguments from him right now. "Sure. I'll be out in the truck."

"SAM?"

No one had ever called her by that name except one man. With her heart thudding out of rhythm, she turned in the plastic seat of the lounge where she'd been waiting for her flight to be called.

Nick came striding toward her in work boots, well-worn jeans and a white T-shirt she could see beneath his jacket. She couldn't imagine what he was doing here, but judging by the dark expression hardening his masculine features, whatever he had to tell her wasn't good.

She rose to her feet, brushing madly at her wet cheeks with the back of her hand. It was too late to hide her face, which had to be glistening from tears she hadn't been able to stave off. "What's wrong?"

He cupped her elbow and ushered her away from the half-dozen passengers seated in the waiting area. She felt his touch charge her body like a current of electricity. His eyes were the stormy slate color of the clouds obscuring the peaks of the Tetons.

"That's what I'm here to ask you. I left my daughter in tears, and discover her mother's in the same condition."

"I didn't mean to cause her pain, Nick."

He must have realized he'd been holding on to her

because all of a sudden he let go of her arm as if it scalded him.

"Why did you turn your cell phone off? She's been trying to reach you."

She shook her head in confusion. "I didn't know. I don't remember turning it off."

"Come on, Sam. What's the real reason you can't come to the mother-and-daughter party next Friday night? I don't buy the excuse that you can't get out of a prior work commitment to spend one night with Jessica. She doesn't buy it, either."

Samantha's thoughts reeled. He was upset because she *hadn't* said yes?

"Are you still too weak from the chemo to try and make plans with her? Are you afraid you'll have to break them at the last minute?"

"No!" No, no, no.

"Then why didn't you give her an answer she can live with? Is there another man who doesn't want you to have anything to do with your daughter?" His mouth had gone white around the edges.

"No, Nick. No. It's nothing like that." *There's never been anyone but you!*

"Then what prevented you from granting her one little wish that would mean heaven and earth to her? By telling her you couldn't come because your law practice keeps you too damn busy, you might just as well have driven a stake through her heart."

His pain was tangible. She shook her head. "You don't understand. I'd give everything I possess to go to that party with her, but I know I don't have the right!"

Her answer caught him off guard. His whole demeanor changed. "Explain that to me," he said in an oddly shaken whisper.

"Nick—I signed away my parental rights to her thirteen years ago. You're her father. I never dreamed you would let me see her, but you did. After your incredible kindness to me, I didn't dare take advantage of that. It would have defied all the laws of decency."

He rubbed the side of his jaw. She'd seen him do it many times in the past when he was pondering something serious. Apparently it was a habit he hadn't lost.

"Didn't you realize I gave you the right when you received the first phone call from Jessica? Don't you know I expected a call from you years before now?"

No—she hadn't known. What was he saying? Had he *hoped* she would call him? Was it possible?

Her eyes filled again. "I realized you'd given me permission for *one* night. I knew I had to fit a whole lifetime into it," she cried. "Being able to have breakfast and go shopping with her this morning was a bonus I never expected. We had such a wonderful time, the last thing I wanted was for it to end. But I thought it *had* to."

His breathing sounded ragged. "She's going to be calling you later today to ask you why you really turned her down."

Joy surged through her body until she could hardly contain it. "Then I'll tell her the truth. That I wanted to come, but because I hadn't cleared it with you first, I wasn't sure if it would be all right to say yes."

A bleakness entered his eyes. "Once you admit that, then it won't be her last request. What will you tell her when she asks you to do something else?"

If he was saying what she thought he was saying, then another miracle had happened, much greater than the news that her cancer had gone into remission.

"Nick, my answer will always be yes unless—"

"Unless what?" he cut in. "Don't make promises you can't keep!" he warned before she could finish.

She nervously moistened her lips. "I can't promise my cancer won't come back. If I got too sick, that would be the one and only thing to prevent me from honoring a commitment to her."

Like a live wire, the possibility of her illness recurring hovered in the air between them. In truth, Samantha still had trouble believing she was no longer on the verge of death. She'd lived with the inevitability of it for too long. Nick's grim countenance reflected her own tortured thoughts.

"Does she know I've been ill?"

He studied her for a long, intense moment. "No. Not if you haven't told her."

A smile broke out on her face. "Then she really wanted to see me?" The news that Jessica hadn't responded out of sympathy or pity thrilled her in ways Nick could never comprehend.

"What do you think?" he ground out like a person who'd reached the limit of human endurance. "She's your flesh and blood."

Samantha averted her eyes. "I may have given birth to her, but that doesn't make me a mother. It would be understandable if she hated me."

"She called you Mom today."

Her head lifted. "She did?"

"Yes." He admitted it with such reluctance, she

knew this situation wasn't of his liking and never would be.

But there was one thing about Nick she could always count on. He possessed an innate honesty that compelled him to be truthful, even if it almost destroyed him in the process.

"Do you want me to tell her? About the cancer, I mean? I'll do whatever you say."

He stood there with his hands on his hips. His eyes searched hers—for what exactly, she didn't know. "It would probably be best if it came from you. Knowing Jessica, she'll be full of questions only you can answer."

She nodded. "I'll tell her when the moment's right. She's an exceptional girl, Nick. You've done the mos—"

"Don't!" He cut her off with brutal finality.

"I'm sorry," she whispered. "I only mea—"

"I know what you meant." He flashed her a wintry smile. "Let's agree Jessica's a gift and let it go at that."

Nick wasn't about to take any credit from her. He wanted nothing from her. She understood that and would stay out of his way.

But he was demanding she be there for Jessica. That's what he'd meant when he'd made the remark about expecting a call from her long before now. As he would come to understand in the years ahead, where their daughter was concerned, Samantha would never fail him.

An announcement came over the loudspeaker. Passengers started getting out of their seats. "My flight's been called. I should be back at my condo in about three hours."

"Don't misunderstand." His silvery eyes flashed a warning that sent chills racing across her skin. "As far as Jessica's concerned, you and I never had this conversation," he informed her. "She was so distraught a little while ago, I have no idea what shape she's going to be in when I get home. She's gotten it in her head she was a mistake."

A mistake!

"I'm not sure if you'll ever hear from her again."

In the next instant his long strides ate up the expanse until he'd disappeared from sight.

Thirteen years ago he'd stormed out of her hospital room declaring that she wouldn't be seeing him again.

Just now he'd said virtually the same thing about Jessica.

Samantha could hear the flight being called one final time, but she couldn't bring herself to walk through the doors.

Without considering the consequences, she reached for her overnight bag and started running out of the terminal.

"Nick?" she cried when she saw his tall physique in the distance. He'd almost made it to his truck. "Wait!"

He wheeled around in disbelief that she hadn't boarded the plane. By the time she'd caught up to him, she was a little out of breath from the exertion.

"Why aren't you on the plane?" Obviously her actions had shocked him.

"How could I leave knowing Jessica believes she's a mistake?"

She heard him curse under his breath.

"Nothing could be further from the truth, Nick, and you of all people know it." Her voice trembled. "I begged you to make love to me. I planned to spend my whole life with you and have lots of babies with you.

"My parents may have seen me as a foolish teenager who'd experimented without knowing what I was doing, and shouldn't be held accountable for my actions, but I *did* have a heart, which I gave to *you.*

"I'd hoped the albums would prove it, but a few pictures and mementos don't tell the whole story. Jessica needs to hear from me how I felt back then, otherwise she'll grow up warped! I couldn't be—"

"Sam—"

"Please, Nick," she interrupted. "Every day for the last thirteen years I've wanted to explain to her what happened. If you'll drive me back to the Elk Inn, I'll get another room. Then I'll call Jessica and tell her I decided not to leave until tomorrow, so we could have more time together. She'll never know you and I talked. I swear it."

He rubbed his jaw again. "That's not going to work."

"Why not?"

"At this point, if there's any hope of convincing our daughter of anything, we need to present a united front to her."

Sam swallowed hard. "Meaning what?"

"Meaning..." His chest heaved. "Her heart might be willing to listen if she discovers you in the truck when I pick her up at Amanda's. The knowledge that she's dealing with two mature people who've put bitterness aside to do what's best for her should go a long way to help her construct a truer picture of our lives."

Samantha fought her tears of gratitude and won. Nick didn't want to see them any more than he wanted to hear her observations about what a terrific father he'd been. He would only tell her you didn't congratulate a father for doing the job he was born to do. In Nick's mind, being a good dad was a given.

Every human being should have him for their role model.

"What about tonight?" she asked quietly.

"Jessica will figure out the sleeping arrangements. Our daughter is nothing if not the busy little homemaker."

He took the suitcase from her and placed it in the truck bed. Forever the gentleman, he walked her around to the passenger side to help her in.

Riding in a truck with Nick was a new experience. Gone were the college days when he did favors for his friends in order to use their cars or motorcycles to take her on dates. He could buy what he wanted now.

As chief ranger of biological research, he held a vitally important job dealing with wildlife problems affecting all of the major national parks across North America. It was a surreal moment for Samantha to be here with him like this.

When she saw the sign that said they were entering Grand Teton National Park, she experienced such a thrill of excitement, she purposely kept her face turned toward the passenger window for fear of giving herself away.

CHAPTER SIX

RIDING THROUGH MOOSE with Samantha Bretton meant Nick had broken every rule in his own unwritten book of rules. But if she was going to show up at the mother-and-daughter party with Jessica next Friday night, he couldn't very well pretend she didn't exist.

Fact one: From here on out, he knew in his gut Sam was going to be part of Jessica's future. An integral part.

Fact two: From here on out, Sam would be an occasional visitor seen coming and going from Moose.

Fact three: From here on out, every ranger would speculate on what was happening between him and Jessica's mother.

More than ever it was imperative he visit Gilly King on Monday. And if that didn't work because the feelings weren't there, then he'd tell Rex Hollister, Pierce's assistant, to go ahead and line him up with his wife's younger sister.

Melanie had recently graduated from medical school and was now practicing pediatrics in Evanston, Wyoming. From the pictures Rex had shown Nick, she was an attractive blonde who loved to get out in nature.

Up until twenty minutes ago, the idea of a blind

date had been horrifying to Nick, but no longer. Not since Sam had caught up to him in the airport parking lot, sounding out of breath and looking a little pale. A part of him had been alarmed because the exertion might have been too much for her.

Another part of him was shaken because he cared so much, he'd wanted to sweep her into his arms and kiss away her tears.

Lord—it was happening all over again. That certain feeling that had gotten him into trouble the first time.

Waves of desire were washing over him. He didn't know how in the hell to fight them, not with her sitting there within touching distance, unknowingly tempting him. He had to do something to fight his yearnings.

While Jessica bonded with her mother, now would be the time to work on the one element of his life that had been missing for too many years. Pierce had been dead right about that.

Nick pulled to a stop in the Tanners' driveway. "I won't be long." Without casting Sam a backward glance, he levered himself from the cab and walked up to their door.

Amanda's brother told him she and Jessica had left with their girlfriends. Nick thanked him and headed for the truck.

Under the circumstances, he decided it might be better if he took Sam to the house first, then went hunting for his daughter. She might have gone to the general store. Then again, she could be at one of the other girls' houses.

He would like to be able to talk to her right now, to tell her something important had happened. In the past he'd fought against letting Jessica have her own cell phone. But Sam's unexpected advent in their lives had already changed things so drastically, he was beginning to think it might be a good idea.

Ever since Leslie had bought a phone for six-year-old Cory, Jessica had wanted one. Nick had been forced to explain that Cory's case was special because he had an irrational fear of losing his father and needed to stay in close touch with him.

Now the joke was on Nick. Though it might not be irrational, he *did* fear for his daughter's happiness. When he'd dropped her off at Amanda's, she'd been deeply upset. They needed to talk.

He climbed back in the truck. "She wasn't there," he said. "I'll take you to the house, then call around to some of her friends."

During the sixty-second drive home, the woman at his side didn't say anything. When he pulled into the garage, she got out of the truck before he could help her. Once he opened the door to the house, she followed him through the kitchen to the living room.

How strange to think of the thousands of times he'd entered his house never dreaming Sam would walk over the threshold one day. Yet it felt so natural for them to be together again, he was stunned by the rightness of it.

At a glance, he spotted several parkas on the couch. Relief swept over him to see Jessica had brought her friends home. He could hear pop music coming from her bedroom.

His gaze swerved to Sam, who must have removed her new sheepskin jacket on the way in. There'd been a time when relieving her of her coat provided an excuse to pull her into his arms and kiss her senseless.

Was that why she'd been so quick to do it herself? Because she remembered? No. *Don't think about that, Kincaid.*

"Just a minute. I'll tell her you're here."

Might as well get the introductions over with now. Hopefully Sam's arrival would only cause a brief wonder, then everything could settle down to…normal.

What was that, anyway? Normal as he knew it was gone forever. As soon as he got a jump-start on a relationship with Gilly or whoever, he would create a different kind of normal. One that was good for him and his daughter.

One that would help him combat the emotions ripping him to pieces right now.

He walked down the hall and poked his head inside the room. Jessica and three of her friends were making posters for what looked like next week's school party. Nick didn't see the photo albums anywhere.

She'd been so distraught earlier, he had a hunch she'd decided not to show them to her friends yet. Jessica wasn't about to share precious information like that if she couldn't be sure of seeing her mother again.

"Hi, honey."

She lifted a despondent face to him. No sign of tears, but her eyes were still red-rimmed. "Hi, Dad."

"Hi, Mr. Kincaid," the girls said in unison.

"Hi, girls. You guys look busy."

Jessica got up from the floor and walked over to him. "How come you're home from work this early?"

"I didn't make it to the dam. Your mother has decided to stay over for another night. She's out in the living room."

His announcement was met with instant stillness.

There was no such thing as magic, but his daughter underwent a profound change, as if all the atoms in her body had suddenly lined up at attention.

"Come and introduce your friends to her before I take them home."

Like a star whose light had finally reached earth, her face gave off a new radiance. She turned to the others. "Do you guys want to meet my mom?"

Surprise dominated their expressions. Eager and curious, they left their markers and posters on the floor and followed Jessica to the living room. Nick watched from a distance.

"Mom? This is Amanda Tanner. Her dad's a ranger. And this is Jenny Hughes, whose dad owns the gas station in Moose. And this is Sandy Grayson. Her dad owns the guest cabins down the road.

"Guys? This is my mother, Samantha Bretton. She's an attorney for the Idaho National Wildlife Federation in Coeur D'Alene, Idaho."

The pride in Jessica's eyes as she showed off her mother told Nick this had to be one of the supreme moments of her life.

Her friends took their own mothers for granted. It was only natural. In Jessica's particular circle, everyone had two parents who were still married to each other and lived together.

Nick's daughter had grown up with good friends, but there'd been a few people in her past who'd labeled her the product of a broken home. The stereotype carried a certain sting.

There was a point in her childhood when she'd mentioned feeling inadequate because she didn't have a mom in the house. Nick understood Jessica's feelings, but was powerless to do anything about them. It seemed to her that the golden kids, the ones with two parents, sailed through life with feelings of superiority and confidence.

So Jessica feared there were those who thought a person with only half a family couldn't possibly reach maturity and expect to be a whole person.

Certain shows on television discussed the pros and cons of being raised in a one-parent home. It was argued that some children might not make the best marriage prospects if they grew up without having had both role models to learn from.

Nick knew some people thought of her as his love child. No marriage, no divorce, only abandonment by her birth mother.

Jessica's journey had definitely been harder than Nick's. Growing up, he'd been viewed by some as that poor boy who'd lost his parents—how tragic it was that he didn't have a father to teach him how to be a man. How tragic to be left with a daughter to raise all alone. That Kincaid boy must have been born under an unlucky star.

Nick had heard it all. So had his daughter, who'd poured out her heart to him in her dark moments. But it didn't matter. So far they'd made it through the growing years just fine. In spite of everything, he and Jessica were happy. That's what counted.

Given the chance to do things over again, he would have made the same choice to keep his daughter with him. If he'd listened to the Brettons, she would undoubtedly have been adopted by a loving couple.

But no one could ever have loved her the way he did. Thank heaven for his uncle Willard, who'd understood his deepest feelings. The man who'd taken over the responsibility of raising him had been a thousand percent behind him when he'd made certain he got custody of Jessica.

Maybe he was looking over Nick's shoulder right now. Nick could imagine him smiling at his little red-headed poppet, a replica of the woman who'd endowed her with those blue eyes and that porcelain skin.

As he watched his daughter interact, he realized this was Jessica's moment in the sun, to brag and preen over her mother's four-year academic scholarship to Harvard, her prestigious law degree.

Do it, honey. Knock 'em dead listing all the accomplishments of the Bretton side of your family. Make them sit up and stare.

Nick knew he shouldn't be enjoying this so much, but he couldn't help it. With every revelation about Jessica's remarkable mother, her friends' eyes grew bigger and rounder.

"Did you know there's going to be a mother-and-daughter party at our school next Friday night?" Sandy informed her. "My mom and I are in charge of it."

"Jessica told me," Nick heard Sam say. "I'll be coming with her. Can we bring food? My daughter makes a fabulous chocolate mint cake from an old Bretton family recipe."

Sandy blinked. "I didn't know that. Sure! The party's potluck. Mom's going to make chili dogs."

"How about if Jessica and I contribute some barbecued baby back ribs, too? They're another family favorite."

"That would be great." Sandy sounded totally shocked.

Nick had problems holding back his laughter.

"Did you know there's going to be a talent show too?" Jenny asked.

Sam nodded. "What are you and your mom going to do?"

"Probably sing a medley from *Fiddler On The Roof.*"

"Don't you love Tevye?"

"Tevye?"

"Umm. The father. You know. 'If I were a rich man...'" Sam's eyebrows lifted expressively. "'Yabba yabba yabba yabba doo.'"

"Oh," Jenny murmured. "I don't know that one."

"There were a lot of songs from that musical. Tevye's was a man's song, anyway." Sam smoothed over the moment. "What about you and your mom, Amanda?"

"We're going to do a gymnastics routine. She did gymnastics in college."

"How exciting!" Sam exclaimed with genuine pleasure. "I can't wait to watch." She turned to Sandy. "Are you and your mom going to perform, too?"

"Yeah. I play the violin. Mom's going to accompany me."

Sam smiled at all of them. "With everyone so talented, it sounds like a wonderful evening's in store. I can hardly wait."

Nick decided it was time to step in. "If you girls want to get your posters out of the bedroom, I'll drive you home."

They hurried to gather up their things. He helped them on with their parkas. Everyone walked out to the Xtera, even Sam. "It was wonderful meeting you girls. See you next Friday!"

As Nick backed out of the garage, the sight of her standing in the doorway leading into the kitchen haunted him. He looked away to discover two pairs of eyes staring at him from the back seat.

Jessica's friends were definitely viewing him in a different light. He was no longer the man of mystery he'd once been. His past had caught up to him.

Nick could hear them having to reconstruct their thinking. It was serious business trying to figure out who Jessica Kincaid really was.... No doubt about it. Sam's unexpected entry into Jessica's life had given them a lot to think about.

Unfortunately, Sam had given him a lot to think about, too.

ONCE THEY WERE BACK in the house, Samantha turned to her daughter. "Is that upright piano in the living room a decoration only?"

A tiny smile bent the corner of her mouth. "Dad's family gave it to us when his uncle Willard died. They said he wanted me to have it because I always liked to make noise on it when we went to his house."

"What a fabulous gift. He must have loved you a lot."

She nodded. "Dad told me I'd better learn to really play it so it wouldn't go to waste."

"And do you?"

"Kind of. In seventh grade I started taking piano lessons from a lady in Jackson. Now the high school orchestra teacher gives me a half-hour lesson every Tuesday and Thursday after my last class. But I'm not very good.''

''Do me a huge favor and let me hear you?''

''Okay. But promise you won't laugh.''

''I would never do that.''

She followed Jessica into the living room and watched her pull some music from the piano bench. After a false start, her daughter played a familiar Beethoven prelude with surprisingly good technique.

''That was terrific! Don't stop. Play something else.''

Soon Jessica had executed an excellent rendition of the ''Shepherd's Song'' from Debussy's *Children's Corner.*

''You have a fine touch,'' Sam declared when she'd finished. ''Let's see what else you've learned.''

With a smile on her face, Jessica moved off the bench so Samantha could look through the rest of her music. Her eye fell on a book of Schubert duets. She drew it out and closed the piano bench.

''Have you learned any pieces from this yet?''

Jessica nodded. ''The 'Marche Caracteristique.' My teacher plays it with me.''

''I bet you had to learn the top part.''

''Yup. How do you know that?''

''Because I took piano lessons from the time I was seven until I was sixteen. My teacher made me learn this piece, too. Come on. Let's see how we sound together.''

For the next little while Samantha had the time of her life playing the lower part of the duet with her daughter. They did several run-throughs to work out the kinks, then pulled off a fairly polished perfor-mance.

When they'd finished, their cry of triumph was drowned out by someone clapping. Samantha turned around on the bench. Nick had come into the living room without them being aware of it.

Earlier, at the airport, his eyes had resembled twin thunderheads. Now they gleamed silver. "I know a gymful of mothers and daughters who'll be green with envy when the Kincaid-Bretton duo takes all the hon-ors."

Jessica ran over and hugged her father. "Can you believe Mom plays the piano, too?"

"I knew she'd taken lessons."

"But your father never heard me play. I'm afraid I gave it up before we met," Samantha confessed. "As of now, however, I repent of every minute I ever cursed my parents and piano teacher for making me practice. I'm in awe of your talent, darling. In fact I'm so proud of you, I can hardly stand it!"

Her daughter's face glowed. "Thanks, but you're the expert."

"No. I haven't touched the piano in years."

"It didn't sound that way to me," Nick said.

"You know what they say. It's like riding a bike. You never forget. Except that there's all the difference in the world between getting around the block in one piece, and winning the Tour de France."

Nick burst into laughter.

Samantha hadn't heard that beautiful sound since before the night she'd told him she was pregnant. Right now a smiling, laughing Nick from the past was too much for her to handle.

Jessica gave her a speculative glance. "How come you decided to stay another night? I thought you had a...date."

A date.

If her daughter meant with a man, Samantha needed to disabuse her of that notion. Jessica was so busy internalizing every bit of information, the last thing Samantha wanted was for her to get the wrong impression.

Nick was the only special man in or out of Samantha's life. To tell her daughter anything else would be a lie, and it would worry her unnecessarily.

"I have a friend named Marilyn May. She might as well be a sister to me. We're that close. She still thinks I'm coming back tonight. I need to call her and let her know I won't be home until tomorrow."

"Oh." Jessica's face brightened. "Are you staying at the Elk Inn again?"

"I haven't made any plans yet."

Nick moved closer to them. "I went to the airport to see if I could catch your mother before she left. Luckily, she hadn't boarded the plane, so we were able to talk. I told her how upset you were."

Their daughter's features froze. "I wish you hadn't done that, Dad."

"I'm glad he did," Samantha interjected, "otherwise I wouldn't have known how he really felt about my going to the mother-and-daughter party with you."

"What do you mean?"

The truth, Samantha. She would always tell the truth from here on out. Once upon a time she'd lied to Nick by not telling him she was underage. That sin of omission had changed the course of history. *Never again.*

''When you were born, I'd made the promise to my parents that I would give you up, so the doctor didn't allow me to see you or hold you after the delivery.'' In the retelling, she found her nails digging into the palms of her hands.

''Soon after your father took you home from the hospital, I had to sign papers giving him sole custody of you. That meant I had no moral or legal rights to see you or be with you ever again. It was the law.'' Sam took a breath.

''But I broke that law by calling him last week and asking him if I could visit you, anyway. He was noble enough to tell you I'd phoned, and to let me come. I didn't know if it was a one-time concession he'd made for me out of the goodness of his heart or not. To be honest, I was terrified to ask for more time with you in case he felt I was trying to take advantage of that goodness.

''It's the only reason I told you I couldn't go to the party with you. Do you understand what I'm saying now?''

''Honey…'' Nick put a hand on Jessica's shoulder because she wasn't talking. ''I couldn't figure out why Sam had turned you down for the party. I must confess it angered me because, like you said, it seemed pointless for her to bring the albums if she had no intention of seeing you again.

''I wanted an explanation from her so I could put a stop to your pain one way or the other. When I learned the truth, it cleared up the misunderstanding. She wants to go to the party with you. *I* want her to go with you.''

Their daughter studied them for a full minute. Samantha could almost hear her brain working. ''If it was against the law to try and see me, but you broke it anyway, how come it took you so long before you did it?''

So much pain and longing echoed in that one question....

''I never wanted to sign the papers, Jessica, but a promise is a promise. Don't forget I lied to your father by not telling him I was only seventeen. When he told me he didn't date cute little freshmen girls, I knew I couldn't reveal the truth. Otherwise he really *wouldn't* have dated me. It was a sin of omission, and it was wrong.

''Your father deserved better. In fact, he deserved the best I could give. I felt that if I honored that promise, then it would be the best I could give. So life went on. He went his way with you. I went mine. I excelled in school and was able to pick the job I wanted after receiving my law degree. But I would be telling a lie if I said that I never looked back.

''A few weeks ago the pastor of my church came to visit me. He asked if there was anything in my life I hadn't resolved. His question set off an explosion inside me like the one that blew the top off Mount Saint Helens. I thought, I hoped, I prayed maybe your father would forgive me if I tried to see you this one time so I could tell you how much I've always loved you.''

Jessica's eyes welled with tears. ''I'm so glad you called.''

"So am I, darling."

Whether it was right or wrong, Samantha opened up her arms. Her daughter came running into them.

Through the red-gold curls she could see the concern in Nick's eyes. During the next heart-to-heart with her daughter, and there were going to be more in the future, thanks to his generosity, Samantha would tell her about her medical history.

"Dad?" Jessica said after finally letting her go. "Can Mom stay here tonight? I'll put her in my bedroom, and I'll sleep on the hide-a-bed in here."

"You two make any arrangements you want. I'm going to run to the dam, and should be back for dinner by six-thirty."

Jessica turned a euphoric face to Samantha. "That means seven-fifteen to seven-thirty."

Samantha chuckled.

"What do you want for dinner, Dad?"

"Tacos will be fine," Nick called over his shoulder. Within seconds Samantha could hear the sound of the truck as he backed out of the garage.

"Mom? What was one of dad's favorite foods when you two were dating?"

"Pizza."

"Besides that? We have it all the time, and spaghetti and tacos."

"Well, he didn't have much money to pay for anything more expensive. Sometimes I provided the picnic if we went boating. Most of the time he and his buddies ate macaroni and cheese in the dorm, and we went out for ice cream. He put up peanut butter sandwiches to take to work."

"Dad still does that." Her brows met together. "Can't you think of anything else?"

"Hmm. Sunday dinner was sacrosanct at my home. Because I knew my parents would be upset if they found out how much time I spent with your father, I never asked if he could come to dinner.

"As soon as it was over and I'd helped with the dishes, I'd drive one of our cars to his work and stay with him until he got off at nine. Sometimes if I could get away with it, I'd take some leftover roast in foil so he could make sandwiches. He often talked about the great roast dinners he ate at his uncle Willard's."

"What kind of roast?"

"Probably beef, since your relatives ran cattle on their property."

Jessica glanced at her watch. "It's three-twenty. If we bought a roast, how long do you think it would take to cook?"

"You don't have one in your freezer?"

"Dad never buys roast. Besides, he uses the freezer to store all his experiments and stuff."

It was Samantha's turn to chuckle. "A beef tenderloin roast cooks up pretty fast."

"If you drove me to the store we could be back in ten minutes."

She bit her lip. "Your father might not like me taking his car."

"I promise he won't care. There's an extra set of keys in the drawer." Jessica dashed into the kitchen for them. "This is so cool. I finally have someone who can drive me besides Dad!"

They both put on their jackets before leaving. Samantha was happy to do her part, but she drew the line at going in the store. She was afraid it might create too much attention. Nick wouldn't like it.

"Tell you what," she said once they'd pulled into the parking area. "While you get the meat and a nice cauliflower, I'll fill the car with gas. It's running on empty as we speak."

"Okay. Charge it to Dad. He has an account there."

"Fine," Samantha said, though she had every intention of paying for the gas herself. "I'll be back in five minutes."

She made a U-turn and started down the road. Buying gas for Nick's car was the least she could do for him. He'd made a miracle happen by allowing her to have a relationship with Jessica. There wasn't enough she could do for him in return.

When she pulled in next to a pump, she closed her eyes for a minute. *If this is a dream, don't let me wake up.*

Someone tapped on the window. She jerked her head around, then pressed the button to lower the glass.

"Hi there." A fortyish-looking man smiled at her with male admiration.

"Hello. Would you fill it with unleaded please?"

"You bet." After he'd put the nozzle in the tank he came back to her. "For a minute I thought Jessica had taken her dad's car on a joy ride."

Uh-oh. "No. I'm her mother."

He grinned. "You look too young."

The man had to be kidding!

"I'm Bill Hughes, a friend of Nick's."

"Oh yes. I met your daughter Jenny a little while ago. She's a lovely girl."

"Thank you. So's Jessica. Are you here on a vacation?"

What to say? "I came to visit my daughter." Before he could ask another question she said, "I'll be back in a week to go to the mother-and-daughter party with her at the school."

"That'll make Jessica's day."

"It has already made mine. How much do I owe you?"

"That's okay. This tank's on me."

Samantha could have argued about it but decided not to. "Thank you very much, Mr. Hughes. It's nice to have met you."

He nodded. "You're welcome. Next time call me Bill."

"I will," she said, doubting very much she'd be seeing him again.

After putting up the window, she swung the car around and drove back to the store. Jessica still hadn't come out yet. While Sam waited, she decided now would be a good time to call Marilyn.

To her dismay she got her friend's voice mail instead of a live person. Samantha left a brief message about her plans and told her she'd see her tomorrow after she arrived at the condo.

As she was putting her phone back in her purse, there was another tap on the window. She turned her head in time to see two rangers in hats standing there studying her. They looked to be in their early twenties. Cute.

"Yes?" she said after lowering the window again.

"Sorry, ma'am. We thought Jessica was driving

Ranger Kincaid's car and came over to give her a lecture before her dad caught her.''

This was probably going to be a regular occurrence until Samantha met everyone in Moose! But she couldn't help wondering if Jessica had a bit of a problem. Most teenagers wanted to drive a car before they were old enough. Did Nick know about it?

"I'm her mother."

"Sorry for the mistake, Mrs. Kincaid." They both tipped their hats and stepped away from the car to their patrol truck.

"Wait—" she called out, intending to correct them, but they took off too fast. Samantha sat back in the seat.

Mrs. Kincaid…

That's what she could have been if—*No, don't even dare think about it.*

"Hi, Mom." Jessica shut the passenger door. "I got everything we needed. What did the rangers want?"

She turned her head toward her daughter and told her about both incidents.

Jessica's mouth broke into a smile. "That's so cool. Everyone thinks we look alike."

Samantha had her answer. Jessica hadn't been doing anything illegal behind Nick's back. They started for the house. "There's only one problem. They called me Mrs. Kincaid."

"That'll frost Dad." But she said it with a grin.

"I'm sure it will," Samantha muttered.

"Don't worry about it, Mom. They're new recruits who don't know anything yet. Dad says they're wet behind the ears."

Her dad was bigger than life to her.

When they carried the groceries into the kitchen a few minutes later, the phone was ringing. Jessica reached for it. "Kincaid residence."

Samantha removed her jacket, then washed her hands and took the paper off the roast. Jessica anticipated her actions and found a pan so it could go in the oven.

"I'd love to baby-sit Cory, but my mom stayed over and won't be going back to Idaho until tomorrow. I'm sorry—"

"Jessica? Tell her just a minute."

Her daughter blinked. "Leslie? Hold on for a sec." She put a hand over the mouthpiece. "What is it?"

"I don't mind if Cory comes over. He's the son of your dad's best friend. I'd like to meet him. I want to be a part of your life, get to know your friends." *I want to be a part of Nick's. I want things I have no right to ask for.*

"Cory's a lot of fun. I'll tell him to bring some of his games."

"Good. I love games."

Her daughter flashed her a smile that reminded her of Nick at his most competitive. "So do I."

She turned back to the phone. "Leslie? Mom says it's fine with her. She wants to meet Cory. Bring him and Lucy over anytime. What? Okay. Just a minute." Jessica handed her the phone. "She wants to talk to you."

Samantha nodded. "Hello, Leslie? This is Samantha Bretton. I've heard a lot about you. All of it absolutely wonderful."

CHAPTER SEVEN

NICK HAD JUST PUT the last soil sample into his carrying case when his phone went off. He glanced at the caller ID and answered. "Hi, Rex. What's going on?"

"My wife's sister drove up from Evanston for the weekend. We thought we'd invite a few friends for dinner. How would you like to come? This is totally impromptu."

"What time do you want me to be there?" He fired back the question without having to think about it.

There was a pause. "Am I talking to the right Nick Kincaid?" Rex asked, sounding as if he didn't quite believe his ears.

"Do you know another one?" he teased.

"Yeah. I know a Nick who wouldn't accept a blind date if you bribed him with a million bucks."

"Oh. *That* Nick. He used to have a problem with his daughter who suffered from separation anxiety. But the problem appears to have been fixed. At least for this weekend. So I'm your man."

"You sound different, you know that?" Rex said in a more serious tone. "For a lot of reasons I'm glad to hear it."

"What time do you want me for dinner?" Nick redirected the conversation. Right now he didn't want to think, let alone talk, about Sam.

"Seven-thirty. Don't worry about my sister-in-law. She's as gun-shy as you are in the being-set-up-for-a-date department. If there's chemistry between the two of you, it's anyone's guess which of you will be the more surprised."

"Message received. Thanks for the invite, Rex. Tell your wife I'm looking forward to it."

He rang off and climbed in the cab of the truck. His watch said twenty to seven. It would take him a half hour to get home. If he hurried, he'd make it to the Hollisters' by seven-thirty or thereabouts. Jessica had probably fixed tacos for her mother. He would enjoy the leftovers tomorrow.

He knew he was dead wrong the second he walked into the kitchen. The smell of roast and everything that went with it assailed him. The kitchen table had been set with a cloth and matching napkins for four people.

On the way to his bedroom he glanced into the living room and discovered towheaded Cory at the piano with Jessica. They were playing chopsticks. Lucy followed Nick down the hall. She sniffed at his pants, which smelled of dam water, sending her into ecstasy.

When Sam unexpectedly came out of Jessica's bedroom dressed in a pair of navy sweats, the kind he liked to wear around the house, his heart missed several beats.

She let out a soft gasp. "You're home! Jessica will be thrilled. She has worked so hard on this dinner for you. The only thing she let me do was set the table according to her exact specifications."

Nick stifled a groan. How could he have been so stupid? Of course his daughter had wanted to impress her mother with this first meal. She wanted to show that she'd grown up to be the perfect little hostess who'd been taking good care of her father all these years. This was something she needed to prove in front of both her parents.

Unfortunately, he'd already committed to Rex and couldn't back out now. He had to think fast to come up with a solution that wouldn't disappoint his daughter or his friend.

"I'll be ready in five minutes. I have other plans for this evening so I'll have to eat quickly."

She didn't flick an eyelash. "Then I'll help her put everything on the table right now."

"Thanks."

His eyes followed her retreating figure before he realized he didn't have time to dwell on the curves she'd retained in spite of her weight loss. While Lucy raced after her, he dashed into his bedroom and took a two-minute shower.

Once he'd shaved and dressed in a pullover and trousers, he phoned Rex and told him not to hold dinner for him, that he'd be there by eight-fifteen at the latest. Being the good man he was, Rex didn't ask questions, only thanked him for the call.

The vegetables and gravy along with the roast were so good, Nick asked for a third helping. Jessica may have done the cooking, but Sam had provided the impetus and the know-how.

Cory's blue eyes looked huge behind the glasses he wore to correct his amblyopia. "How can you eat that much?"

"Like Popeye and his spinach, rangers have to eat lots of meat and potatoes to keep up their strength," Sam explained.

"But I like pizza," Cory said, sounding a little worried before he took another bite from the slice Jessica had warmed up for him.

Sam smiled. "Everyone loves pizza, Cory. Nick ate it almost every day at college. All that protein and calcium in the cheese gave him big muscles and beautiful white teeth."

"Really?" Cory stared at Nick with new appreciation.

Nick was afraid to look at Sam, who'd just given Cory a lot to think about. In the process of making him feel good about his limited food preference, she'd brought up a whole host of intimate memories better left in the deep freeze.

He pushed himself away from the table and walked around to hug his daughter. "That was the best meal I ever tasted. Thanks, honey."

"You're welcome."

"It was out of this world, darling."

"Thanks, Mom."

Jessica looked happy.

Obviously Sam had told his daughter he was going out. To his amazement she seemed all right with it, otherwise his departure would have robbed her of the joy of the moment.

"Where are you going?" Cory asked.

"To the Hollisters'. They're having a party."

"Mom and Dad already left for their house."

That news didn't surprise Nick. Rex and his wife must have figured the more friends around, the easier this blind date would go. "Are you going to sleep over at our house tonight, sport?"

"Yup. I brought my sleeping bag. Lucy'll be good."

"Terrific. See all you guys in the morning."

"We'll be quiet in case you want to stay uncon-scious till ten, Dad."

"I appreciate that. Good night."

Because the Xtera needed gas and Nick couldn't fill it up until tomorrow when he took Sam to the airport, he drove the truck to the Hollisters', who lived a couple of blocks away.

Pierce had parked his Grand Cherokee in front of the house behind an unfamiliar Chevy Tahoe. It probably belonged to Evanston's newest doctor.

Rex's wife showed him inside and introduced him to her sister, Melanie, a tall blonde who was attractive in an athletic kind of way. It looked as if everyone was at the dessert stage of dinner. Though Nick was stuffed, he didn't dare refuse the apple pie à la mode.

Except for Pierce and Leslie, no one knew Sam was in Moose. Though Nick could depend on the Galla-ghers' discretion not to say anything about it, the co-incidence of Melanie visiting her sister at the same time was amazing to say the least.

The evening turned out to be a pleasant one. Mel-anie was laid-back, yet interesting to talk to. Nick found the Hollisters' latest home movies of a family trip to Cancun with their eight- and nine-year-olds en-tertaining.

But before they'd finished viewing everything, Pierce received an emergency call from headquarters at the same moment a couple of the younger park rangers appeared at Rex's front door. Everyone assem-bled in the foyer to find out what was wrong.

It seemed a semi had plowed into one end of the Moose visitors' center following a high-speed police chase. The rangers had gotten involved when the truck didn't stop at the entrance to the park.

"That's a new one for the books," Pierce muttered. "We're on our way."

Nick eyed Pierce. "We'll go in my truck."

"Do you want us to run your wives home?" one of the rangers asked.

"I thought you guys knew I'm not married," Nick told them.

"Whoops. Today we saw your Xtera in front of the store and thought Jessica was in the driver's seat. That is until we went over to talk to her and met her beautiful mother." *What?* "I called her Mrs. Kincaid by accident. Sorry."

Oh hell. Did the idiot have to blurt it out for Melanie to hear? Nick turned to her. "I'll call you tomorrow before you leave for Evanston."

"That's okay, Nick. I'll be leaving early, but it was nice to have met you."

AT EIGHT IN THE MORNING, everyone tiptoed down the hall to the front door as prearranged. Cory hurried out to Leslie's Grand Cherokee with Lucy and got in front. Samantha stood on the front porch and breathed in the cold air while she waited for Jessica to put the note she'd written to her father under the fridge magnet.

This morning like yesterday was overcast. Mist shrouded the peaks of the Tetons. She didn't think the temperature had dipped to freezing, but it had to be close to it. Not the greatest weather for flying, but no new storms had been forecast.

"Dad came in at five, so I shut off his alarm," Jessica informed her.

If Nick hadn't come home from a party until this morning, then he had to be involved with a woman who mattered to him. The knowledge shouldn't have hurt Samantha, but it did. In fact, she felt shattered, but she couldn't let her daughter know it.

Jessica pulled the door shut before they both walked to the car, where Leslie Gallagher stood waiting. With her stylish, light-brown hair and hazel eyes, Cory's new mom was a stunning woman, Samantha thought. She imagined they were about the same age.

The other woman had been so easy to talk to on the phone that Samantha was already prepared to like her. When Leslie gave her a spontaneous hug instead of a handshake, Samantha felt as if she'd gained a new friend.

Leslie took her suitcase and put it in the rear of the car while Samantha and Jessica climbed in the back. The heater was going strong. It felt good.

Once they were off, Leslie said, "Guess what, Cory? In just a minute you're going to see a sight you've never seen before."

Hugging his dog, he peered at her from behind his glasses. "How come?"

"Because I don't think an eighteen-wheeler truck has ever driven straight into the wall of the Moose Visitors' Center before."

"You're kidding!" Jessica cried.

"Nope. That's why Pierce and your father didn't get home until five this morning. There was so much cleanup to do, the poor things will probably sleep till late this afternoon."

"Oh my gosh!" Jessica blurted the moment the center came into view. It did look like a war zone to Samantha, with all the yellow police tape and cars and rangers milling around keeping tourists away.

Sheets of plastic protected the gaping hole in the end of the building. The damaged semi had been moved to the side parking lot. There was already a construction crew on the site.

"What a mess!"

"You can say that again, honey." Leslie patted Cory's arm.

"How come the driver rammed into the building?"

"Your dad said he was a bank robber from Jackson who killed the real driver to get away from the police. By the time he reached Moose, the police and rangers had him blocked so he couldn't go forward or backward, so he drove into the center."

"Is he dead?"

"No. He's at the hospital being treated for cuts before they take him to jail."

Samantha leaned forward. "Was anyone in the center hurt?"

"No. None of the skeletal crew were in the reception area at the time of the accident."

"That was a blessing." The thought of anything happening to Nick made Samantha ill. On the other hand, the fact that he hadn't been out with a woman all night made her so euphoric she wanted to shout for joy.

"You're right," Leslie murmured, sounding shaken by the threat to her husband's safety. Who could blame her?

Jessica bit her lip. "Thank goodness Dad's and Pierce's offices are down on the other end."

"Can we go look inside?"

"We don't have time, Cory honey, but your father will show us around later. Right now we need to take Samantha to Grayson's so she can book a cabin for next weekend. Then we're going to have breakfast in Jackson before we take her to the plane."

Cory looked over his shoulder at Samantha. "I wish you didn't have to go home today. Will you play Dragon Ball Z with me again when you come next weekend?"

"I'd love to," she exclaimed before Leslie could say anything. "Maybe we could all go to a movie in Jackson on Saturday after the school party. And later, you could come to my cabin with Lucy. We'll play games, eat pizza and have another sleepover."

"Goody! Can I, Mom?" he begged.

"Are you sure?" Leslie asked Samantha, eyeing her through the rearview mirror. "After being up all night with the girls, you may be too exhausted."

Samantha appreciated the other woman's concern. Undoubtedly Nick had told Pierce and his wife about her medical history.

"We're positive, aren't we, Jessica!" she declared in an attempt to reassure Leslie she was fine. Getting involved in her daughter's life was the greatest thing that had happened to her in thirteen years.

Jessica looked starry-eyed. "It'll be perfect."

"How come you have to go home today?" Cory demanded.

"Because I've got a court case in the morning to prepare for."

"Did somebody do something bad?"

"They *want* to. I'm asking the judge for an injunction to stop loggers from building a road."

"What's an injunkshun?"

"It means I want him to tell those people 'No, you can't build a road there.'"

"Where do they want to put it?"

"In the Kelly Creek area."

"Where's that?"

"In the Wild Clearwater country in north-central Idaho. They call it the Yellowstone of Idaho. Every time a new road is built, it ruins the habitats of the animals, and brings people who pollute the clean air and water. More roads mean more mining, all of which destroys the rivers and streams."

"Dad says that's really bad."

"Your father's right, Cory. We all have to fight to preserve the environment."

Jessica eyed her mother. "Dad could use you to fight for the Endangered Species Act."

"Why hasn't he hired an attorney before now?"

"The funding has been cut off except for necessities. Pierce has asked the governor to do something about getting extra money for one. I'm a reporter on the school newspaper staff covering issues that Teton Park has to deal with," Jessica told her.

"Good for you! My daughter the nature activist!"

Leslie chuckled. "Living in the park is turning me into one, too."

"Isn't it unfortunate that everything always comes down to money," Samantha mused aloud. Nick had to be frustrated out of his mind.

"Look, Mom. There's Grayson's! I'll get Sandy to

ask her dad to give you the corner cabin. It's the biggest one, and has a picnic table along the window where we can play games.''

Samantha's gaze swerved to the grouping of white-trimmed guest cabins, very rustic and cozy-looking with curls of smoke rising from some of the chimneys. The Tetons formed a breathtaking winter backdrop. She couldn't wait to stay here.

She never wanted to leave....

NICK CAME AWAKE all of a sudden, which was strange because the house seemed quiet as a tomb. He glanced at his watch. One-thirty?

Sam. She was supposed to be on the noon plane!

His adrenaline surging, he jackknifed into a sitting position and checked his alarm. It was pushed in. He distinctly remembered setting it for eight o'clock before collapsing into bed after the all-nighter at the visitors' center.

Had he heard it go off and then gone back to sleep?

Pulling on the bottoms of a pair of gray sweats, he hurried out of the room. The bed in Jessica's room was made up, with no sign of Sam or her suitcase. Further investigation proved no one was in the house.

His daughter had left him a message in the usual place.

Dear Dad, Leslie came and got all of us in her car. We've gone to Jackson to have brunch at the Moran Grill, then we'll take Mom to the airport. Cory wants to go ice-skating later, so we might do that. When you get up, there's plenty of roast to make sandwiches, and there's chocolate mint cake in the fridge, too. Enjoy your day. Love, Jessica.

Nick reread the note. *Enjoy my day?*

What daughter was this?

Certainly not his little guardian of hearth, home and family. Not the little worrywart who until yesterday needed to know his every move ahead of time if it was at all possible.

He couldn't ever remember having this kind of luxury to be alone in his own house, knowing Jessica was feeling totally secure away from him.

Security.

That's what Sam had given their daughter by entering her life. But if she didn't stay in remission, the thought of what it could do to Jessica was too terrible to contemplate.

Nick bowed his head. Right now he'd be ungrateful to entertain negative thoughts. He'd done too much of that since the moment Sam had signed over their daughter to him. That kind of thinking got you nowhere.

Seize the day, Kincaid. He was a free agent for a few hours. He intended to make the most of them.

Before another minute passed he needed to call Melanie. But when he reached for the receiver in the kitchen, he couldn't bring himself to punch in the Hollisters' number. What would he say to her if she hadn't left yet?

You're a very nice, attractive woman who will make some lucky man a wonderful wife?

Maybe it was a blessing she'd overheard the ranger talk about Jessica's mother being in Moose. Melanie wasn't looking for a man with baggage. At least this way she wouldn't view last night's experience as a personal rejection.

Better to leave it alone and wait to thank Rex and his wife tomorrow when things were back to normal.

There was that word again. He shook his head. There was nothing normal about anything. Who was he kidding?

What he ought to do was call Gilly King. If she were free for lunch tomorrow, then he would avoid wasting time driving out of his way to see her, only to discover she wasn't there.

He headed for his bedroom where he kept a master list of phone numbers. After sinking down on the side of the bed, he picked up his cell phone and dialed the Mammoth ranger station.

The ranger who answered said she was off duty, but she'd be back on first thing in the morning. If Nick wanted to leave a message, the other man would make sure she got it.

Nick gave him his name and number asking her to call, then he hung up.

Normally he'd be starving by now, but for some reason he couldn't understand, he wasn't that hungry. He went to the living room for the Sunday paper, but the headlines with their usual attacks against the president bored him.

He threw it down on the coffee table, deciding to take a shower. Once he'd dressed, he would drive the car over to the gas station and fill it up so he could take off early in the morning.

Twenty minutes later he pulled up to one of the self-serve pumps. When Bill Hughes saw him from the doorway, he walked over. "How are you doing, Nick?"

"I'm good. How about you?"

"Can't complain."

"When Jessica's mother asked me to fill the tank with gas yesterday, for a moment I thought it was Jessica at the wheel. You could have knocked me over. Now I know why your daughter is such a little beauty."

Bill was the second person to tell him Sam had been driving around in his car yesterday. With her red hair and blue eyes, she was impossible to miss. Certainly Nick hadn't been immune to her charms the first time he'd seen her in the Lory Student Center. She'd stood out like a heavenly scented candle glowing in a dark room.

"Excuse me a minute, Bill," Nick muttered. He removed his hand from the gas hose and got back in the car to turn on the ignition. One glance and he could see the gas tank no longer registered empty. He hadn't even noticed on the drive over!

Jessica knew where he kept an extra set of car keys. She must have prevailed on Sam to drive them to the store, and Sam had realized it was almost out of gas. Nick had assumed they'd walked to the grocery store.

He turned to Bill. "Did she charge it to my account?"

"No. She tried to pay me cash, but I told her to forget it."

"That was very nice of you, but I'll take care of it now." He pulled a twenty dollar bill out of his wallet and tucked it in the chest pocket of Bill's uniform.

Nick could tell Jenny's father was dying to ask

questions, but he managed to refrain. It was just as well, since Nick was in no mood to answer them. In twenty-four hours, Sam had made a shambles of the ordered world he'd taken years to build.

"Thanks, Bill. See you later." He shut the door and drove off. Without knowing what he was doing, he ended up in Pierce's driveway.

To his surprise his friend's garage door suddenly opened and he saw the taillights of his truck flash red.

Nick honked so they wouldn't collide.

Pierce stood on his brakes. In the next instant he jumped down from the cab and walked out to the car. He shot Nick an ironic grin.

"We'd really make history if one of our young rangers happened to drive by and see the latest in a series of car-truck accidents within park boundaries. It would get back to Lewis Fry from the cable network, who has already sensationalized last night's story to the limit of his ability."

A sound of exasperation escaped Nick's throat. "I should have phoned first, but I didn't know I was coming over here until I pulled in your driveway. Now that I think about it, I left my cell phone on the night-stand."

"That explains why I couldn't reach you."

Sensing something was wrong, Nick sat up straighter. "What's up?"

Pierce's blue eyes studied him for a moment. "Jess admitted to Leslie that she turned off your alarm so you could sleep."

"That little monkey." She'd never done anything like that before. But then Sam had never been in Jessica's life before. Her presence had turned his daughter's life inside out just as thoroughly as his. "Leslie shouldn't have had to worry about getting Sam to the airport."

"My wife wanted to do it. It gave them a chance to get acquainted. When I couldn't reach you on the phone a few minutes ago, I thought either you were still dead to the world or…you were at the Hollisters'."

Nick stared back at him as they communicated without words. "Now you know."

"Yup. In that case, how would you like to go to Jackson? The kids should be through ice-skating by the time we get there. Cory wants to get hamburgers at Shiver's. I thought we'd join them."

"I'll drive," Nick said without having to think about it.

"Give me one second." Pierce moved his truck back into the garage, then joined Nick. "Let's get out of here."

"I owe Leslie for this."

"No you don't. Samantha booked a cabin at Grayson's for next Saturday night following the school party." Nick's body quaked. Sam was coming for the whole weekend? "She has already asked to let Cory sleep over with her and Jess. He was ecstatic when he told me about it on the phone.

"My son has always been crazy about your daughter. Now it seems Samantha has made a real hit with him, too, which is no small feat as we both know. Since he's all excited about it, Leslie and I have decided we're going to enjoy a mini honeymoon at the house."

Nick cleared his throat. "That's good. You two need it and deserve it."

"With Jess taken care of for the weekend, it looks like you'll be free to do whatever you want for a change."

Whatever I want. I wish I knew what that was.

You'd better figure it out fast, Kincaid. Otherwise you're facing the weekend from hell.

CHAPTER EIGHT

As Jessica entered the kitchen from the garage ahead of Nick, they both heard his cell phone ringing.

"That's probably Mom! She promised to call and let me know she got back to Coeur D'Alene safely. I'll get it!" Jessica was off like a shot.

He glanced at the clock on the wall. Seven-thirty. While they were eating hamburgers, Cory had informed Nick that Sam's plane had taken off at one. She would have been home quite a while by now. Did her friend pick her up, or had she left her own car in the airport parking lot?

According to Cory, he and Jessica had prevailed on Leslie to stay and watch the plane leave. Pierce's son was full of admiration for Jessica's mother. She'd taught him a new version of chopsticks on the piano and could beat everyone at his Space Raiders game. *And* she'd said pizza was good for growing boys who wanted to be rangers.

The disturbing realization that every thought in Nick's head had to do with Sam drove him to his lab to check out the latest soil samples for spores. Hopefully the first series of dam flushings had eradicated the problem.

He'd just opened his carrying case when Jessica said, "The phone's for you, Dad. I left it in your bedroom. It's Gilly King returning your call. Is it okay with you if I call Mom on *our* phone?''

What? No third degree to find out why he'd called Gilly in the first place?

"Go ahead." Jessica was so consumed by thoughts of her mother, nothing else seemed to register right now. Like daughter, like father?

The question haunted him all the way to his bedroom. He reached for his phone. "Hi, Gilly. How are you?"

"Hi!" She had a little-girl voice that was cute and deceiving because she was one tough ranger. "I'm great! The question is, how are you? The news about the semi crashing into the visitors' center is all anyone can talk about around here."

It took him a second to remember there'd been a disaster last night. Other things had been on his mind. Another woman had filled his thoughts.

"You'd be amazed what a mess it made. Too bad there has to be a funeral for the driver of that rig. He was just trying to do a day's work when he was attacked."

"Isn't it always the culprits who seem to walk away without a scratch?"

"You've got that right."

"Obviously you were trying to reach me about something. What's going on?"

"How would you like to have lunch with me tomorrow? I'm going to be in the general vicinity on business."

"Lunch? I haven't had an invitation to lunch in so long I can't remember. I'd love it!"

"What time would be good for you?"

"Twelve-thirty?"

"All right. I'll pick you up at the ranger station and we'll drive to the Park Street Grill in Gardiner."

"Sounds terrific, Nick. Thanks for calling."

"My pleasure. See you tomorrow."

He hung up. That was easy enough. Too easy?

What in the hell is wrong with you, Kincaid? Did you want her to give you a hard time? Were you hoping she would tell you she was involved with someone else, but thanks anyway?

In a vile mood, he headed back to his lab. As he passed Jessica's room, he could see her on the bed, lying on her stomach with her legs up, ankles crossed. She moved them back and forth while she chatted happily with her mother.

He'd raised his daughter not to eavesdrop on other people's conversations, so took his own advice. But it almost required an act of nature for him to keep moving to the other bedroom. He could picture Sam on a bed in much the same position, her red-gold curls a lick of flame in the lamplight.

No sooner had he prepared some new slides than Jessica breezed into the room. "Dad? There's something important I have to ask you, but I don't want you to think it's because I don't love you."

His mouth grew taut. "I know you love me, honey. Just tell me what it is you're trying to say."

"How would you feel about me spending Thanksgiving with Mom and my grandparents in Denver?"

One of the slides fell to the floor and broke.

"Mom told them about seeing me, and they want to meet me."

He rubbed a hand over his face.

Like the big volcano that was building beneath Yellowstone Park—one that would make Mount Saint Helens look like a firecracker when it blew—the world he'd known with Jessica was starting to crack with a burst of steam here, a new geyser there, a hot lava bed suddenly visible where no lava bed had ever been before.

"If I go to their house, then I'll be able to meet my two great-grandparents from my grandfather's side, who are still living. They're too old to travel, but they'll be at my grandparents' for dinner.

"Dad, if you don't want me to go, I won't. But since the family has already invited us to Gillette for Thanksgiving, I thought maybe you wouldn't mind going alone this once. What do you think?" His little girl was so excited she had to catch her breath before continuing.

"Mom understands completely if you say no. She said the way her parents treated you was so unforgivable, she's not assuming anything. It's just that she wanted me to know she'd rather be with me than anything else this coming holiday."

Nick stifled a groan. He had to admit there'd been a time when he'd considered the Brettons' actions inhuman.

Nevertheless, having been a parent himself for thirteen years, and especially now that Jessica was a teenager, he understood to a greater extent where they'd been coming from when they'd learned their seventeen-year-old, not even out of high school yet, was pregnant.

These days Nick didn't see life in black-and-white, the way he once had. The fact that Sam had chosen to seek out her daughter whether her parents cared or not proved how independent she'd become.

It also indicated that her brush with death had softened their hearts to the extent they would welcome Jessica into their home, if only for their daughter's sake. The love of a child made you do a lot of things you never thought you would.

"Is your mother still on the phone?"

"No. She had to get off. Tomorrow she's got a big case to present in court, and she needs to work on it. Because she stayed over to be with me an extra night, she'll be up late preparing."

"What kind of case?" he asked before he could stop himself.

Jessica told him what she'd learned from Sam. "Next week Mom's going to bring me some copies of decisions she has won for the federation. I can use them to help document next month's school article on the ESA. She knows a ton of stuff, Dad. It's fantastic!"

It was fantastic all right. Fantastic that until ten days ago his cousins and their kids had made up the sum total of Jessica's family. With Sam's phone call, that world had expanded to include grandparents and great-grandparents.

Nick would have given anything if his own parents could have raised him and had the opportunity to know Jessica. So how could he deny her the experience of meeting her flesh and blood from Sam's side of the family?

"If you want to plan to spend Thanksgiving with her, it's fine with me, honey."

"You're the best, Dad." She gave him a hug. "Mom will pay for my flight to Denver and back."

He stiffened. "I think I can afford to send my daughter on a trip."

"Mom said she knew you would say that. She hopes you'll let her do it because it would make her feel more like a parent and she loves the feeling."

Sam had the knack of getting to him and breaking down his defenses the way no one else could except his own daughter.

When he'd first seen Sam in the student center on campus, she'd had *freshman* written all over her. For several days he'd fought his instant attraction to her, yet that hadn't put her off. She'd seen it as a challenge. Who else would have used such a forceful approach and simply drop all her books next to his chair?

Her phone call on Halloween had had the effect of those heavy texts, exploding like a hundred-ton bomb when they reached the floor of the quiet library. *Boom!* There she was in his face again, up close and personal.

He remembered her words—"I've battled with cancer and have won this round, Nick. Will you let me see my daughter?" It had been a fait accompli before he could think of an exit strategy.

If she handled herself in court the same way, the opposition didn't stand a chance. No one did, least of all their vulnerable daughter, who was more like her mother than either of them knew.

Only now was Nick beginning to realize just how similar.

AN ODD NOVEMBER warm spell prompted Samantha's rowing instructor to get everyone out on Coeur

D'Alene lake for one more session before class resumed in the spring. The sun at high noon kept the chill out of the air, but the denuded trees let them know autumn was fast fading into winter.

Samantha hadn't thought she would live to see another one. At this time last year she'd had no hope of meeting her daughter in the flesh. She'd assumed that opportunity would have to wait until the next life.

Now, unbelievably, she was flying to Jackson Hole tomorrow afternoon to be with her adorable Jessica. Nick would be there!

The following weekend she would be taking her daughter to Denver to meet the family. While they were in Colorado, Samantha intended to show her all around the college town of Fort Collins, an hour's drive from Denver.

While she was counting her blessings, she heard the instructor say, "We're coming in to shore. Secure your oars."

In a few minutes everyone had climbed out of the boat and said their goodbyes until next year. Samantha drove Marilyn back to the hospital, where she worked in the pharmacy.

Before her friend got out of the car she turned to Samantha. "I'll be in front of your condo tomorrow at one to take you to the airport."

"Thanks a million, Marilyn."

"You don't need to thank me. I'm so grateful Reed is giving you the time off to come to Phoenix after Thanksgiving, you'll never know. If you're there for the first week, I feel like I can make it through."

"Of course you're going to make it through! You're

a survivor like me!'' She'd decided to take the pastor's words to heart. *Think of this as permanent remission.*

They stared at each other. ''Those are beautiful words, Samantha Bretton. Wouldn't it be amazing if it were true? I'd love to get to know that daughter of yours.''

Samantha brushed tears from her eyes. ''You will. I promise.''

''I'll hold that thought.''

Once her friend got out of the car, Samantha headed to work without stopping at the condo to change clothes. Since she didn't have to see a client until tomorrow morning, she could hibernate in her office for the rest of the day. There was a lot of paperwork to finish up. More importantly, she'd promised Jessica some material for her next school newspaper article.

Ever since she'd learned that Nick had given his permission for their daughter to go to Denver, Samantha's feet hadn't touched the ground.

Before her transplant, she'd bared her soul to her parents where Jessica was concerned. They'd wept tears to realize she'd suffered for so long in silence.

Then the truth came out that they too had grieved, because she was never the same Samantha after that. Their fear grew when none of her relationships with men worked out.

That conversation had acted as a catharsis for her pain. Samantha had learned that her parents had done a lot of soul searching in private. They'd worried about causing irreconcilable damage by forcing her to give up her baby.

Though she'd assured them it had been her decision

when all was said and done, they'd still blamed themselves.

Now that they knew she'd had contact with Jessica, and could see the joy it brought her, they not only accepted this new state of affairs, they were excited and eager to meet their only grandchild. They'd even gone so far as to suggest Samantha invite Nick, too.

Much as she would love to do that, Samantha felt she couldn't. She'd already asked too much of him. Besides everything else, the history between her parents and Nick had all been negative.

Though she already considered him the man she most admired on this earth, her regard for him knew no bounds because he was unselfish enough to let Jessica spend the holiday away from him. Just contemplating his first Thanksgiving without her had to be a wrenching experience.

That's how she knew what a fabulous parent he was. He put Jessica's happiness and welfare above his own. Samantha could only hope she would always do the same, consciously or otherwise.

TWENTY-FOUR HOURS LATER she drove her rental car into Nick's driveway. She'd bought the best baby back ribs she could get from the butcher in Jackson. Now she and Jessica could cook up a storm before they had to be at the high school at seven.

While she was opening the trunk, Nick came out the front door dressed in jeans and a dark-green polo shirt defining his broad shoulders. She was so surprised to see him, she found herself staring and had to look away.

"Hello, Nick." The words sounded breathless, even to her ears.

"Hi. How was your flight?"

"Less bumpy than last time. The weather seems as clear here as in Coeur D'Alene."

"It's been beautiful the last two days. Perfect for tonight's party. Jessica will be relieved to know you made it on time. Her bus hasn't pulled up yet. Let me help you with those groceries."

"Thank you," she whispered. He carried the sacks in the house. With her heart thudding, she followed him into the kitchen. After removing her jacket, she put it over one of the chairs. "Do you mind if I get started cooking? The ribs will take a couple of hours."

"I'll help you. What do you need?"

"A big roasting pan and a large bowl to mix the barbecue sauce."

He pulled the items from the cupboard. "How high do you want the oven?"

"Three hundred fifty degrees."

"Done. What else can I do?"

Go away, Nick.

He wasn't supposed to be here. She couldn't handle it when he was this close to her. It brought back too many memories. From the first moment she'd seen him, she'd wanted him in all the ways a woman could want a man. That hadn't changed.

He smelled good, just the way he used to. He looked good. In fact he looked so much better than good, either he needed to leave right now or she did. This house, this village, this state wasn't big enough to hold both of them. Not the way she was feeling.

"Mom?" Jessica came bursting into the kitchen

from the front door. Sam had been laying out the ribs in the pan. She turned to hug her daughter without using her hands. They both laughed.

"Dad! What are you doing home this early?" Jessica left her mother's arms to give her father a kiss on the cheek. He'd been lounging against the counter with his arms folded, watching Samantha.

"Today I made a concerted effort to be here in case your bus was late."

"It took forever. As soon as I wash my hands, I'll be in to start the cake."

The minute Jessica left the kitchen Nick said, "What time does your plane leave on Sunday?"

Sam's hand shook as she poured the vinegar into the cup. With that one question, she knew he wanted to know her plans because he'd made some of his own. Big ones, depending on Samantha's cooperation. The lucky, lucky woman, whoever she was.

Don't worry, Nick. I'm going to help you out.

"I have to be at the airport at noon, so I'll bring Jessica back here at eleven-thirty. Between now and then I'll try to take perfect care of her, so please feel free to do whatever you want."

For some reason her comment seemed to annoy him, because she could feel a certain tension coming from him. "Jessica can always reach me on my cell phone."

"Of course." Sam opened a couple cans of tomatoes. Why didn't he say this to their daughter? What was he hanging around the kitchen for?

"When are you going to tell her you're recovering from cancer?"

She slowly lifted her head to look at him. So *that's*

why he lingered. He was worried about Jessica's reaction. Naturally he was. Sam had been worrying about it, too.

"I'd planned to have a talk with her after we dropped Cory off at his parents on Sunday morning, but if you don't think it's a good time, please tell me."

He pursed his lips. "There's no good time to have a serious conversation like that."

Jessica had to be told at some point, and he obviously wanted to be there for her because it's the way he was made.

"I tell you what. Sunday morning I'll casually suggest Jessica phone to let you know what time to expect her. That way I'll find out whether some emergency cropped up that prevented you from being available. If that's the case, I won't say anything to her until I'm sure you'll be there to talk to after I've gone, even if it means I have to stay at Grayson's until Monday before flying back to Coeur D'Alene."

He rubbed the back of his neck. "I don't anticipate anything preventing me from being at the house when you bring her home, but—"

"But we both know the unexpected can happen," she interjected. "Last week that semi tried to tunnel through the visitors' center, and you had to be gone all night helping with the cleanup. I understand. So if anything else unforeseen should arise, be assured I'll take care of her."

Nick started to say something, but Jessica chose that moment to come back to the kitchen, ready to get busy cooking. His pewter eyes sent Samantha a private thank-you.

You don't need to thank me for anything, Nick. She

knew how much love and concern he had for their daughter.

More than ever Samantha realized the sacrifice he'd made to let her into Jessica's life. It had been a huge risk that opened all of them up to more hurt and pain, depending on how everything was handled. Yet he'd been willing to do this for Jessica's sake. Samantha's heart ached with love for him.

Their daughter walked him to the door leading to the garage. While he gave her a big hug goodbye she said, "Have fun with Gilly, Dad. Don't worry about Mom and me."

Gilly. What a cute name. No doubt the other woman lived up to it, otherwise Nick wouldn't be interested.

Stop it, Samantha. What Nick did or didn't do had nothing to do with her. She'd lived without him for thirteen years. She could live without him for thirteen more, and thirteen more after that.

"I'd love to be a fly on the wall when you play your duet."

His comment produced a broad smile on Jessica's face. "Nobody knows we're going to do it. We'll perform last. I can't wait!"

"You can tell me all about it on Sunday."

"I promise!"

Samantha refused to watch him leave. It was bad enough he was taking her heart with him. When she heard the garage door open she turned to Jessica. "I forgot that I parked the car in the driveway."

"Don't worry, Mom. It's on the side behind the truck. He takes the Xtera when he goes on a date."

"Do you like this Gilly?" Samantha could have bit-

The Harlequin Reader Service® — Here's how it works:

Accepting your 2 free books and mystery gift places you under no obligation to buy anything. You may keep the books and gift and return the shipping statement marked "cancel." If you do not cancel, about a month later we'll send you 6 additional books and bill you just $4.69 each in the U.S., or $5.24 each in Canada, plus 25¢ shipping & handling per book and applicable taxes if any.* That's the complete price and — compared to cover prices of $5.50 each in the U.S. and $6.50 each in Canada — it's quite a bargain! You may cancel at any time, but if you choose to continue, every month we'll send you 6 more books, which you may either purchase at the discount price or return to us and cancel your subscription.

*Terms and prices subject to change without notice. Sales tax applicable in N.Y. Canadian residents will be charged applicable provincial taxes and GST. Credit or debit balances in a customer's account(s) may be offset by any other outstanding balance owed by or to the customer.

If offer card is missing write to: Harlequin Reader Service, 3010 Walden Ave., P.O. Box 1867, Buffalo NY 14240-1867

NO POSTAGE
NECESSARY
IF MAILED
IN THE
UNITED STATES

BUSINESS REPLY MAIL
FIRST-CLASS MAIL   PERMIT NO. 717-003   BUFFALO, NY

POSTAGE WILL BE PAID BY ADDRESSEE

HARLEQUIN READER SERVICE
3010 WALDEN AVE
PO BOX 1867
BUFFALO NY 14240-9952

Play the Lucky Hearts Game

and get...

2 FREE BOOKS
and a FREE MYSTERY GIFT...
YOURS to KEEP!

yes! I have scratched off the silver card.
Please send me my *2 FREE BOOKS* and
FREE mystery GIFT. I understand that I am
under no obligation to purchase any books as
explained on the back of this card.

Scratch Here!
then look below to see
what your cards get you...
2 Free Books & a Free
Mystery Gift!

▲ DETACH AND MAIL CARD TODAY! ▲

© 2002 HARLEQUIN ENTERPRISES LTD.
® and ™ are trademarks owned and used by the trademark owner and/or its licensee.

336 HDL D34Y   135 HDL D35J

FIRST NAME   LAST NAME

ADDRESS

APT.#   CITY

STATE/PROV.   ZIP/POSTAL CODE   (H-SR-10/04)

Twenty-one gets you
2 FREE BOOKS
and a *FREE MYSTERY GIFT!*

Twenty gets you
2 FREE BOOKS!

Nineteen gets you
1 FREE BOOK!

TRY AGAIN!

Offer limited to one per household and not valid to current Harlequin Superromance® subscribers. All orders subject to approval.

ten her tongue off for asking the question, but it came out of her mouth before she could prevent it.

"Yes. She's really cute."

Nick didn't date cute little freshman girls. Sure he didn't.

It was a good thing Samantha had chosen that moment to pour the contents of the bowl over the ribs because it slipped from her hands. No harm done, thank goodness.

"H-has he been dating her for a while?" she stammered before putting the pan in the oven.

"No." Jessica got the eggs out of the fridge. "He took her out for the first time on Monday when he went over to Yellowstone on business."

Samantha's pulse rocketed. Monday was his first time with the other woman?

"She's a ranger who transferred there from Teton Park after a maniac ranger named Dave Cracroft started harassing her."

"Ooh. That doesn't sound good."

"He's in jail right now waiting to stand trial."

"You're kidding!"

"Nope. He tried to kill Pierce and could have killed Dad at the same time because they were both together when Pierce got shot. It was right after a tornado swept through part of the park."

A shudder rocked Samantha's body.

"You can't believe all the terrible things that happened. Dave tried to get Leslie to go out with him. Then Pierce fired him and everything went wrong."

For the next little while Samantha listened in fascination and horror as her daughter recounted the events surrounding their lives. That horror intensified when she heard about the manhunt for Cracroft, who needed psychiatric help, and how Pierce had captured him.

There was an incident with a grizzly bear in the Teton high country that almost took Dave's leg off. Nick had fired the shot to bring the bear down. Leslie, a former photojournalist, had caught the whole thing on film. The thought of the danger they'd all been in made Samantha shiver again.

"Dave was jealous of Pierce. He accused him of being interested in Gilly and getting her transferred from the park. But Pierce loved his first wife, who'd died in a plane crash, and he never liked any other woman until Leslie came to work as Cory's nanny."

Samantha had already learned how Leslie had ended up in the Tetons. While in hiding from her stalker ex-fiancé, who was a psychopath, she'd fallen in love with Pierce.

Attempting to digest everything Jessica had just told her, Samantha couldn't understand why Nick had waited until last week to start dating the female ranger. If she was so cute, what had taken him so long to ask her out?

For that matter, why wasn't he married? It should have happened a long time ago.

Then she gave a self-deprecating laugh. People had asked her the same question, not only to her face but behind her back. "Why haven't you found a wonderful husband by now? Why is a lovely, intelligent woman like you still alone?"

Samantha knew exactly why she hadn't settled down and never would. She was doomed to love one man who wasn't available to her. That wasn't the case with Nick.

The more Samantha thought about it, the more she decided Nick had stayed single because the love he and their daughter shared was enough. When he wanted a woman like this Gilly, he didn't have to marry her to satisfy his needs.

Nick Kincaid was the kind of man who would always have his pick of women, if that was his desire. But it was obvious he had never let an outside relationship, no matter how intense or involved, infringe on the life he'd built with Jessica.

Maybe he was waiting until their daughter got married before he decided to take a wife. That made the most sense. Nick had a scientific mind. He was a methodical man, the kind who planned and met his goals, never deviating from a course once it was set.

Samantha had never known anyone so resolute in his thinking. Because of that single-mindedness, he'd raised Jessica to be the most wonderful girl in the world.

"Darling? I brought us a present to wear to the sleepover."

Jessica was ready to put the cake in the oven, but they had to wait for the ribs to brown. Her eyes sparkled when she looked at Samantha. "You mean pajamas?"

"You're close. There's a woman who sews for your grandmother from time to time. I asked her to make us old-fashioned matching nightgowns and bed caps like the Ingalls women used to wear in *Little House on the Prairie*."

Jessica let out a shriek of delight. "Where are they?"

"In the sack with handles in the back seat of the car."

"I'll get it!" On her way out of the kitchen she paused long enough to throw her arms around Samantha. "I love you so much, Mom."

"That's only a hundredth part of how much I love you."

"PIERCE?"

The chief was on the phone with another ranger. He took one look at Nick and motioned him inside his office while he finished up the call.

Nick complied and sat down in one of the chairs facing the desk. He'd been out in the field all week and hadn't come into headquarters at all. The place looked pretty much back to normal now that the remodeling was complete, following the accident.

Being a Friday evening, most of the staff had left the building. Pierce was staying on as part of the skeletal crew so he could take all day Saturday as well as Saturday night off to be with his wife.

Thank heaven for Pierce. Nick needed to talk to him or he wasn't going to make it through the next ten minutes, let alone the weekend.

Once Pierce had hung up, he stared at Nick. "You look almost as bad as you did on Halloween. I thought you were on your way to West Yellowstone."

Nick grimaced. "That was the plan. Yesterday afternoon I changed my mind and called off the date with Gilly."

Pierce sat forward in his swivel chair. "How did she take it?"

"Like a trooper. There's something wrong with me, Pierce."

His friend studied him for a long time. "You can't force feelings if they aren't there."

"It's not even about feelings. At this point nothing excites me."

"Since when?"

"I don't know."

"Yes you do. Let's face it. You've never had to share Jessica before. Your whole world has revolved around her. Suddenly you've been given a little time off. Though it was something you've always wanted and needed, you wouldn't be human if you weren't a little hurt that Jessica's so happy with Sam."

"That makes me some kind of a monster, doesn't it."

"No. It makes you human like the rest of us. For thirteen years you've had the sole responsibility for your daughter. Now her mother has entered the picture, giving you a little space. But you don't have anything to fill the void yet."

"*Void* is the right word," Nick muttered. "Here I am floundering, wondering what foot to put in front of the other, while my daughter is off to a party with her mother, having the time of her life. You know what's the irony of all this?" he cried. "I couldn't have gone to that party even if Sam *weren't* in Jessica's life!"

"That's true. Leslie would have taken her, and you would have been content until Jessica came home to give you a debriefing. The difference is, your daughter is making memories with her mother, memories that until now she only made with you. That has to hurt.''

"It does," he admitted. "She's a new person, Pierce. Happier. No matter how hard I tried, I couldn't do that for her.''

"No. Because you're not her mother.''

"My daughter has been transformed by the knowledge that Sam loves her and wants her in her life. How do I get over my anger and jealousy?''

Pierce sat back. "The same way you got over your pain years ago. The same way I got over mine after Linda died. Time is the great healer. Time plus the knowledge deep down in your soul that Jessica's life is better for having Sam in it.''

"Somewhere inside of me I know you're right, but every time I think about Sam and what she did to us…'' Nick couldn't finish the thought.

After a pause Pierce said, "So you still haven't forgiven her.''

Nick put his head down. "I sound like a bastard, don't I.''

"No. You sound like a man who never fell out of love. But before you go on torturing yourself over the fact that she couldn't have loved you and do what she did, just remember one thing.

"Sam was a vulnerable seventeen-year-old girl, not much older than Jessica is right now. She was an only child with an intelligent mind, a daughter doted on and loved by her parents and grandparents. It was asking a lot, maybe the impossible, for her to have gone against their combined advice and wishes.''

Maybe it *was* asking the impossible. Nick buried

his face in his hands, not knowing what to believe anymore.

"Nick?" His head came up. "Do you think your anger goes deeper than Sam?"

"What do you mean?"

"Perhaps you never forgave your parents for dying, and took it out on Sam for refusing to marry you."

That was exactly what it was like. He'd needed her so badly, and she'd shut him out forever, too. "You're in the wrong field of work, Pierce. You should have been a psychiatrist."

His friend's grin was lopsided. "You know what they say about psychiatrists. They can help other people, but when it comes to themselves, they're as clueless as the next person."

"Well, you've given me a hell of a lot to think about. In repayment, I'm sending you home to your wife. I'll stay on duty till morning. There's a pile of paperwork on my desk I need to start plowing through. No time like the present to get it done."

"I can't let you do that." Pierce was trying to pretend the offer didn't excite him, but he failed miserably in the attempt.

"Go on. Get out of here," Nick ordered. "You'll be doing me a big favor and you know it."

"I *do* know it," his friend said. "That's the only reason I'm leaving."

"It's not the only reason," Nick teased him. "But I'm glad you're going willingly, otherwise I might be forced to take drastic steps."

Pierce chuckled before he got up from the chair. "Let's touch base Sunday night."

Sunday night.

Nick looked forward to it and dreaded it at the same time. It was anyone's guess how life at the Kincaid house would be once Jessica heard about her mother's recent illness. No matter what, their daughter was headed for a new emotional crisis.

CHAPTER NINE

AT TEN AFTER ELEVEN Sunday morning, Samantha pulled the rental car into the Gallaghers' driveway. "It's been so much fun, Cory. We'll have to do it again soon."

"Yeah! Thanks!" He got out of the car.

"Bye, Cory!"

"Bye, Jess."

He opened and closed his hand, his manner of waving. Samantha thought he had to be the cutest boy in the world.

When he darted to the front door of the house with his sleeping bag and the games he'd brought with him, Pierce and Leslie were there to open it for him. Lucy bounded out on the porch and jumped all over Cory, licking him. It was a precious sight.

"Thank you!" the Gallaghers called to Samantha.

"You're welcome!" she answered before raising the window.

A final wave and they were off to Nick's house a couple of blocks away. The nice weather had held. It was cold, but beautiful. The Tetons were so gorgeous, she couldn't believe they were real.

"I wish you didn't have to go back to Coeur D'Alene," Jessica mumbled.

If she meant *ever*, then her darling girl wasn't alone.

Samantha's heart constricted with emotion. She loved her daughter so much it hurt. "I know how you feel. But only five days from now we'll be in Denver together. Your grandparents can't wait to meet you, and that's the truth."

"I can't wait to see them, either."

Jessica was such a mature, honest, open, loving girl. She accepted explanations without condemning people. Her positive outlook on life and her ability to forgive were revelations.

Samantha had to hope all those wonderful qualities would help her daughter deal with some news that was going to upset her.

It would be impossible to know how Samantha's confession would affect Jessica. Only time would tell. Unfortunately, Nick would have to bear the brunt of the initial fallout after she left for the airport.

Rather than drive around, Samantha decided to take Jessica home and talk to her in the car. Her daughter's phone call to Nick earlier in the morning indicated he would be there waiting for her.

Once they reached the driveway Samantha set the brake, but she didn't turn off the motor. They needed heat.

"Darling? Before you go in, I want to tell you something about myself." Her daughter's expressive blue eyes flew to hers, alert to some nuance in Samantha's voice. "Almost two years ago I was diagnosed with multiple myeloma, a cancer of the body's plasma."

"You've got *cancer?*" In that moment her daughter seemed to fall apart.

Samantha reached out and took hold of her hand. "It's in remission now."

The tears gushed from her eyes. "What does that mean?"

"It means that my transplant and chemotherapy worked. The cancer has been halted."

"You promise?" she cried, her voice throbbing.

"I wouldn't lie to you."

"Is it gone forever?"

The zero hour had come. "I can't promise that. For some people, it never comes back. I'm hoping I'm one of those people, but no one knows for sure."

Jessica was trembling. "But you don't have it now?"

"No, darling."

Her daughter looked at her as if she didn't believe her. Samantha reached out and pulled her into her arms. "I swear I'm not sick right now," she whispered into her red curls.

Jessica was sobbing. Samantha continued to hold her. "You need to know I'm doing everything possible to keep it from coming back. I have too much to live for. I have a daughter to get to know. We were the hit at talent night, weren't we?"

Jessica wasn't listening. Samantha let her cry it out. News like this, especially when it was your mother, took time to process. That's what Jessica needed. Time, and possibly some professional help if she suffered too long.

Finally she raised her head and sat back on her own side of the car. Her eyes seemed to take up her whole tear-ravaged face. "How did you know you had cancer?"

"I got a pain in my ribs and had it checked out."

"When did it happen?"

"A year ago last February."

"Was it awful?" she whispered in a shaky voice.

"Yes."

"Were you supposed to die?"

"Yes."

"But then you didn't?"

"No."

"How come?" She sounded like Cory just then.

Samantha took a deep breath. "No one knows the answer to that. It could be because of a lot of reasons. I'd like to believe my body is good at fighting disease. I inject myself with medicine to keep the protein down, and I've been doing things to help me stay mentally and physically strong."

"Like what?"

For the next few minutes Samantha told her about her martial arts and rowing classes, her meditation sessions, the qigong therapy.

"You've done all that?"

"All that." Samantha nodded. "I have good friends who are also recovering. We do things together to stay positive."

"Is your friend Marilyn one of them?"

The whole truth, Samantha. "She's my best friend, and she's still fighting her cancer."

Jessica looked sick. Her face went whiter. "When did you get better?"

"About a month ago my blood test showed my protein level was back to normal."

Samantha watched as her daughter continued to digest everything in her mind. Suddenly she cried, "Oh my gosh! You're going to be late for your plane! Pop the trunk so I can get my things!''

Before Samantha could tell her not to worry about the time, Jessica scrambled from the car. ''Thanks for everything, Mom!'' she said before hurrying around to the rear end.

Nick must have been watching from the window because he came out of the front door with a solemn expression that gave his rugged features a slightly chiseled look.

Just as Samantha slid from the driver's seat to help, Jessica darted toward the house juggling two pans, her suitcase and her sleeping bag. She whipped past her father as if he weren't standing there, and disappeared into the house.

Their eyes met. Nick looked ill. Samantha's heart almost failed her as he stepped over to the car ''What do you want me to do? Shall I stay or go?''

He closed the trunk. ''Go.''

Samantha had never felt so helpless in her life.

''I HATE MY MOTHER, Dad! I never want to see her again!''

While Nick had waited for the endless weekend to be over, he'd imagined every reaction from his daughter but this one.

He'd honestly thought she would say that she wanted to live with Sam from here on out because no one knew how much longer her mother had before the cancer might come back.

For the last thirty-six hours he'd been searching his soul to see if he had what it took to let his daughter go if that was her deepest desire. The thought of shared custody greatly pained him, but Jessica had to come first here.

He'd assumed there would be the inevitable side effect of Jessica fearing she might get cancer, too, since she was Sam's daughter. So many worries had bombarded him.

Yet this strange reaction was something he hadn't considered when he'd made up his list of possible traumatic scenarios. Naturally her emotions were violent at the moment. He'd expected that. But he hadn't imagined that his daughter could say she hated Sam and didn't want to see her again.

That didn't make any sense to him, unless she was more his child than he'd realized. He thought of last Friday night, when Pierce had asked him if anger over his parents' death had compounded his pain when Sam wouldn't marry him.

Perhaps Jessica couldn't forgive Sam for not marrying him, thereby denying her the chance to live with a mother and father like all her friends. Perhaps that was where her anger was coming from.

Nick was a scientist and he tried to look at this situation objectively. Some ingredient was missing in this experiment. Some essential element that would change the whole equation. He would have to be patient and work it again and again until he discovered what it was.

He rubbed Jessica's back while she sobbed her heart out on the bed. They'd been here many times before in their lives, each one seeming the darkest to his daughter. But this time was different.

"She doesn't love me, Dad."

Jessica sounded so heartbroken he was at a loss

what to say. Since he patently knew that statement wasn't true, all he could do was continue to watch and wait for the elusive piece of information to manifest itself.

"I'm not going to Denver," she declared. "I don't want to meet my grandparents. Will you call her tonight and tell her for me?" Her question came out half muffled by the pillow.

"Why didn't you tell her that yourself while you were in the car?" Nick prodded.

"There wasn't time."

He didn't buy that. "She would have stayed over another night."

"I didn't want her to. I wanted her to leave."

After a long silence he said, "I'll do whatever you want, honey."

"Thanks, Dad. I love you so much!" She sat up and hugged him hard enough to squeeze the air out of his lungs. "I'm glad she's gone. We'll go back to being just the two of us. We never needed anybody else."

My adorable little liar. If Jessica could see her own glittering smile, the pain in her eyes.

"Let's drive to West Yellowstone and have an early dinner at the Lariat Hotel!" She rolled away from him and got off the bed. "I'll pay with my baby-sitting money." The same money she'd been going to use to pay for Sam's hotel room two weeks ago?

Nick made a path through his hair with his fingers while he watched her pull some bills from the top drawer of her dresser. She slid them in the pocket of her jeans.

He knew agony drove his daughter's abrupt movements. He had to do something to alleviate the worst of it. Maybe a drive *was* a good idea.

"I'm ready to go whenever you are."

"Great! Give me a sec."

While she headed for the bathroom, he grabbed his cell phone and jacket, then locked up the house.

She joined him in the kitchen wearing her jacket. Together they walked out to the car and took off.

He knew better than to ask about the party. All the joy his daughter had experienced with her mother over the weekend had been canceled out in the last hour by the news that Sam was a cancer survivor.

Cancer…the terrible word. One many people in the twentieth century didn't even dare say aloud. Some people thought if you had it, it meant you were bad in some way. The disease was shrouded in mystery. Nick's own great-aunt hadn't been able to talk about it; she'd referred to it as "*that* disease."

Jessica was a product of the twenty-first century, yet cancer still struck such fear in her heart, she couldn't deal with it.

At some point they would have to talk about it, but right now his daughter was like a trout in the Snake River. One minute the innocent thing had come up to the surface for a meal. In the next instant a hook had grabbed her by the throat. Going into survival mode, she was taking the line out as far it would go.

Nick would have to reel her in, but with great care and skill, to make sure he could remove the hook without damaging her more than she already was.

She broke the silence some time later on the outskirts of West Yellowstone. "How was your date with Gilly?"

"I called it off."

"I thought you might."

He lifted one brow in surprise. "How come?"

"If you'd wanted to take her out, you would have done it a long time ago. The only reason you went to lunch with her was to stop me from hoping you and Mom might get back together."

Good grief.

"Admit that's what you thought I would want, Dad. You were single. She hadn't married. It was perfect."

The blood pounded in Nick's ears.

"But you don't need to worry—I don't have any big dream like that. Mom didn't love you enough to marry you the first time, and she didn't love me enough to bring me those albums before she got cancer.

"She had to be dying to do that. Even then, it took her pastor to open up her conscience while she was lying in that hospital bed. It was his job not to let her die until he could tell her how to make things right with the baby she'd abandoned. He probably told my grandparents they'd better shape up, too, since they're getting real close to dying.

"Now I know what my Sunday school teacher meant about deathbed repentance. It doesn't work because it's too late. Mom is thirteen years too late to tell me she's sorry," his daughter declared, dry-eyed.

The essential element had just surfaced. Nick's patience had won out.

He pulled off to the side of the road beneath some pines, where a couple of squirrels were playing, and turned to his daughter. Her profile could have been carved out of granite.

"Jessica? Look at me."

When she complied, he barely recognized the hard veneer.

"You've got everything right except for two things."

"What?" she retorted abruptly.

"Her pastor didn't visit her in the hospital. When he happened to stop by her condo, your mother was already in remission."

Jessica gave a little gasp and her chin started to quiver. The first sign of a crack.

"When she told him she'd won her bout with cancer, he advised her that if she had anything left in her life to resolve, to do so. That it might make her so happy, her spirit would fight to keep her cancer from coming back. That's when she called me. Would you like to hear what she wanted to say to the pastor?"

His daughter slowly nodded.

"'I want to go back thirteen years to that hospital room and beg you to bring our daughter to me so we can be a family, Nick.'"

Jessica bit her lip. "What did you tell her?"

"That it was too late."

"What did she say then?"

Nick would never forget. "Your mom said, 'I know, but I had to take the risk. Thank you for not cutting me off. Tonight when you're kissing your children, give Jessica an extra squeeze. She won't know it's from me, but *I* will.'"

Sam had said some other things too. Private things meant only for his ears.

"For thirteen years your mother honored her promise to me to stay away, even though you and I both know it was the last thing she wanted to do.

"When she realized she was going to die, she could have asked her parents to find me. She could have begged me to bring you to the hospital so she could look at you one time before she died. But she didn't do that because she knew it would be utterly cruel and unfair to you.

"It wasn't until a miracle happened and she'd been given a second chance at life that the pastor's words gave her the courage to approach me. Even though she knew it would be breaking the law, so to speak, that's how strong her drive was—the drive of a mother wanting to be with her child."

Tears glistened in Jessica's eyes, removing the last trace of the veneer that had made her look so foreign to him.

"She didn't seek you out simply to tell you she was sorry for giving you up, Jessica. She wants to be your mother in every sense of the word, but she can't promise you she'll live forever. Her greatest concern was that you know the truth about her medical history in case the disease comes back."

"Do you think it will?"

Nick had asked himself that question too many times in the last few weeks. "No one knows the answer. We have to live by faith."

After a troubling silence, Jessica murmured, "Dad? I'm sorry if I hurt you when I said she didn't love you enough to marry you. I didn't mean it."

He reached out to tousle her curls. "I know you didn't, honey. But it's the one thing you said that *is* the truth. And I'm convinced the only reason she hasn't married before now is because she has been grieving over you.''

''Are you still in love with her?''

He'd been waiting for that question. ''No,'' he said without hesitation. ''I *can't* be. Love has to be fed. The question is, do you want your mother as a permanent fixture in your life? She told you the truth about herself today so you could make up your mind once and for all. But Sam's a big girl now. If you decide you only want to see her when *you* feel like it, she'll understand. If you determine it would be too painful to continue the relationship with her, then she's prepared to leave you alone. It's up to you where things go from here.''

''Honestly?''

Nick thought he understood what she was really asking. Though it would kill him, it was up to him to help her out. ''Honestly. Even if it means you would like to live with her for a while to make up for lost time.''

''You would let me do that?'' she cried.

His gaze had returned to the road. ''Whatever brings you the most happiness.''

''Dad? Could we just get a hamburger and then head home? I want to call Mom. She should be at her condo by the time we get back to Moose.''

Though Nick realized she would always harbor fear in terms of her mom's ability to fight off cancer, it seemed Jessica's fundamental concerns had been about a mother's love. With everything straight in his daughter's mind at last, there would be no stopping her.

How was he going to handle it when she decided

to move to Coeur D'Alene for a while? Nick's chest felt as if a giant boulder was inside it, the kind that came crashing down the mountain when the earth suddenly shifted beneath the Grand Teton.

IT WAS DARK by the time they reached the house. While Jessica rushed to her room to phone Sam, Nick closed the door to his bedroom to call Pierce on his cell phone. His friend picked up on the second ring.

"Nick?"

"Thank heaven you answered."

"I was expecting a call from you before now."

"Jessica and I have been to West Yellowstone and back."

"Then she's in worse shape than I feared."

"For once you're wrong. I'm afraid *I'm* the one falling apart here. Can you talk?"

"As long as you want."

Without preamble Nick told him everything. "I wouldn't be surprised if Jessica asks to move to her mom's after Thanksgiving to finish out the school year there."

"Did Sam say anything about that?"

"No. I'm reading between lines. But I know my daughter, Pierce. All the signs are there. She's got big plans. That's why I'm calling you. How would you feel if I took a leave of absence from the park until June?"

He could almost hear his friend mulling everything over. "Are you thinking of transferring to another park on a temporary basis?"

"You're reading my mind. Great Smoky Mountains National Park is having a problem with the inroad of rainbows and browns on the brook trout. That's one of my areas of expertise. I could work out a trade with another ranger who would live in my house, I'd live in his."

"You know I'd fix anything for you, Nick, but I think you're jumping the gun here."

"Maybe. But if I'm right, I need to have a backup plan in place or I'm not going to make it."

"I hear you. I had my own backup plan when Cory was being so difficult. If he hadn't learned to love Leslie, I would have been forced to move us to my parents' house in Ashton." A deep sigh escaped his throat. "I tell you what. Tomorrow I'll put out a feeler and see what happens."

"I knew I could count on you."

"For what it's worth, I'm hoping you're wrong about everything. Temporary or not, our whole family will be devastated if you and Jessica leave. To lose my best friend, even for a season..."

"Now you know how I felt when you told me you might have no choice but to leave the park."

"Dad?"

Nick got up from the bed. "I've got to go. Thanks for being there for me, Pierce. Talk to you tomorrow." He hung up.

"Come on in, honey."

The door opened. Jessica's face was as alive as a bubbling Christmas tree light. "Mom's on the phone. She wants to talk to you."

Steeling himself for what was coming, he reached for the receiver by the side of his bed. "Hello, Sam."

"Nick—" Every time she said his name in that breathless voice, it took him back thirteen years and nailed him to the spot. "Is Jessica on the phone with you?"

His daughter was standing right next to him. "No."

"Then I'll make this quick. Jessica seems to have taken the news better than I thought she would. Tell me the truth. Is it an act?"

"No."

"Thank heaven," she whispered. "Are you still all right about her coming to Denver for Thanksgiving?"

"Yes."

"I'll prepay her ticket and let you know the details of her flight in a few days."

"That'll be fine."

"Nick?"

"Yes?"

"I understand you'll be in Gillette with your cousins for the weekend, but Jessica is hoping you'll meet us in Fort Collins on Saturday so we can show her around."

Sam's suggestion that he join them in Colorado was such a far cry from his assumption that she wanted to discuss Jessica living with her, the shock of it staggered him.

"She's afraid to broach the subject for fear you'll say no, so I told her I would ask you. From her viewpoint it's understandable she would like to be with both of us when she sees where we once lived and dated. I realize it's unorthodox, but since our relationship was unique, anyway, does it really matter? In order to satisfy our daughter's curiosity, would you be interested in doing this for her sake? I've never been back. Have you?"

He swallowed hard. "No."

"We could stay overnight at a hotel and drive to Denver on Sunday to catch our flights. Will you think about it and let me know?"

Jessica was watching his face, studying his expression. If she'd put her mother up to this as some kind of test, and he said no, his daughter might think he hadn't meant it when he'd told her he wasn't in love with Sam.

As for Sam, she would have seen through Jessica's manipulations, but was in the unenviable position of not wanting to thwart their daughter in any way yet. Especially when Jessica had handled the news about her medical condition as well as she had.

Nick understood that the reality of Sam being united with their daughter was still too new, too sweet and heady to start setting limits.

But when the trip was over, the two of them would have to establish ground rules so Jessica wouldn't be able to get away with this again.

"I don't have to think about it, Sam. The answer is yes. I'll let you and Jessica make the arrangements. Here she is." He handed his daughter the phone.

He couldn't tell if the smile Jessica flashed him was one of relief or of secret satisfaction. Maybe it was a combination of both. She was starting to remind him of the Sam who'd once beguiled him.

He headed for the kitchen. Though he was craving a beer, he opted for cola. The last thing he wanted was for Jessica to see him drinking something stronger than soda and jump to the conclusion that he wasn't as in control of his emotions as he pretended to be.

But the minute he pulled it from the fridge and popped the lid, he realized he was allowing what his daughter might or might not think to manipulate him again. Hell—if he felt like a beer, he was going to have one.

He set the can down with a jolt, spilling cola on the countertop.

"What's wrong, Dad?"

Muttering under his breath, Nick wheeled around to discover his daughter in the entry dressed in a white gown and nightcap, like something from the pioneer days.

"Do you like it?" She came all the way into the kitchen and modeled it for him. She looked charming, adorable.

"I love it, honey."

"Mom had these made for us."

A vision of Sam in the same outfit ran through his mind, setting his pulse pounding without his permission. "I bet nobody's sleepwear at the party was as original."

"Nope."

"How did the duet go over?"

"Mom said we were sensational."

Nick could imagine. "Is that what you thought, too?"

She nodded. "All the mothers wanted the recipe for the barbecued ribs and the cake. Mom wrote them out without needing to look anything up."

"Does that surprise you?"

She grinned. "No. Mom's amazing. She knows more stuff about environmental issues than anyone else. When everyone found out what she did for a living, they wouldn't leave her alone.

"She and Pam Royter's mom got talking about the

snowmobile problem in the parks. Mrs. Royter asked her to come and speak to the Wyoming Sierra Club meeting in Sheridan the weekend after Thanksgiving.''

He took a swig of cola. ''Your mother's a busy attorney. I doubt she'd be able to get away for something like that unless it was planned months ahead of time.''

''Mom said she would have come, but she has to be in Phoenix that weekend.''

''Phoenix?''

Jessica's expression sobered. ''Her best friend, Marilyn May, is recovering from breast cancer and is going in for another chemo treatment. She wants Mom to be there.''

This time when he set the can down, cola burst out of it like an eruption from Old Faithful geyser.

CHAPTER TEN

SAMANTHA'S SENSE OF having done this before was so strong, her body felt weak as she, Jessica and Nick got out of the rental car and started walking around the corner to the Lory Student Center in Fort Collins.

It was eight-thirty, not ten o'clock on a cold winter night. It was the Thanksgiving recess, not the end of exam week before Christmas vacation. But in all other ways, tonight was like the night when the word *happiness* had been erased from Samantha's vocabulary.

This was the painful part.

Up until now the three of them had enjoyed driving around Fort Collins. They'd visited favorite old haunts—the schools Samantha had attended growing up, the building where her father had had his law firm, the Hilan Apartments, where Nick had lived. The campus building where he'd worked as a security guard, Samantha's former home, her friends' houses, the reservoir where they'd picnicked and water-skied. *And made love.*

But her father had sold their family's thirty-five-foot luxury cruiser when they'd moved to Denver. No evidence remained at the marina to remind her or Nick of those stolen hours of rapture in the bedroom of the cruiser her parents had never used. Only Jessica herself, the fruit of their union.

"Where were you sitting when Mom dropped her books, Dad?"

Samantha turned toward the spot where Nick was looking. A few students were studying, but the basement wasn't as full as usual.

He walked over to the table in question and put his hand on the empty chair. It probably wasn't the same one, but it could have been.

The only difference between then and now was the fact that Nick was thirteen years older, more attractive than ever in his sheepskin jacket, and Samantha was more in love with him than she'd thought possible. The pain of loving him and not being able to do anything about it was almost unbearable.

Nick flicked his gaze to hers. His eyes weren't as dark as a thunderhead or as silvery as a cloud's lining. Their color was somewhere in between, which told her little about what he was really thinking. "I would say we've done it all."

"Except for our favorite dessert, I agree."

A smile twisted his mouth, making Samantha's insides flutter as if a hummingbird were trying to escape. "Let's go."

He drove them to the Cache-Poudre strip mall, where the name of the shop was different, but the ice cream was still the same—rich and velvety. The three of them ordered double fudge with marshmallow.

Thanks to Jessica, the day had been spun out to its maximum length. Now it was time for everyone to go to bed. Samantha's spirit rebelled, but there wasn't anything she could do about it.

Outside the hotel room mother and daughter shared,

Jessica kissed her father good-night before running inside, claiming she was anxious to take a shower.

Nick's room was across the hall. To Samantha's surprise, he lingered at the door. "She's as transparent as glass."

Samantha chuckled softly. "You know what they say about a child's dreams."

His eyes played over her features. He seemed to be looking for something that was eluding him. "It didn't take much to make our world go round back then, did it?"

A flood of emotions swamped her. "No. Those months were the happiest of my life."

"And mine." His voice sounded husky. "What do you say we complete the picture for her? For old time's sake," he added. "Come here, Sam."

Suddenly her legs felt like mush. "I don't think—"

But that was as far as she got before he pulled her into his strong arms. "If you've forgotten how, don't worry about it. You didn't seem to have a problem the night I kissed you outside the center. I'm sure it'll come back to you with a little practice."

"Nick—" she cried before his mouth closed over hers. At the first touch of his lips, a voluptuous warmth stole through her. She'd dreamed about this so many times, it seemed like an extension of her desires.

Her mind had never forgotten anything about him. Neither had her mouth or body, which molded to his in the old, remembered way.

It was a revelation to Samantha that a decade and more had gone by without any contact, yet here they were, embracing like young lovers who'd never been apart. But there was one difference. Nick was kissing her with more primitive force than she remembered, a kind of refined savagery that reminded her they weren't kids anymore.

She felt anger in his kiss, too. That was a new element.

Only one person could have put it there. Pain and guilt over what she'd done to destroy their perfect love drove her to tear her lips from his.

She lowered her head, afraid to look into his eyes and read the accusation there. "Thank you for a wonderful day, Nick. Good night."

Relieved to go inside the room and shut the door, she lay against it while she attempted to catch her breath. She had an idea Jessica had been a spectator, but her daughter knew how to be discreet and was giving her the space she needed.

On Thanksgiving night Samantha's mother hadn't been as subtle. "You're still in love with Nick, aren't you," she'd said.

"Yes."

"Is there any chance…?"

"No, Mom. No chance at all. You don't do what I did to Nick and expect him to go on loving me."

Today's visit to Fort Collins had been the result of Jessica's manipulations. They may have taken a walk through the past for their daughter's sake, but that kiss at the door had been for Samantha's sake. Nick's way of letting her know she'd ruined something so precious they could never get it back.

"But after all this time he's still single, honey. Doesn't that tell you anything?"

"Yes. That he has devoted his life to Jessica and his career. And obviously he has forgiven me enough to let me have a relationship with our daughter. Her happiness is the most important thing to him. But Nick's still young, Mom. Only thirty-three. Some men don't marry until their thirties or forties. One of these days, when the time is right, he'll fall hard for a woman, maybe even start another family. But he'll make sure his daughter is happy and secure first.''

There was a long silence before her mother said, ''Did you speak to Nick about some sort of arrangement so Jessica can spend part of the year with you in Coeur D'Alene?''

The minute she raised the subject, Samantha disabused her of the notion. ''No, Mom. They're too close. Jessica would never be happy away from her father except for a short holiday visit like the one we're having now. No matter how much she loves me, Nick will always come first with her.''

Nick was their daughter's raison d'être. Her hero. Samantha could never be envious of that fact or resent it. Little did Jessica know he was Samantha's raison d'être, too. He always would be.

''One thing I've learned about Nick in the short time we've been together is that it would kill something inside him if he had to let her go for any length of time.''

Her mother's eyes grew dim. ''Your father and I should have given our permission for you to marry him. We should have helped give you and Nick the best start possible, especially with Jessica on the way.''

Samantha hugged her tightly. ''Don't do this to yourself. It's not your fault. I would have married him if he'd ever talked about marriage before I told him we were going to have a baby. I didn't want to end up like Brenda's sister."

"We know now that you wouldn't have," her mother said with tears in her eyes. "Nick has been a superb father. Jessica's such a marvelous girl. Your dad adores her."

"As I told you on the phone, Jessica's a gift. I want to be worthy of her love and Nick's trust. That's why I'll never take advantage of the situation."

"You're as noble as Nick."

"No, Mom."

"Yes, and so courageous in ways that still astound me. I'm proud to be your mother. I love you, darling."

"I love you, too. Did you know Jessica's already crazy about you? She's convinced your genes are the reason she decided to join the newspaper staff.

"I happen to know she's going to read all those novels you're sending home with her. She wants to be able to connect with you on your level. At the mother-and-daughter party, she bragged about her grandmother Bretton's post-graduate degree in English literature. You would have loved it, Mom."

Their weekend had been glorious. On Friday Jessica had gone to the country club with her grandfather for lunch. Then he'd taken her downtown to his law firm to show her around—just the two of them.

Friday night the whole family had visited with the great-grandparents, who'd come to Thanksgiving dinner the day before. The weekend had been a voyage of discovery for Jessica and a time of great happiness for the Bretton household.

But Samantha's happiness was marred by the day in Fort Collins spent with Jessica and Nick, which had turned bittersweet with one kiss. It had been the fitting end of a visit to where their great love affair had begun and flourished until Samantha had ruined everything.

After today's experience, she felt it was possible for them to be friends for Jessica's sake.

It was more than Sam could have ever hoped for. Therefore she had no right to be upset that tomorrow Jessica and her father would go back to the Tetons, and she wouldn't be seeing them for another couple of weeks.

Marilyn needed her in ways no one could understand unless they'd been fighting cancer, too. Samantha wanted, needed to be there for her friend, but already she felt the ache of separation from the two people she loved most in this world.

A FRESH BLANKET OF SNOW had turned Jackson and the whole Teton range into a fairyland. Before Nick did anything else, he had to clean a ton of white stuff off the Xtera sitting in the airport's short-term parking area.

Once they drove out to the connecting road, he noticed few cars were moving. The plows had yet to clear the highway.

Halfway to Moose his cell phone went off.

"I bet that's Mom."

Nick's heart raced at the mention of Sam. With the taste of her lips still fresh on his, he couldn't think, couldn't concentrate. "It's Pierce," he said after checking his ID. His friend had amazing timing. Disappointment swept through him that it wasn't Sam.

"Oh." Jessica sounded just as upset.

"Her flight left Denver after ours, honey. She'll call when she can."

He had no idea if Coeur D'Alene had been hit by the same storm. No doubt his daughter was picturing her mother knee-deep in snow with no one to help her. The hell of it was, since their plane had landed, that same picture had been emblazoned in Nick's mind.

For so many years he hadn't known where Sam lived, and he'd long ago convinced himself he didn't care. Now that he *did* know where to find her, he still shouldn't care and it still shouldn't matter. Not after the way she'd abruptly broken off that kiss—a kiss he'd needed so badly, he'd risked everything for it.

He was damn sure she hadn't given him a second thought after waving them off at the airport with a cheery goodbye!

For Jessica's sake she'd walked through that doorway to the past with him yesterday. During the long, excruciatingly painful ordeal, she'd exhibited a sangfroid he would have given anything to possess.

Such composure, feigned or real, had to be dynamite in the courtroom. The opposition wouldn't know what was going on in her head.

Nick clicked on after the fourth ring and said hello.

"Uh-oh. The trip to Fort Collins should never have happened."

Nick gritted his teeth "You've got that right."

"Where are you?"

"Eight minutes from home."

"Why don't you and Jess stop by our house first? Because of the storm, Leslie's sister and her family decided to fly back east tomorrow. The kids would love it if Jess came over. While they're playing in the snow, you and I can talk. Much as the selfish part of me doesn't want to tell you this, the feeler I put out has produced results if you're still interested.''

''More than ever.''

''That's what I was afraid of,'' his friend muttered. ''See you in five. Thanks.'' He hung up.

Jessica regarded him with curious eyes. ''What's going on?''

''Pierce wants us to drop by on our way home. Leslie's family won't be going back to New Jersey for another day. Cory needs you to help him and his cousins build a snowman.''

She studied him closely. ''You and Pierce were talking about something else.''

Her radar was lethal. ''It's just ranger business, honey.''

''What kind?'' she persisted.

Might as well lay the groundwork now. ''Remember a few years ago when I recommended keeping minimum flows instream for cutthroat trout habitat? To make sure they didn't get on the endangered species list?''

''Sort of.''

''Well, there's a ranger like myself working in Great Smoky Mountains National Park who's having problems because there's an inroad of non-native trout endangering the brook trout. Since the plan I instigated seems to be working, maybe I can help *him* out.''

''Clear back in Tennessee?''

Yup. Clear back and far away from your mother. New scenery. New people. New women.

Nick expelled the breath he'd been holding. After kissing Sam, after feeling her warm, curvy body in his arms again, the idea that any other woman could fulfill him wasn't in the realm of possibility.

"Would you have to go there?"

Jessica displayed curiosity, not anxiety. Since Sam's appearance, a monumental change had come over his daughter.

"I couldn't do much good from here. Assessing the impact and extent of a species invasion requires hands-on experience before coming up with a solution. I'd have to determine how many of what species are present in the water, what habitats they occupy and what they eat, their rate of propagation and so forth."

"How long do you think it would take?"

"That's hard to say. Six months maybe?" At this point he was swimming in deep waters.

"When would you have to go?"

Nick paused. "That all depends on you."

Her eyes widened. "I'm ready whenever you are. It would be cool to go to school in Tennessee. I've never been there."

Nick almost lost control of the car. "What about your mother?"

"She'll fly out to see me on weekends and holidays, so it doesn't matter where I am."

Until she wants you with her for longer than a few days at a time.

They'd just pulled into the Gallaghers' driveway. Pierce had already cleared it with the snow blower and was now working on a path to the front door.

Cory left the big ball of snow he was rolling with his cousins, and came running over to the car, with Lucy in pursuit.

Maybe Pierce was right and Nick had jumped the

gun on this one, but these were early days yet. Who knew how things would change once Sam got back from Phoenix?

"Honey? Don't mention this to anyone yet. I'm only toying with the idea."

"I won't. Does that mean you don't want Mom to know, either?"

Naturally, a mother was different.

"I would never presume to tell you what to discuss with her."

Jessica leaned over to kiss his cheek, then opened the door and jumped out. Whatever was on her mind, she didn't intend to share it with him. Nick watched the other children drag her through the snow. Their shrieks of excitement resounded in his aching heart.

"TEN DAYS SINCE THE CHEMO and you're sitting around the pool eating watermelon. I think you're a fraud, Marilyn May."

Samantha's friend smiled from her chair beneath the umbrella. "The nausea's gone."

"What about the weakness?"

"I'm feeling stronger today. Maybe not quite enough for rowing."

"Come spring and you will be."

Marilyn stared hard at her. "I've decided to stay in Phoenix and work at a pharmacy here, but you're the first person I'm telling."

Samantha had seen it coming. "Your family's going to be overjoyed."

She nodded. "Knowing you've united with your daughter makes me realize we have to take advantage of these second chances we've been given. I've lived away from home long enough.''

''I'm going to miss you,'' Samantha whispered.

''I'll miss you, too, but there's always the phone and weekend visits.'' Her friend studied her closely for a moment. ''Something's going on with you, Samantha. I've sensed it for a couple of days. Don't hold back on me because you think I'm too sick. I'm not, and even if I were, it wouldn't matter. We've been through too much together to keep secrets.''

The tears Samantha had been suppressing ran down her cheeks. ''Oh, Marilyn. I'm so afraid.''

''Of what?''

In a burst of emotion, she told her about the trip to Fort Collins and Nick's fiery kiss at the door. ''Now he's thinking of transferring to Great Smoky Mountains National Park in Tennessee.''

Marilyn blinked. ''When?''

She wiped the moisture off her face. ''Soon, I think.''

''How long have you known about this?''

''Since the night I called Jessica to make sure she got home from Denver safe and sound.''

''This has been on your mind for almost two weeks and you never said anything about it until now? Shame on you,'' Marilyn chastised her, but she said it with all the affection in the world.

''I couldn't do that to you.''

''Well, I'm well enough now, so tell me—did Jessica say he'd been thinking about it for a long time, or did it come out after kissing you?''

''I don't honestly know. But I'm sure the idea of leaving the Tetons never entered his head until I came along and destroyed the beautiful world he'd created for him and Jessica.''

''You know better than that, Samantha Bretton. As you've told me so many times, he's a scientist who never acts impulsively. He considers all the possibilities first before carefully making a move. There's no way he would have told his daughter you wanted to meet her if he hadn't thought it all through first and decided it was for the best. He knew the risk he was facing, and he took it.

''Sounds like he decided to take another risk and kiss you to see if the old fire was still there.'' She cocked her head. ''Was it?''

''You know it was! I couldn't believe I was back in his arms again, but the longer the kiss went on, the more I could feel an edge to it.''

''Hunger, you mean? Longing for what you took away from him?''

''No, Marilyn. It was anger.''

Her friend's eyes trapped hers. ''Are you sure? Or are you just assuming everything, like you've always done?''

''I don't think so. Otherwise why would he be ready to pull up roots and move to the other side of the continent?''

''What did Jessica tell you, exactly?''

''That another ranger hasn't been able to solve a problem with the native fish being eradicated. They need someone with Nick's expertise to go there and help. It could take six months.''

''Then it's just a temporary thing.''

Samantha shook her head. ''No, it isn't. Nick might

have told Jessica that to pacify her, but I know what it means. For once his nobility has backfired on him.''

"What do you mean?"

"Isn't it obvious? He isn't as ready to share Jessica with me as he thought he was," she cried in pain. "I never meant to cause all this trouble, Marilyn. Now I don't know what to do.

"Jessica assumes I'll fly out to Tennessee to be with her every weekend. You should hear the plans she's made. Yet that's exactly what Nick is hoping to avoid by moving so far away. I'm sure he's thinking along the lines of a once-a-month visit.

"So far he's been civil to me, but if I try to satisfy my daughter's wishes, he'll end up despising me, and could stop the visits altogether. The trouble is, if I don't fly out there every Friday night, Jessica's going to think I didn't mean it when I told her she was my life.''

"You're jumping to conclusions. In the first place, he hasn't gone anywhere yet. And if he does, it could be a case of him really being needed for a temporary period. It's possible the decision has nothing at all to do with you. He might even welcome your help if he has to work long hours on the weekends, too, and doesn't know people he can trust to be with Jessica.''

"Possible, but not probable, Marilyn. This was no coincidence. Nick loves the Tetons. He and Pierce Gallagher are close, like you and me. It's where he has made his home with Jessica. Nothing in the world except a threat to his happiness could make him leave paradise, because that's what it is.''

She buried her face in her hands. "I've posed an

enormous threat, and now I don't know what to do about it.''

''Don't do anything. Haven't you and I both learned that after we've done all we can do, the rest is up to providence? Leave it alone for now. You act as if you're guilty of something.''

At that remark Samantha's head came up. ''What do you mean?''

''Jessica came into this world because two people loved each other. You behave as if you're the one wholly responsible for everything that happened.''

''I am, Marilyn.'' Her voice hardened. ''I'm the one who lied to Nick. I'm the one who begged him to make love to me.''

''I *knew* it!'' Marilyn sat forward. ''You're still stuck in that old groove. Listen to yourself! You talk as if Nick didn't have a say in the matter. What is it going to take to convince you he could have told you *no?* This paragon you've put on a pedestal had a weakness. It was *you!* As far as I'm concerned it's still you. Why else would he have put his heart on the line once again to kiss you outside your hotel room door? So help me, Samantha, if you tell me you're to blame for *that,* then I'm going to pick you up and throw you in the pool!''

The idea that Marilyn would try it in her condition was so ludicrous, Samantha started to laugh.

Her friend grinned. ''What do you know. I think we've achieved a breakthrough.''

''Of sorts,'' Samantha conceded. ''I'll admit I didn't put a gun to his head.''

''All right—we're making progress. Now let's take that thought a little further. No gun was pointed at his head when he told Jessica you were trying to make contact with her.''

She sucked in her breath. ''Agreed.''

''In other words, he acted as a free agent where the most important decisions of his life were concerned.''

''You've got me there, counselor.''

''*So…* it makes no sense that he suddenly wants to zap himself and Jessica to the other end of the universe unless he's falling in love with you all over again. Be honest with me. You're the one who stopped kissing him before he was ready to let you go, right?''

Samantha bit her lip. ''Yes.''

''Which means you were exhibiting perfect Bretton form.''

''What do you mean?''

''You know exactly what I mean. The same Bretton form he remembered in that hospital room. A woman without an Achilles' heel.''

Samantha averted her eyes.

''I realize that sounded cruel,'' Marilyn murmured. ''I only said it because I love you like a sister. Don't you know I want you to see the situation for what it might be? But you can't do that without taking off the blinders. I thought it was time I helped you do that.''

''And I thought I was here to help *you.*''

ON FRIDAY AFTERNOON Nick trained his binoculars on two skiers he'd sighted above the Gros Ventre Campground area. The only way they could be on that slope was if they'd been airlifted in by helicopter earlier in the day. He'd climbed from his truck and walked to the spot where it would land to pick them up.

Last winter a law had been passed limiting forest

service commercial helicopter permits so there'd be no overflights of the Teton range. The wolverine and lynx populations used this portion of the high mountain territory for denning.

Somebody had deliberately broken the rules. He would wait until the helicopter landed to pick them up, then issue a citation before informing the forest service the pilot in question needed to be fired.

While he was reporting the incident to headquarters, another call came in on his cell phone. It was Jessica. The bus must have just dropped her off from school. No doubt Sam had arrived from Phoenix and his daughter was calling to tell him their plans.

This was the weekend he'd been worried about. By the end of it, he would probably hear that she'd decided to live with her mom for a while. Nick had had no appetite for several days now.

He rang off with Sally, who would leave the information on Pierce's desk, then he phoned Jessica. "Hi, honey."

"Hi."

Such a dull, lifeless voice when he was expecting exuberance warned him something had gone wrong. "What's the matter?"

"There was a bomb threat at the Phoenix airport. It could be a terrorist thing. No planes can fly in or out. Mom went back to Marilyn's house to wait."

His eyes closed tightly. "Is your mother all right?"

"Yes, but she doesn't think she can fly out until tomorrow, and she said she really has to get back to Coeur D'Alene after being gone from work this long. S-so it looks like I'm not going to get to see her until next weekend."

He could tell Jessica was fighting not to break into tears. Unfortunately, he could hear the helicopter in the distance.

"I'm sorry, honey. Why don't you go over to Cory's and wait for me? I'll be home as soon as I can."

"How long?"

"Six o'clock?"

"That's too long. Hurry, Dad."

"I promise, honey."

After he hung up, he phoned Leslie. To his relief she was home. When he explained the situation, she said she would take care of everything. No sooner had they quit talking than the helicopter touched down.

Nick made his approach. He told the pilot to shut off the motor and climb out.

"Cut me some slack, will ya? My buddies are just having a little fun away from work for a couple of hours."

"That little fun may have cost the lives of several animals this park is supposed to protect. If enough guys like you have their way, there won't be a park one day. Let's see your ID."

"You're really going to write us up?"

"That's right."

By this time the other two men, probably in their late twenties, had approached on their skis.

Nick shook his head. "You guys know better. You've violated the National Environmental Policy and Forestry Management Acts. I need to see your ID."

Unlike the pilot, they didn't say anything as he issued their citations. He gave each of them a copy, then tipped his hat. "See you in court." He waited until the copter was airborne before heading back down the mountain to his truck.

There'd been quite a few incidents with heli-skiers and snowmobilers already this winter. Because the park didn't have the funds to hire an attorney who could prosecute these cases to the full extent of the law, guys like this probably wouldn't lose their jobs. Worse, they'd be back again, knowing the law lacked the teeth to do any lasting damage to them.

At quarter to six Jessica phoned him again. She'd been at Leslie's, and now was home waiting for him. Five minutes later he pulled into the garage expecting she would come running. Instead he found her dry-eyed in the kitchen making dinner. Something had changed since Sam had phoned her earlier.

"Those tacos smell delicious. I'll join you in a minute." After freshening up, he hurried back to the kitchen and helped her put everything on the table.

"Is the airport still closed?"

"No. Just before you drove in, Mom phoned to tell me she's going to get a flight to Coeur D'Alene tonight."

"I'm sorry, honey. I know how much you were counting on seeing her."

She nodded. "Dad?"

He knew what was coming next. She was going to ask if she could fly to Coeur D'Alene in the morning to be with her.

"Yes?"

"When Cory asked me why I was crying and I told him, he said, 'Why don't you ask her to be your nanny?'"

What? "Honey—"

"I knew you'd say that, but I bet Mom would do it. Then it wouldn't matter if we had to go to Tennessee."

He didn't know whether to laugh or cry. "Did you mention this to your mother on the phone?"

"No. I was waiting for you to get home so we could talk about it first."

"Jessica—aside from the fact that it just wouldn't work, your mother has a career she can't walk away from."

"She could be an attorney here or in Tennessee."

Good grief. He should never have mentioned transferring. It seemed to have given her ideas. "It isn't that simple, honey."

"But what if she said yes? I think Cory had a great idea."

Nick pushed himself away from the table and got to his feet. "Cory's a six-year-old boy who needed someone to look after him while Pierce was at work. Leslie answered the ad in response to that need. Our situation isn't the same thing at all."

"Yes it is. You always tell me I need someone to look after me while *you're* at work. And Mom's my mom!"

Nick eyed his daughter. "You're grown up enough to understand why your mother couldn't live in the same house with us."

After the way Sam had torn her mouth from his the other night, she wouldn't put herself in the position of letting it happen again. As for Nick, he couldn't promise that he wouldn't reach for her whenever she was around. That's what was killing him. She was his sickness. An addiction.

"I didn't mean in the same house, Dad. If she stayed at Grayson's the way Leslie did before she married Pierce, wouldn't that be all right?"

"No, honey."

"Why?"

"Because this is our world, not hers. She has her own life, her own friends. I'm sure she has a fabulous condo. You saw your grandparents' home and know the kind of background she comes from. To live here would be giving all of that up. It isn't realistic to even consider the possibility, honey."

"She said *I* was her life. What if she were willing to move here for my sake?"

"No matter how much she loves you, I can promise you she wouldn't do it. Trust me on this."

Her cheeks splotched with color, Jessica jumped up from the table. "You hate her, don't you. I bet you wish she had died."

In all these years Jessica had never talked to him this way. "You know better than that."

"If I could live with her, I would!"

He quaked inside. "Has she asked you?"

"No. She said she never would because I belonged with you and it would hurt both of us too much to be apart from each other."

Nick stood there planted to the floor long after Jessica ran to her room, sobbing.

CHAPTER ELEVEN

DUE TO HER EXERCISE and meditation class after work, Samantha didn't get back to her apartment until nine Monday night. She'd needed that time to get herself centered again.

Not only had it been difficult to tell Jessica she couldn't see her until the weekend, Samantha had a doctor's appointment at eight-thirty in the morning. He would draw blood for her first test since she'd gone into remission.

She wouldn't be human if there wasn't a part of her that feared her protein level had gone up again. But the mental and physical discipline she worked on to keep herself in positive mode had taken hold.

After her shower she climbed into bed with a new brief to study. Three pages into it the phone rang. It was her parents calling to wish her good luck at the doctor's in the morning. They'd offered to fly to Coeur D'Alene and go with her, but she'd assured them this was routine and she was fine.

Deep down inside, she admitted that the idea of their coming would somehow place more importance on the appointment than was warranted. Marilyn had agreed that Samantha would be better off to treat this like she would a trip to the dentist.

After she'd studied another fifteen minutes, the

phone rang again. She checked the caller ID. It was Nick's call. Suddenly, her chest felt tight.

"H-hello?" she stammered. How incredible that just knowing he was on the other end made her as nervous and excited as a schoolgirl.

"Hi, Sam. Forgive me for phoning so late, but there's something important I need to discuss with you. If this isn't a good time, let me know what time we can talk tomorrow."

"Anytime is a good time if you need to get in touch with me. Go ahead."

"When did you last speak to Jessica?"

"Last night about seven. She called me from her friend's house." Samantha slid out of bed, unable to lie still. "What's wrong?"

"Jessica didn't go to school today. She woke up with a stomachache, so I stayed home with her. Tonight she told me she knows she's too sick to go to school tomorrow."

Samantha pressed a hand over her heart. "It's because I couldn't come last weekend, isn't it. I could hear her disappointment, but by the time the planes were flying again, I had to get back for a case I've been working on."

"You had no control over that bomb alert," he stated tensely. "Jessica knows that."

"It still doesn't make the news any easier to bear. I promised her I would come this Friday and spend the weekend. Do you want me to call her tonight and reassure her? I would have done that, but I barely got back from my exercise class and was afraid you might not want me disturbing you."

"Aren't we past the point where you need to worry about my reaction to your dealings with her?" he said.

"No, Nick. I want to operate by your rules. You're Jessica's father."

"You're her mother," he retorted. "That gives you rights, even if it means phoning her in the middle of the night if you deem it necessary."

When Nick sounded this upset, she had difficulty reading between the lines. "Tell me, what's wrong?"

He gave a muffled exclamation—whether of pain or exasperation, she couldn't tell. Probably both. "Over the weekend Cory put it in her head you could be her new nanny."

An incredulous laugh escaped Samantha's throat and tears welled in her eyes. Dear, darling, adorable Cory.

"My reaction exactly. The idea is ludicrous! But she doesn't really get that, so I've tried to explain in terms she'll understand. I'm forewarning you now so you'll be forearmed when you get here on Friday."

"Nick—"

"I credited our daughter with being more mature," he stated, "but she's still a child with a child's propensity for seeing only what she wants."

"Nick." She cut him off before he could say anything else. "You've misunderstood my reaction."

Marilyn's observation had been all Samantha had been able to think about since she'd left Phoenix.

If Samantha had let nature take its course that evening at the hotel, would there have been a different outcome? Would Nick have admitted that he was still in love with her, too? By halting that kiss, she might have sabotaged a second chance at happiness because of another false assumption.

Maybe it still wasn't too late to correct the damage. She had nothing to lose.

Taking another huge risk, she said, "I think Cory's suggestion is absolutely brilliant."

Nick's gasp of shocked surprise was everything she could have hoped for, and more.

"I knew I loved that little boy. Now I know why." She wiped her eyes. "Since the moment my secretary told me Jessica was on the phone and I realized you'd told her I wanted to meet her, I've dreamed of living and practicing law in Jackson Hole so I could be near her.

"Because I deal with wildlife issues, I've taken the bar exam to practice in four Western states, one of them being Wyoming. My boss at the federation is aware of my situation and is already prepared that I might leave Idaho if it means being in closer proximity to our daughter.

"Cory might just as well have pulled the idea right out of my heart. But if you're planning to transfer to Tennessee and live there, then there's no point in this discussion, so—"

"I'm not going to Tennessee," he interrupted her. Now it was her turn to let out a quiet gasp. "I was only considering the possibility because I believed you were intending to ask Jessica to live with you for the rest of the school year. It…seemed a good idea at the time."

Samantha's instincts had proved correct. Nick couldn't handle the thought of being without his daughter. Their bond was too great. In his pain, he'd thought a change of scene would help him to deal with their separation, if it came to that.

"I'm sorry if I caused you any worry. Let me make it clear once and for all that I have no desire to disrupt the life you've made with Jessica. She would never want to live with me if it meant being away from you. She worships the ground you walk on, Nick." *So do I.*

"Sam—"

"Don't say it!" she cried as her fears took over once again. "I know what I want is asking the impossible. You said it on the phone the first time—it's too late. You've made your own wonderful life with Jessica. I may be her mother, but I don't have the right to come along and rip apart everything you've created.

"Please be assured I would never have made the suggestion to you or Jessica about moving to Jackson. It's only because you told me what Cory said that we're having this particular conversation. It'll remain our secret.

"Please Nick—be honest with me. I need to know what you really want in terms of my seeing Jessica. I'll accept and be grateful for whatever you decide."

While she waited for his answer, perspiration broke out on her body.

"What I want is for our daughter to be happy," he said at last. "She has let me know in the most graphic of ways that she wants you around all the time. Anything short of that won't satisfy her.

"Since you want to be with her every bit as badly, and it would be asking too much of you to commute back and forth, I have no problem with you moving to Jackson."

Samantha had to hold the phone away for a moment so he wouldn't hear her cry of joy. He *had* forgiven her. And maybe Marilyn was right. Maybe he wanted her in his life again.

When she'd gathered her composure she said, "After you get off the phone, will you tell Jessica that when I come on Friday we'll look through the real estate listings together? On Saturday she can help me go house hunting. I—if you could join us, we'd love your input."

She could almost hear his mind mulling over the suggestion. "Provided there are no emergencies, I'll be there." She hugged her free arm to her waist for joy.

After another pause, he added, "I must say you've come up with a novel cure for Jessica's stomachache. There's no doubt in my mind it will do the trick. Good night, Sam."

"Good night," she whispered.

On Friday morning she called the doctor from her office to find out the results of her test. The nurse put her on hold for a minute, then came back. "Everything's normal."

"Thank you."

It seemed the pastor's words were prophetic. *Matters of the heart have a strange and powerful effect on the body's ability to fight disease.*

ON SATURDAY AFTERNOON the Jackson Realtor walked Samantha and Leslie back to the living room of a charming two-story log home.

"One of the features I find most attractive about this house is the glassed-in deck," the man said.

"Even if it's twenty degrees below zero outside, you can sit in the hot tub and look at the Tetons in total comfort. In summer, you can remove the windows and enjoy an open deck."

There were many wonderful aspects to the house, not the least of which was the loft, where an enchanted Cory leaned over the balcony and waved to them. He and Jessica had gone upstairs to explore, and had never come down.

"I'll be outside if you need me," the Realtor added.

"What do you think?" Samantha asked Leslie when they were alone.

She smiled. "With that large office and its own private entrance, it's perfect for your law practice. I don't believe anything else we've seen today compares."

"I agree. I'm still pinching myself to believe a house like this is available right here in Jackson. In good weather Jessica could walk from the high school if she had to."

"Pierce will be coming any minute to take us to dinner and a movie. He knows a lot about construction and can tell you if the house is in good shape."

"His opinion will be worth everything. I wouldn't put down earnest money otherwise."

Nick had told her on the phone he would try to make it, but an emergency had cropped up at the last minute. He'd phoned Jessica to tell them he'd be late. The news had come as a blow. Samantha had to fight hard not to show her disappointment.

"I don't think you'll have to worry about anything being faulty," Leslie said. "It's too new."

Samantha didn't think so, either. She wanted the house. The vaulted ceilings gave a feeling of space she craved. Her contemporary furniture would fit right in.

With three bedrooms and three baths, her parents and Marilyn would be able to stay in comfort when they came for visits. Every window looked out on a breathtaking view of the Tetons.

"Please can we get this house, Mom?" Jessica called out. "The loft is perfect for sleepovers!"

"Please buy it!" Cory echoed. "Lucy will love the stairs!"

Both Samantha and Leslie chuckled.

"When we have parties we'll soak in the hot tub, and then make popcorn and bring it up here." Jessica chatted away. "The bedroom has a window seat. It's big enough to sit in while you read and look out at the trees."

That was another plus. The property bordered the national forest.

"Dad!" Cory cried out all of a sudden.

"Hi, sport!"

He'd seen his father coming through the door before the rest of them. Like a shot he rushed down the stairs to hug Pierce.

"You've got to see Jessica's house!" He started pulling him toward the staircase. "We're going to sleep upstairs and have parties. Jessica says I can bring Cameron and Logan."

After the ranch-style houses they'd lived in, Samantha realized a two-story house was a genuine novelty.

"You've already bought it then?" another deep male voice inquired.

Samantha spun around to discover Nick on the

threshold. She went weak just looking at him. It had been so long. Weeks.

He'd changed out of his uniform and wore a brown cashmere sweater with darker brown trousers. He was so handsome she couldn't catch her breath.

"Not yet," she said in a voice that sounded way too shaky. "Leslie suggested you and Pierce take a look around first. Maybe you'll see a problem I don't. I've never bought a house before. It's quite different than a condo."

"Guess what, Dad?" At this point Jessica had joined them. "There's an office for Mom, and a barn out in back. We could bring some horses from Gillette next spring."

"I think you're getting a little ahead of yourself, honey." His gaze swerved from his daughter to Samantha. She glimpsed a vaguely anxious expression in his eyes that surprised her. "Are you ready to take all this on?" he asked her.

"Yes. Jessica said she would teach me to ride. But it's a moot point if you think I should keep looking."

"Come on!" Their daughter grabbed his hand. "You've got to see everything. Did you know there's a shop in the garage? It would make the coolest lab for you."

"Is that right?" At this point the lines were blurred in Jessica's eyes. *What's mine is yours.* It was very sweet, very touching, really. Nick wasn't unaffected by the situation, but Samantha would give anything to know what he was really thinking.

For one breathless moment, she found herself visualizing the three of them living here as a family.

"Much as I'd like the grand tour, honey, we don't

have time right now. Did you forget Marsha Gardiner's birthday party?''

''Oh my gosh!'' She put a hand to her mouth.

''I thought it had slipped your mind. I'd forgotten about it, too. Amanda called the house to see if you wanted a ride. I told her I'd bring you. I've got your present.''

Jessica eyed both of them with a pained expression. ''I don't want to go.''

''Sure you do, darling. It'll be fun,'' Samantha declared. ''Call me when you're through and we'll pick you up.'' She'd spoken for Nick, too, hoping he didn't mind.

''Where you will be?''

''At Grayson's.''

''But you flew all the way from Coeur D'Alene to be with me.''

''Jessica—it's only for a few hours. Pretty soon I'm going to be living in Jackson. So go on, and have a blast!''

''Okay.'' She gave her a hug.

Nick glanced at Samantha, an unreadable expression in his eyes. ''I'll see you back here in a little while.''

''The Realtor has another appointment right away. Why don't you meet me at Grayson's instead? I'll show you the brochure.''

''Sounds like a plan.''

Samantha followed them to the front door and waved as they drove off. Just then Pierce and his family stepped out of the garage. The Realtor stood a little distance apart from them.

She waited till the Gallaghers came up to her. Pierce had his arm around his wife.

"Well?" Samantha asked in a quiet voice. "What do you think?"

"You already know my opinion," Leslie said.

Pierce's blue eyes lit up with his smile. "I think it's a great house. Go for it." Cory gave a little jump in the snow, he was so excited.

"I'm excited too, Cory." The little boy had no idea just how much.

"Come and have dinner with us," Leslie urged. "We'll call Nick to join us."

"Thank you, but I want to drop by a hardware store and find some paint and wallpaper samples to take to the cabin. I would like Jessica to be able to decorate her own bedroom."

"Your daughter will be in heaven."

"She won't be the only one."

"For eight years I've watched Jess grow up," Pierce commented. "There's a new glow about her since you came into her life. I'm happy about your plans to move here."

Her eyes glazed over with tears. "Coming from you, that means a lot." Pierce's opinion carried a great deal of weight with Nick.

They all hugged before Pierce helped his family into the car. Once they drove away, Samantha approached the Realtor. "I'd like to make an offer."

AFTER DROPPING JESSICA off at the party, Nick headed back to Moose. Since his phone call with Sam the other night, his world had changed. She'd asked for his help and she was going to get it, because he'd decided to face the truth about himself.

For thirteen years he'd been stuck in a time warp. No woman since Sam had ever made him want a permanent relationship. Her image had always been before his eyes.

Raising Jessica had made it impossible for him to forget her mother. Now, incredibly, Sam was back in his life, saying and doing all the right things, hooking her womanly tentacles into him deeper and deeper.

She was going to be living here for good. Translated, that meant as long as her cancer stayed in remission.

What am I going to do about you, Sam? I can't go on like this any longer.

If the memory of their love had prevented her from finding someone else, then he intended to wring that admission from her. Otherwise why was she willing to move to his world?

Their conversation on Halloween would forever be burned in his memory. She'd told her pastor she wanted to go back in time so the three of them could be a family.

If she'd meant it, then that explained why she hadn't stopped him from kissing her outside her hotel room. She could have turned away in time, using Jessica as an excuse. Instead, she'd launched herself into his arms and had kissed him with the kind of hunger he'd never felt from her before.

So why, in the middle of such intensity and rapture, had she unexpectedly wheeled away from him, leaving him bereft?

It was time he found out, but he needed to be smart

about it. One thing was certain. He couldn't handle another rejection.

As one of his favorite college professors had taught him, don't try to fight or alter nature. It doesn't work. You have to let it take its course if you want to see the true pattern of things emerge and develop. Then learn from it.

That's what Nick intended to do with Sam. He wouldn't fight his feelings. Instead he would let things take their natural course and see what happened.

If nothing did, then he would have learned from the experience and could finally move on.

The drive to Grayson's seemed to take forever. They kept the place well-lit for their guests. Out of the corner of his eye he saw Sam at the door of her cabin. She was juggling a pile of things as high as her head.

Without hesitation he pulled off the road and levered himself from the car to help her. "Sam?"

He must have startled her, for everything she was carrying fell to the porch with a loud thud and she spun around. If his eyes weren't mistaken, she'd lost color.

"Nick! I didn't realize you were there." She seemed to have difficulty swallowing.

"I'm sorry to have frightened you. I thought you heard me coming on the path." He hunkered down to gather the wallpaper books. When he stood up, she was struggling with the lock.

"Let me." He took over and jostled the key into the opening until it gave. A little oil would fix the problem.

Once they were inside the warm, rustic room she

cried, "I swear I didn't drop those samples on purpose!"

Her response stunned him. He put the books on the pine picnic table arranged beneath a picture window framed with red-and-green-plaid curtains. "Did I accuse you?"

"After what I did to get your attention years ago, you would have every reason to think so," she said in a trembling voice. "Here you've been going along all these years minding your own business, and now I've turned up again like a bad penny."

His brown brows formed a bar. "Is that how you see yourself? A bad penny?"

"Yes. That's what I was. A willful teenager who threw herself at you. I was always the one who made you do things you didn't want to do. Lying to you about my age was unforgivable, but I was afraid of losing you."

Nick had heard all this before, but he had the advantage of being older now.

Hopefully maturity and fatherhood had helped him put emotion aside long enough to read between the lines and hear what she was really saying. If he bided his time, he might find the answer to the one question that had eaten him alive.

She stood behind an easy chair, clutching the corner. "To call you out of the blue after all these years and ask to see our daughter... I shouldn't have told you about the cancer."

He rubbed the back of his neck, trying to understand. "Did you feel you needed the excuse?"

"No! After the first lie I told you, I vowed I would never lie again. If I hadn't made that promise to myself, I wouldn't have said anything to you about my illness. I would have just phoned to tell you I wanted to see my daughter, and hoped you might let me.''

"If that's true, why didn't you call years ago?"

Sam averted her eyes. "Because I was afraid you would see me as the same needy girl who kept putting you in a position of having to deal with me, one way or the other. It wouldn't have been fair to you. I was never fair to you."

"So what you're saying is it took the prospect of escaping death to override your fear of approaching me again?"

She shook her head. "No. It was the pastor's unexpected visit at the condo. When he asked me if there was anything I needed to resolve, I thought that, because I'd suffered remorse over my sins for so long, maybe it was a sign that I'd finally been forgiven.''

Nick's throat constricted as he heard her anguish. "I had no idea you felt such tremendous guilt."

"I didn't know, either. Not in the beginning. It took months after Jessica was born before the numbness went away enough for me to feel anything again. Then the pain and guilt descended in full force.

"When I talked to my old pastor in Fort Collins, all these feelings came out. I admitted lying to you about my age. I'd lied to my parents about the amount of time I spent with you. I'd had a sexual relationship outside of marriage. I'd given up my baby.'' Tears gushed down her cheeks.

"The pastor told me I was forgiven. That it was my job to forgive myself and make the best future I could from there on out. He promised me that in time the pain would lessen, and he could think of no better outlet to assuage it than to pursue my studies.

"So I left for Boston with the determination to be the top student in my class. I studied day and night. It's all I did. Throughout undergraduate school I couldn't think of dating. I didn't feel worthy yet.

"Later on things got better. The guilt subsided. I went out with several guys in law school. I tried to like them, but after a few dates the idea of a relationship turned me off. It was such a relief to finally get my degree and move to Coeur D'Alene, where there wasn't the pressure from friends to go on a blind date, or meet somebody's brother."

Nick could relate to that.

"Life was good, but there was a void."

He could relate to that, too. But he still had to hear why she'd refused to marry him.

"Sam—if you loved me enough to lie to keep me, to lie to your parents so you could continue in the relationship with me, then what held you back from saying yes to my proposal?

"The baby book you made is proof you had the instincts to be a wonderful mother. Your parents wouldn't have disowned you if you'd decided to marry me the day you turned eighteen. So what was really going on in your head when I couldn't change your mind in that hospital room?"

Her face took on a tragic cast. "Haven't you been listening to me?"

"Every word," he declared through gritted teeth. "You've suffered a lot, that's clear, but I'm still waiting for an answer."

He could see a shudder run through her beautiful body. "It wasn't because I didn't love you, Nick."

He stiffened. "You could have fooled me."

"It was just the opposite!" she cried. "I realized I loved you too much. I'd lied to get you and keep you. Brenda's older sister did the same thing to hold on to her boyfriend. He left her after they'd been married only six months! Her life was a mess after that, and her parents ended up raising her baby. I couldn't bear to be like her and trap the man I loved into marriage if he didn't really want me. I'd already lied to you about my age and felt sick with shame."

Nick's heart was racing. "You never told me about your friend's sister. I thought those ideas came from your parents!" He could barely remember the girl, whom he'd been introduced to on only one occasion. After finding out Sam was still in high school, Nick had realized she'd kept her friends from meeting him so he wouldn't learn the truth.

"They did, but I wouldn't have listened to them if I hadn't already seen what happened in Brenda's family. They would have financed her college, but the divorce devastated her. She lost interest in school and old friends. Eventually she left home and got into drugs. Her rare visits to see her child had to be supervised, increasing her parents' emotional burden.

"There was resentment and tension from the other siblings. The father of the baby never came around because he'd never loved Brenda's sister in the first place. I was convinced you would end up despising me and would leave me after we were married. I couldn't bear that."

"Sam, you would never have turned out like that, and I would never have left you."

"Maybe not. But I could understand my parents' fear that my dreams to become a good attorney with a successful career would be jeopardized by getting married so young. You have to understand that because they're socially prominent, I was afraid to be an embarrassment to them.

"But more than that, I was terrified you felt like you had to marry me, and that one day you would leave me. It would have been the punishment I deserved for not telling you the truth about my age."

She wrung her hands. "In the end I wanted to do the noble thing, so I set you free, but my heart died that day."

"So did mine," he whispered.

You have your answer, Kincaid.

"Perhaps now you understand why I don't want you to think I'm trying to manipulate you or the situation with Jessica. I'll never lie to you again. I've found out life's too short to be anything but honest."

He took a fortifying breath. "In that case, I want to know what your plans are for the future."

A wistful smile curved her mouth. "Since I found out I have a future to look forward to, you have no idea how just hearing the word makes me feel."

"I'm sure I can't imagine," he murmured. She'd been to hell and back. It tore him apart thinking about that. It tore him apart to know she'd loved him so much she'd sacrificed everything to let him be free.

"My plan is to live near our daughter so we end the commuting. Taking airplanes is a disruption we can all live without."

Amen to that.

"My parents will come often to visit. I'm hoping to get my friend Marilyn here, too. As for Jessica, she can't spend every weekend with me, and she won't want to once things settle down. I don't expect to see her every spare moment, and I'm not going to encourage it. Frankly, I'd like to be here as a backup for you."

Backup? "I appreciate that."

"Thirteen years is a long time to shoulder all the responsibility, Nick. No matter how much you adore Jessica, there are times when you're sick, when you need to travel, when you want a…a breather."

"You mean a date?" he demanded.

A blush crept up her neck into her face. "Yes. From now on I'll be here to help out. Because you're a ranger, I can't imagine any kind of a visitation schedule we could come up with that would work."

He folded his arms. "You're right. Too many emergencies arise, over which I have no control, like the one this afternoon. Besides, our daughter's old enough to decide these things for herself."

"I agree. You've been such a wonderful father, Nick. I know you don't want to hear it from me. But please let me say it just this once. She's a remarkable girl, and all of the credit goes to you."

His heart gave a fierce kick. "Jessica inherited her mother's protoplasm. It gave her a head start."

Sam laughed softly. "Spoken like the scientist you are. You love it here, don't you."

"Yes."

"I love it here, too. The Tetons have a majesty that speaks to your soul. Today I put money down on the log house. You know what sold me? The view of the Grand Teton from the office window. This is God's country.''

It was a fact. Another fact was that one of His most beautiful creations was standing in front of Nick right now. "Do you think you're going to want to set up your own law practice, or work in an established firm?''

Her eyes ignited, making them an even more intense blue. "I'm glad you asked that question. I—I have a proposition for you.'' Her voice faltered.

"What's that?'' Any attempt to tamp down his excitement over being here with her like this failed.

"Since you have a lot of influence with Pierce, do you think the park might hire me to be their legal representative?''

Just when he thought she couldn't do or say anything else to surprise him... "He'd welcome you with open arms, but there's no funding to pay you a salary.''

"I know. The thing is, I don't need one.''

"Sam—''

"Hear me out, please? My maternal grandparents left me an inheritance of five million dollars. I've already given half away to cancer research. Since I found out I have a second chance at life, I know where I want the other half to go. A fund could be created that would last for many, many years. It would be anonymous, of course. I'd be paid the normal salary for a park employee.''

With a surge of emotion he grasped her shoulders, drawing her close. "You would give away that much money to work for the park just so you could be with our daughter?'' He could hear his own voice shaking with emotion.

Her eyes filled with tears. "Yes. I don't want to be anywhere else ever again."

Nick had difficulty swallowing. "Sam…" In the next instant they were in each other's arms. He needed her kiss more than he needed air to breathe. This time she gave him the response he craved without pulling away. Her beautiful mouth and body were his for the taking.

"Dad? Mom?"

Jessica's timing couldn't have been worse.

"Hurry and unlock the door! I'm shivering out here!"

For once it was Nick who was forced to relinquish the luscious mouth clinging to his. Samantha's protesting moan made his heart leap.

CHAPTER TWELVE

NICK UNLOCKED THE DOOR before Samantha could even begin to think about moving her limbs. Jessica rushed in, bringing the freezing air with her.

"How was the party, honey?" he asked.

"It was fun. What have you guys been doing?"

He shut the door. "Your mother and I have had things to discuss."

The way he moved in slow motion as he removed their daughter's coat and draped it over the end of the couch, Samantha knew he too was having difficulty pulling himself together after their explosion of passion.

There was no question she'd shocked him with her proposal. If she did become the park's attorney, she would make up part of Nick's inner circle.

Outside of marriage, that was about as up close and personal as you could get to the man you adored. When Marilyn heard about this, she could never again accuse Samantha of being inscrutable.

She gave Jessica a hug. "I thought you were going to phone us to come and get you."

"Sandy's mom offered to bring a bunch of us home."

"That was nice of her."

Jessica nodded before tucking her hands in the back

pockets of her jeans. She eyed both of them expectantly. "What happened at the house after I left this afternoon?"

Nick flashed their daughter a mysterious smile reminiscent of the old Nick who used to love to surprise Samantha with little treats. When he looked like that, her bones melted. "The answer is sitting over on the table."

"Oh my gosh!" she cried the minute she recognized the wallpaper samples. "You bought the house!"

Samantha smiled at Nick. She couldn't help it. Their daughter was in heaven. "I made an offer, but I think we can safely assume it's ours—mine," she amended. "One of those books has some Waverly prints like the ones you admired in the upstairs bedrooms at your grandparents' home."

To Samantha's joy, Nick walked to the table with her. They sat down on either side of Jessica, who'd already started poring over them. For the next hour all three of them became amateur decorators, expressing their preferences like any normal family.

"I like this one best!" Jessica had her eye on a small print of tiny blue flowers against a white background. She'd gone back to it again and again.

"It'll be perfect in that upstairs bedroom with the window seat. We'll have to buy you a big four-poster bed and an armoire."

"I can't wait!"

"We'll shop for them online and have them shipped."

"I wish we could do it tonight."

Moments such as this were so precious, Samantha

held her breath for fear it was a dream that would disappear the longer she tried to hold on to it.

"Look at that, Dad!" Jessica had turned to the last page in one of the books. It displayed a tiny all-over print with a border done in a charming horse motif.

"It's cute."

Samantha thought it was very cute. "I can see it in the guest bathroom between the office and the door leading out to the barn."

"That'll be perfect!" Jessica's sparkling blue eyes dazzled her.

When Nick's cell phone rang, there was a collective moan of protest. Samantha held her breath while he answered it. *Please don't let it be an emergency.*

She saw him grimace before he said, "I'm on my way."

"What's wrong, Dad?" Jessica had just taken the words out of Samantha's mouth.

"A tourist hit a moose on the Teton Park Road. Sometimes the animals use it as a corridor to migrate at night, but the ranger summoned to the accident says this moose looks sick. It could be disoriented and that's why it wandered onto the highway. I have to investigate. See you tomorrow, honey."

After giving Jessica a kiss, he shrugged into his jacket. His glance flicked to Samantha. "I'm glad you're here."

"I am, too," she said in a whisper.

Their daughter let him out of the rental cabin. That was good, because Samantha wasn't capable of moving one foot in front of the other. Just then Nick had sounded as if he really meant it. She'd felt a lingering warmth in his regard. She longed to bask in it forever.

Her thoughts darted back to that first precarious moment when they'd seen each other in the foyer of the Elk Inn. One arctic look from him had shriveled her. She couldn't believe how different the situation was tonight.

"It sounds like your father has just given you more information to put in one of your newspaper articles. How's your latest one coming, by the way?"

"Thanks to something you said in one of your cases about the foresight of enlarging the Wild Clearwater country, I've almost finished it. The headline will read Yellowstone and Grand Teton, One park? Extravagant Concept or Visionary Thinking?"

"That's an attention grabber if I ever heard one! Bravo!"

Jessica sounded so savvy, Samantha couldn't wait to tell Nick. Being around Leslie Gallagher had rubbed off on her. Maybe Samantha and Nick were wrong and their daughter was going to grow up to be like Pierce's wife, a former staff journalist for the *New York Chronicler.*

On the other hand, Jessica showed signs of being a dedicated conservationist who'd been absorbing her father's philosophy. Whatever she ended up doing, it was going to be exciting to watch, because her analytical thinking exhibited real brilliance.

Overwhelmed by emotion, since at this time last year Samantha hadn't expected to survive the winter, she hurried to the couch to turn it into a bed for Jessica.

"After you've slipped on a nightgown, I want to hear about the party."

"We watched the old version of *Freaky Friday* and had pizza."

"That was a fun movie. After the way I've been twice mistaken for you, we would probably be able to pull off a mother-daughter switch and no one would notice."

"Except Dad. Did he like the house?"

Amused that the child was vetting the parent, Samantha decided honesty was still the best policy. "I'm sure he did, but mostly we discussed how things would work once I'm living here practicing law."

"Dad has to plan everything out, even though he rarely sticks to it."

"But he gets points for trying, right?"

"Right! Marsha always says she wishes she had a dad like him."

"Your father's one in ten billion."

Jessica studied her for a long moment before she removed the locket around her neck. "Want to see what I put in this?"

Samantha's heart raced as she opened it. Her daughter had added a picture of Nick. The very serious look brought his handsome features into sharp relief. Yet it underlined his male beauty, which reached out to her like a living thing.

"Cory took it at the wedding last month and gave it to me."

Sam had to clear her throat before a sound could escape. "It appears Leslie is turning him into quite the amazing little photographer."

Her daughter nodded. "I think Dad looks sad. Don't you?"

"Yes. It's not every day your best friend gets married."

Jessica flashed her a perplexed glance. "He and Pierce didn't lose each other."

"Of course not. But when two people marry, they cling to each other. It's so special, everyone around them feels it."

"Do you wish you'd married Dad?"

Oh Jessica...

The truth, Samantha.

"Yes."

SODIUM CYANIDE POISONING. All the signs were there. Slobbering, bleeding from the nose. As soon as Nick studied the stomach contents and ran tests on the blood and liver of the moose, he'd have viable proof.

How in the hell had it been poisoned? Moose were plant eaters. He surmised the poor cow had probably found some tender willows in the snow, and had accidentally caused the spring of the hidden 'coyote getter,' or M-44 as they called it, to discharge the poison capsule.

Using the flashlight, Nick followed the animal's split hoofprints through the snow into the forest. Every so often he discovered scat, the long round pellets, and traces of the animal's vomit.

Toxic fumes created when the moisture in its mouth activated the dry poison had killed it before the Jeep had crashed into it. Nick shuddered to imagine the animal's terrible agony before it died.

Almost every day he encountered evidence of man's destruction. Though there were laws on the books, the park had little money to enforce them. Nick couldn't help but consider Sam's proposition.

He shut his eyes for a moment. Her generosity and legal expertise would be a godsend.

"Nick?"

At the sound of Pierce's voice he stood up and turned. "How come you're not home in bed?"

"On the way home from Jackson, I checked in with dispatch and heard you suspected we have a poisoned moose on our hands. I thought I'd drive over and see what you found."

"Sodium cyanide."

"Damn."

Their breath curled in the freezing night air.

Like Nick, Pierce grieved over every treacherous human act against the wildlife they put their lives on the line to protect.

"If I had the money, I'd track down the person who did this and make certain he or she was sent away for the duration. It's times like this I wish I believed in the lottery and could use the winnings for something truly meaningful."

A half moon had come up over the Grand Teton, bathing them in enough light for Nick to see the lines of tension in his friend's face.

"What if I told you I know someone who holds the winning ticket for two and a half million dollars, and is ready to give it to us, no questions asked?"

Pierce let out a bark of laughter. "Then I would say you've been going heavy on the Jack Daniels tonight."

"Do you smell alcohol?"

His friend sobered. It was starting to dawn on him Nick was being serious. "Run that by me again."

"You heard me the first time. However, there is one small catch." Pierce stared at him as if he'd never seen him before. "It all has to stay in the family, so to speak."

"What are you talking about?"

"Sam."

"I don't understand. Speak English."

"She wants a job only you can create for her. The job we've needed doing around here since day one."

"You're joking…" His head reared back. "Lord, you're *not* joking. Her family has that kind of money?"

Nick nodded. "Her grandparents. No one can ever know. Once the funding's in place and the superintendent informs you, then you would have to open up the job to all who want it. The board will have to vote on the best candidate."

"Which Sam would win hands down."

"When she comes in for the interview, you'll see she's a force of nature."

They studied each other for a full minute before Pierce said, "I take it Cory's going to be sleeping in that loft in a few weeks."

"And riding his own pony next spring. Jessica has it all planned out."

Pierce cocked his head. "When's the wedding?"

"I don't know. Right now I'm letting nature take its course and I'll see what happens."

A silence ensued, followed by a whoop that filled the forest. Before Nick could react, Pierce gave him a bear hug that would have knocked the wind out of him if he'd been a smaller man.

"Chief?" One of the younger rangers came running through the trees, kicking up snow. "Is something wrong?"

"Nope." Pierce tried to hide the ecstatic grin on his face. "A private joke, but I appreciate the concern."

"Sure."

As soon as the other man was out of earshot again he said, "Let's go to headquarters and work out the details right now."

"I'll drop by my lab first, then meet you there."

"Good. In the morning we'll all have breakfast together at my house. I'll take Sam aside and have a chat with her before she leaves for Coeur D'Alene."

Nick felt dazed. "You realize what this means if everything comes together...."

"*I* do," Pierce muttered, "but I know for a fact it hasn't hit *you* yet."

"THE MOVING VAN'S HERE, Mom!"

It wasn't too soon for Samantha, who'd had to forgo spending Christmas with her daughter, and had flown into Jackson only this morning, her last commuting flight.

Until now there'd been too much to do in Coeur D'Alene. Besides getting ready for the move, she'd had to go over important cases with the lawyer hired to replace her at the federation. She had yet to be interviewed though by the U.S. Attorney General's office in Cheyenne for her job with the park. That would happen on Monday.

With only two days before New Year's, she still had

a house to put together before her parents arrived tomorrow afternoon. She was determined to see the New Year in with her daughter and Nick, having put down her roots here for good.

Jessica and Nick had spent Christmas in Gillette with relatives. School was out for the break, and Jessica was dying to help. Samantha had never seen anyone so excited, except herself, of course.

The painting and wallpapering had been done. She'd bought some new furniture, all of which was now in place, including the pieces for her office, her daughter's bedroom and the guest bedroom.

Samantha greeted the driver at the door and gave him a quick tour of the house so he and his partner would know where to put things.

First off the truck came the endless string of boxes containing the law books belonging in her office library. A euphoric Jessica called Cory on the new cell phone Nick had bought her for Christmas. She told him to hurry over as soon as his mom could drive him.

The two of them were like brother and sister. Samantha couldn't have loved him more if he were her own flesh and blood. She loved the people who made up her daughter's world. She loved Nick, whom she hadn't seen for two weeks! If he didn't show up soon, she didn't know how she was going to stand it.

For the next fifteen minutes the movers brought in more boxes marked for the various rooms. Then came the furniture. Samantha turned up the heat to compensate for the freezing air entering through the open doorway.

"Oh my gosh!" Jessica cried out when the black Steinway baby grand was wheeled in on a dolly. She turned a glowing face to Samantha. "You didn't tell me you had a piano like this!"

Samantha just smiled and told the men to set it up in the corner of the living room next to the stone fireplace and inner wall, away from any windows. While they were attaching the legs, she heard voices outside, among them Nick's. She thought she would faint from the thrill.

"Dad!" Jessica pulled him inside the living room. "Look!"

"I'm looking," he said, but when Samantha chanced a glance in his direction, their gazes collided, sending a shock wave through her system. "Welcome home, Sam."

"Nick—" It was the only word that would come out with any coherence.

In the background Sam noticed Cory and realized he and his parents had also arrived. Everyone was dressed in casual clothes, ready to go to work. No one looked better in a T-shirt and jeans than Nick. Being a ranger kept his body fit and well-defined. It was a body she'd once known intimately.

Waves of heat suffused her face at the memory. She quickly turned her head away, but feared Nick had read her mind.

"Oh my gosh!" their daughter exclaimed again.

"Oh my gosh" pretty well described Samantha's emotions right this minute, but Jessica was referring to the large, heavy hutch, which came in two pieces. Samantha told the movers to set it up in the dining room. The bottom half was a bombé style with drawers. The top had been styled in an eighteenth century Flemish motif with glass doors and shelves. The painted exterior was an off white with tiny blue flowers.

"It looks just like my wallpaper!"

"Genes don't lie," Nick whispered from somewhere behind Samantha.

"No," she said, slipping a trembling arm around Jessica's shoulders. "Blue and white has always been my favorite color combination. When I saw this in a furniture shop in Amsterdam years ago, I had to have one just like it. Wait till you see the blue-and-white Delft plates that go inside it."

Jessica literally squealed in delight.

Next came the hand-carved, oval oak table and matching dining room chairs, then the living room furniture—two matching love seats, a coffee table, two easy chairs, end tables and lamps, all of light wood and white fabric in a contemporary design.

The driver approached her. "We're all through except for this last box, which isn't marked."

"Those are some personal things that belong in my bedroom."

"I'll take it." Nick reached for it and disappeared, leaving Samantha with nothing more to do than sign the form.

"Thank you for everything."

"You're welcome, ma'am. It's a beautiful house. What I'd give to live at the foot of these mountains."

She smiled. "That's why I'm here," she said before closing the door.

Cory came running. "Mom said for you to come in the kitchen. She's made a picnic."

"You've got the greatest mother in the world. Come

on, Jessica. I don't know about you, but I'm starving!''

THE MASTER BEDROOM on the main floor featured a superb view of the Tetons. Nick's gaze took in the Italian provincial decor. For a moment he focused on the queen-size bed Samantha had brought from Idaho, the bed she'd slept in alone all these years.

His heart hammered in his throat. As if it were yesterday, memories of nights they'd spent in the bedroom of her father's cruiser flooded through his mind.

When he heard Leslie calling him to lunch, he turned his eyes away and pulled the last item from the box. Out came a black, leather-bound book. Curiosity took hold of him and he opened the cover.

Sam had kept a journal. He knew he shouldn't be looking at it, but he couldn't help it. Sinking down on the bed, he opened it to the first page.

Coeur D'Alene, Idaho
February 7
Today I found out I have cancer.

Nick felt the statement slice through him like a knife.

My doctor advised me to keep a journal to record my feelings. He said the process of writing them down would help to keep me sane.

Sane? What's that? I went to him for a pain in my ribs and was tested for a kidney infection. But some lab work revealed that my protein level was elevated. The doctor told me it could be related to a cancer called multiple myeloma, a disease I've never heard of.

But he didn't believe I had it because I'm only twenty-nine. The patients he has seen with this disease are normally in their fifties or older. I have to see an oncologist tomorrow for more tests.

Like a person at the scene of a fire, horrified yet mesmerized, Nick turned to the next page.

February 9
I learned the horrible truth today. I have MM, a cancer of the body's plasma cells. After reading about it, I looked at myself in the mirror a few minutes ago and can't believe what's going on inside of me.

Plasma cells are present in the bone marrow and make up five percent of it. They are responsible for the production of antibodies when the body is dealing with infection.

Cancerous plasma cells build up in the marrow, interfering with normal immune response. They invade and damage the bone, causing tumors to form. Myeloma cells travel to other parts of the body, causing further tumors.

My mind keeps flashing back to a movie Nick and I once saw on video called *Fantastic Voyage*. A team of scientists in a miniature submarine were injected into the bloodstream of a human body through a hypodermic needle.

I remember the frightening moment when the body's alarm system summoned the antibodies.

Nick was remembering that moment, too, but at the time he'd laughed.

> They began attacking the sub, sending it flying through the aorta away from the heart with the speed of an F-5 tornado.
>
> Right now I can visualize the insides of my own body turning traitor, releasing those dreaded myeloma cells. They're going to fill me with tumors. It's hideous, but the doctor says I'm not ready for therapy because they haven't invaded my bones yet.
>
> He says I have to have a transplant sometime within the next six months to a year. For now I have to watch and wait for the disease to progress.
>
> All I want to do is cry. I can't believe this is happening to me. I want normal back. I want everything back I've ever taken for granted. I want Nick. I want our baby.

Dear God. Nick's eyes closed tightly for a moment before he could bring himself to read on.

> *February 11*
> Today I'm trying to learn everything I can do to fight it. I've been reading about other victims who've pursued a number of alternative remedies—the most important being training in meditation and the martial arts. Imagine me learning martial arts!
>
> *June 15*
> The training has stopped me from going insane.

> For the first time in five months I'm feeling much stronger mentally and physically than I did before my diagnosis. I believe it's keeping me from needing active therapy. The doctor thought I would need a transplant by now.

Nick shook his head, marveling over her indomitable will. Riveted to every word of pain pouring from her soul, he digested the next few entries.

> *August 20*
> Today I learned my IGG protein is on the rise. I've been taking a conservative approach to the disease, deciding I would smolder as long as possible. But the time has come to start the treatment. I have no other option.

Sam's pain and fear drove Nick to his feet while he continued to read.

> *August 23*
> I've begun treatment using VAD and Decadron with Aredia.

> *September 29*
> I've had five ports installed into my superior vena cava. But they have no blood return and are infected. I feel like I've got the flu. I get a raging fever every time they give me another dose of Aredia.

> *October 30*
> The Decadron made me go into a dive after the last dose of the cycle. My hair is falling out. I'm

so horribly fatigued and nauseated by the chemo. Thank God Nick can't see me now. Thank God he was spared this.

Great heaving sobs came out of Nick.

December 3
The doctor says I have a staph infection. He removed the Hickman port and put in a femoral line to collect my stem cells.

January 10
I'm so physically sick. But it doesn't compare to the pain I suffered when I lost Nick and the baby in a matter of seconds. Those papers from Judge Sarkins stating that I'd given up all rights to Jessica brought me such exquisite pain, I'm surprised I've lived long enough to undergo this ordeal.

Sam, sweetheart…

February 4
I've had my transplant. My doctor won't tell me if the torture I've gone through has been for nothing because my protein level is still high and my IGG level is at 2750.

April 21
Because of possible exposure to infected people and germs, I'm still being forced to take a leave of absence from my job. I've been staying at Mom and Dad's house while I get over this emotionally and physically draining experience.

They are saints.

July 10
My goal is to continue injections of Interferon and increase my physical therapy so I'll feel stronger again. As soon as I can manage it, I'm going back to Coeur D'Alene.

August 16
I'm back at work. Marilyn May, a recovering breast cancer patient who's been attending qigong with me, has talked me into joining the rowing club with her, through Northern Idaho College. It will provide me another outlet requiring a mental and physical discipline that I hope will help me think with more clarity on the job.

September 18
Everyone in the rowing class is great and tells me I look wonderful, but I see myself in the mirror. This thirty-one-year-old face and body have been through hell. Marilyn says I'm beautiful. She's another saint. I love her better than a sister.

My hair has grown back, a little thinner than before. I'm keeping it shorter to hide the white hairs creeping in among the red. At some point I'll need to start using a rinse.

October 16
I've been back on the job for two months, working a law case for the Idaho Conservation League to ensure that the state and the Environmental Protection Agency enforce the Clean

> Water Act. There's a specific drive to recover salmon and steelhead to the rivers polluted by the mines and other factors.
>
> This case reminds me of the many long talks Nick and I used to have about saving and preserving the wilds. His ideas have always had a great influence on me.

Moisture bathed Nick's cheeks. He came to the entry marked October 29. The date held particular significance for him, since it had been written two days before her phone call to him.

> By some miracle I'm still here. It appears my cancer has gone into remission. I just learned the news this afternoon.
>
> Maybe it's a coincidence, maybe it isn't, but tonight the pastor of my church came to see me....

His eyes could barely read the rest for the blur.

> Nick will either tear up my letter or hang up on me. No matter. I have to try, otherwise this life has made no sense at all....

He wiped away the tears with the back of his arm. His biggest problem now was to face Sam and pretend he hadn't trespassed on the secret part of her soul.

Hurriedly he placed the journal in the bottom of the box before putting back the jewelry case and bedside radio she'd packed on top of it. After leaving it on the floor by the other boxes the movers had brought in, he left the bedroom.

Before he joined the others, he needed to get his emotions under control. Using the entrance to the office down the hall, he let himself outside and breathed in the frigid air.

Before, whenever he'd looked up at the Tetons, he'd always felt an accompanying loneliness that was at once awesome and inexplicable. It took Sam's heart-wrenching outpourings for him to understand why.

The realization that he hadn't been the only traveller along the seemingly endless, solitary path of suffering brought healing to his wounds. Now his whole soul yearned to heal hers.

He would wait until the next time they were alone. That wouldn't be until her job interview was over, and her parents had gone back to Denver.

Only a few more days, Kincaid.

CHAPTER THIRTEEN

A RECEPTIONIST CAME OUT of the attorney general's office. "They're ready for you now, Ms. Bretton."

"See you in a little while, Dad." Samantha's father had flown to Cheyenne with her to keep her company. She kissed his cheek before entering the conference room full of men.

The attorney general invited her to sit down before he introduced himself and his two assistants, then the governor of Wyoming who was sitting in on the board in an advisory capacity, and the superintendent of Yellowstone and Teton Parks.

"I understand you already know Pierce Gallagher, the chief ranger of Teton Park."

"Yes. It's a pleasure to meet all of you."

"Everyone here has looked over your impressive résumé, Ms. Bretton. Before you came in, it was the consensus of the group that we find out why you would want to fill the new position being created as a special assistant to the U.S. Attorney General's office in Teton Park. With your sterling credentials, you could go into private practice and name your price.

"As you're probably well aware, we've stipulated this is a lifetime career position. You're thirty-one years old, which means you could give thirty-four years to this office. That's a definite plus, since many of the programs in the park are ongoing and need continuity under one guiding hand.

"On the other side of the coin, you're young, attractive, single. Naturally we're concerned that your plans could change. Can you give us any reason to help us not be concerned that unexpected circumstances might cause you to leave prematurely?"

Samantha nodded. "That's a very fair, understandable question. In the first place, I have a thirteen-year-old daughter who lives with her father, Nick Kincaid, the chief ranger for biological wildlife in Teton Park. I've bought a home in Jackson Hole to be near her, and plan to live there and work out of my office for the duration of my life. The only thing that would change my ability to keep working would be if my cancer comes back. I'm in remission and pray that I remain healthy.

"As for my reason for wanting to serve the park, it was Jessica's father who taught me about the sacredness of wildlife. His ideas influenced me to study the kind of law that would help to protect it.

"Nick used to talk about the impact of machines in nature—aircraft overflights, for example—and how they endanger so many species of animals. Working for the Idaho Wildlife Federation, I've come to appreciate what he meant.

"When you're out in the woods, it's the sound of silence that makes the forest such a desirable, even spiritual, place to be. Lovers of the outdoors expect to find that silence in our national parks. It's my opinion the animals and the plants are God's gift to man. It's man's obligation to take care of them. That means we protect them by removing any menace to them in the air, in the water, in the land.

"Gentlemen, I would deem it an honor and a privilege to fight for their right to exist as creation intended, whether it be in Teton Park or elsewhere."

After she'd finished, there was such a long silence she worried that her admission about being a cancer survivor must have spooked them. But it didn't matter. If she didn't get the job, she was glad the money would be there for someone else to fight for the park.

She would always be able to run her own law practice and continue the struggle for the preservation of the environment by representing private citizens and groups.

To her surprise, the superintendent started clapping. Soon everyone joined in. The attorney general got to his feet. He looked around, then smiled at her. "It appears the vote is unanimous. Welcome aboard, Ms. Bretton."

Thank you, her heart cried. She was one step closer to Nick.

"Thank you. I'm thrilled."

Samantha stood up and shook hands with each of them. When she came to Pierce, he squeezed her palm extra hard. "I'll hug you later," he whispered.

"MARILYN? How are you feeling today?"

"Better and better. At this rate I'll be looking for a job in another few weeks."

Samantha moved the receiver to her other ear. "That's wonderful! When you're well enough for that, you'll come stay with me to celebrate."

"I'm counting the hours!"

"Do you think you can stand a little more good news?"

"I already know you got the job."

"How could you have heard that? I just returned from Cheyenne with Dad a few minutes ago and haven't told anybody but Mom."

"Hey—it's *me* you're talking to. Of course you got it, you silly goose! It was a foregone conclusion. What I'm waiting for is the *big* news."

"The kind you're talking about may never come." Samantha's voice trembled.

"Want to bet? If Nick didn't want you around all the time, you'd be commuting to Tennessee on a limited basis instead of living in Jackson."

"That still doesn't mean he—"

"Oh, for heaven sake," Marilyn interrupted. "You didn't survive for nothing. Right?"

There was no one in the world like Marilyn. "Right. Thank you for being the greatest friend on earth."

"I was just going to say the same thing to you. Call me tomorrow and give me the latest chapter and verse."

"I will. I promise."

The second Samantha hung up the phone she heard, "Honey?" When she turned, she saw both her parents standing in the doorway of her bedroom.

She could sense a certain tension coming from them she hadn't felt when she'd first walked into the house. Her adrenaline surged. "What's wrong?" she cried in alarm. "Has something happened to Jessica or Nick?"

"They're fine," her mother assured her. "While you were on the phone, your cell phone went off. We thought it was probably Jessica calling from school to see if you were back from Cheyenne yet, but it was Dr. Blake.''

Dr. Blake?

A cold sweat broke out over her body.

''Apparently he was on vacation when you phoned to get the results of your last blood test. Whoever gave you the information was reading from the first results.''

Samantha's stomach lurched.

''While he was reviewing your chart today, he noticed the latest results weren't in, so he called the lab. For some reason, those results never reached his office. He says these things happen, but it's very rare.

''Anyway, he's calling the lab at the hospital here in Jackson to arrange for the blood work. If possible, he's going to see if they'll fit you in before closing today. He said to give it fifteen minutes, then phone over there to find out.''

Oh no.

Her father smiled. ''You're going to be fine, honey.''

Her mother walked over and put her arms around her. ''You've felt marvelous for several months and have never looked more beautiful. Don't worry about another routine blood test, darling. Too many miraculous things have happened for your happiness to be taken away now.''

Samantha loved her parents. They'd always been positive about her illness. Her fight had been their fight. But this time things were different. The stakes were too high—she had everything to live for.

She eased away from her mother. ''I don't know about that, Mom. All I asked was to see my daughter again so I could tell her how much I love her. That wish has been granted and much more.

"The mistake at the lab is probably a sign that I went too far when I wanted Nick, too. Maybe—" Her voice broke.

"Samantha Bretton!" Her father spoke to her as he had when she was a little girl who didn't want to get back on her bike after she'd fallen. "Over two months ago you were given a clean bill of health. That hasn't changed, and it isn't going to.

"Call the lab. If they're ready for you, we'll drive you over and wait for you. The number is on the pad in your office. Let's go."

Her limbs felt like lead as she followed them down the hall. Each time in the past she'd been able to call on the reserve of faith deep inside to get her through the blackest periods.

But that was before she'd accomplished what needed to be done. Now that she'd had the reunion with her daughter, did it mean she'd run out of blessings?

When she reached for the phone, the answer came with full force. She could almost hear the pastor telling her to look upon her remission as permanent, and treat it as a rebirth.

That was what she was going to do. What she *had* to do.

"JESSICA? Over here!"

Nick's daughter had been walking toward the school bus with her friends. The second she heard her dad's voice she came running to the car and got in.

"Did Mom get the job?"

"There was never any question about that, but now it's official."

Pierce had called to tell him about the reverent ovation after Sam's eloquent speech. Between her conviction that it was a sacred duty to protect wildlife, plus her statement that she was a recovering cancer patient, there hadn't been a dry eye in the room. It had brought the members of the board to their feet.

The news that she'd given Nick the credit for guiding her along her chosen path was a little present Pierce tacked on at the end of the conversation for him to savor. Though Jessica had already told Nick the same thing weeks ago, and he'd read the words for himself in Sam's journal, hearing his best friend repeat them stirred his emotions more than ever.

"Do you think she's home yet?"

"I'm sure of it. I thought we'd drive over and congratulate her." Surprise her would be more like it. Nick didn't care if her parents were still at the house. The desire to see Sam had turned into a burning need.

Jessica didn't know about the money her mother had anonymously donated to enable the park to always have an attorney in residence. One day when his daughter was older, he would let her know what a truly rare and remarkable woman Sam was.

"There's Grandpa's car. They're home!"

He pulled in the driveway and they both got out. The blood pounded in his ears while he waited for Sam to answer the door.

"Maybe they can't hear the bell. Mom gave me a key so I could always let myself in." Jessica got it out of her purse. After she'd unlocked it, they went inside. "Mom? Grandma?"

Nick frowned. "Maybe they decided to grab a bite to eat in town. Let's check the garage."

To his disappointment, the new green Pathfinder Sam had bought over the holidays was missing.

"Heck. I'll call Mom on my cell phone and we'll drive wherever they are." In a minute Jessica said, "I got her voice mail."

"She probably turned the phone off for her interview and forgot to turn it back on."

"I guess."

Nick heard a dejected Jessica leave a message for her mother to call back as soon as she could. After she hung up she said, "Dad? Can we go look for them? Maybe they're at Shiver's."

She was reading his mind. "Good idea. We'll get a hamburger at the same time."

He purposely drove them on a circuitous route through the downtown area of Jackson in the hope of spotting Sam's car, but there was no sign of it.

"Grandpa said he wanted to get a sheepskin jacket like Mom's before they flew back to Denver. Maybe she drove them over to Western Outfitters."

"That's possible. We'll see if we can spot them."

When that failed to produce results, he drove them to Shiver's on East Broadway for a meal.

"Let's order takeout. Then we can eat on the way back to the house," Jessica suggested.

Nick agreed. He was as anxious as she was to find Sam.

Ten minutes later they started down Broadway. Near Willow Street a couple of cars pulled out into the evening traffic from the parking area of St. John's

Medical Center. One of them was the latest model green Pathfinder.

Nick's blood turned to ice water.

Jessica was busy eating her hamburger and hadn't noticed. It was just as well, since he didn't want to alarm her.

To play it safe he stayed several car lengths behind, but there was no doubt it was Sam at the wheel. He'd caught the glint of red-gold in the dying rays of the winter sun before it had dipped below the horizon.

Why had Sam gone to the hospital with her parents? Why hadn't she told him that she had an appointment scheduled?

Oh, no.

Why now? Why today on the heels of her trip to Cheyenne? She'd accepted the job offer. It was official. She wouldn't have followed through if there'd been any question she couldn't do it because of failing health.

Had the flight been too much for her? Had she been working too hard, trying to get settled, and reached the verge of exhaustion?

He would never forget the entries in her journal, the descriptions of what her physical suffering had been like, not to mention her mental and emotional agony.

"Dad? Don't you want your hamburger?"

"I'll eat when we get to the house."

"What's the matter? You look kind of sick."

Nothing escaped his daughter's eagle eye. "Today I verified that the moose had been poisoned."

"That's awful. When you find out who did it, Mom'll be able to prosecute them."

"I'm counting on it, honey." *I'm counting on living the rest of my life with her. I'm planning on us both living a long, long time.*

Nick followed Sam to her home. If she knew he'd been driving behind her, she showed no evidence of it. The garage door went up and the Pathfinder disappeared inside.

Once again he and Jessica went up to the front door, but this time his daughter unlocked it and they entered the house without ringing the bell. "I'll wait for you in the living room," he said before she ran off to find her mother.

He glanced around. Sam had Mrs. Bretton's flair for decorating. The house reflected elegant taste without being ostentatious. He'd never guess she'd barely moved in. Paintings had been hung. She'd placed art books on shelves and tables next to pots of azaleas and poinsettias.

Nick realized that Sam had never done anything in her life that he didn't love except reject him in order not to trap him.

What was the old saying? Set something free. If it doesn't come back, it was never yours to lose.

I was always yours, Sam. He'd never wanted to be set free. *Now you're back in my life, I'm going to keep what's always been mine.*

"Hi, Nick. You remember my mom and dad, of course."

Sam's steady voice sounded too in control for whatever she was hiding. He turned in her direction. She'd come into the room with her parents and Jessica. She made a sensational picture in a tailored green suit with a green-on-white print scarf. Professional, yet feminine.

He shook their hands. "It's good to see both of you again. You don't seem any older." It was the truth. "I find it hard to believe thirteen years have passed."

Nick saw pleading in their eyes, particularly in Mr. Bretton's. They wanted and needed forgiveness for their role in keeping him and Sam apart.

"Let's agree to forgive the past," Nick said.

"You've grown into a wonderful man who has raised a beautiful daughter." His voice shook. Not from age, but emotion. Something was wrong. Nick could feel it in every atom of his body. It was tearing him apart.

He smiled at his daughter. "Jessica's always been a joy,"

"Of course she has," Mrs. Bretton cried softly, hugging her granddaughter around her neck.

He turned back to gaze at Sam, studying her features for any sign of distress. There was none. She was a master at hiding her feelings when she needed to. He wasn't about to let her get away with it this time.

"After the board concluded their meeting, Pierce called me. I hear congratulations are in order."

She nodded. "For better or worse, I'm the new park attorney."

What was she telling him? Was she talking about the job being more than she could handle? Was she talking about her health?

"This calls for a celebration." Nick stared at Jessica. "You won't mind if I steal your mother for a little while, will you? Pierce and Leslie have planned a small surprise. I've been ordered by the chief to deliver her to their house, then I'll bring her back.'' He turned to Sam's parents. "Is that all right with everyone?"

"Of course," Mrs. Bretton replied. "We'll have loads of fun here, won't we, Jessica?"

As she nodded, her grandfather said, "You two go on. This is a red letter day for the park. We'll watch out for our Jessie."

Our Jessie...

Who would have ever dreamed up a scenario like this? One look in Sam's eyes and Nick knew she was remembering another night long ago when her parents had dismissed any possibility of him marrying their daughter.

"If you'll get your coat, we'll go."

Sam kissed her daughter's cheek before leaving the room. Jessica walked him to the front door. "Have a good time, Dad."

"You can't *not* have a good time at the Gallaghers." He tousled her curls. In a moment Sam joined them, wearing a fitted black cashmere coat. She was so breathtaking, words failed him.

"Let's go."

They stepped outside. Though it was only a few minutes after six, it felt like midnight. He helped her into the car before going around to the driver's side.

Once they reached the main road leading to the park he said, "You didn't sign on with the park anytime too soon. I've got a case you can dig your teeth into right now."

The conversation he intended to have with her

couldn't take place until after they'd reached their destination, so he'd decided to talk shop instead.

"Tell me about it."

"A moose was accidentally exposed to poison meant for a coyote and it died. I traced the animal's prints back to the source and delivered a citation to the ranch owner. He said I couldn't prove anything, and even if I could, nobody would do anything about it because everybody knows coyotes are a nuisance."

"What kind of evidence do you have?"

Nick spent the next few minutes giving her the gruesome details.

"I'd say that man's in bad trouble. From what you've told me, I'll be able to prosecute his case as a felony under the Lacey Act. It carries heavy penalties including imprisonment and fines. When word of that gets out to the other ranchers in the area, it should make them wary."

"That case was just for starters. I've got more I need to tell you. One involves some guys I caught heli-skiing where the wolverines are denning. The other is a real problem. We're still searching for the person who killed two large adult mule deer east of the Kelly Road.

"I discovered them the other morning. They'd been killed for their trophy size antlers. One buck had been shot and his antlers removed. The other deer was dead, but its antlers were intact, probably because someone came by, causing the poachers to run away."

"That's horrible."

He nodded. "Pierce has put out a bulletin through the Park Watch and Jackson Hole Crimestoppers. A five thousand dollar reward has been posted for information leading to an arrest.''

Sam let out a heavy sigh. "Killing beautiful, gentle animals in cold blood for a wall trophy is one of the most appalling crimes I can think of.''

Nick grimaced. "I agree. What's worse, every time it happens, the gene pool for the mule deer population is diminished. As I said earlier, the park has needed someone like you in the worst way.''

I need you in the worst way.

"Fortunately, the funding is in place so there can be an advocate for wildlife for many years to come, no matter who it is," she said in a quiet aside.

Shut up, Sam. You're terrifying me.

"Didn't we just pass the Gallaghers'?''

"We're not going to Pierce's house.''

Her head jerked toward him. "I thought you said they were having a little party.''

"I lied.''

CHAPTER FOURTEEN

SAMANTHA *had* been right!

There was a new aggressiveness, a kind of steely determination about him that reminded her of the old, confident Nick. After all the years of wishing she could be with him again, after all these weeks of suppressing her longings in front of him, was it possible he was finally going to let down his guard and tell her how he felt about her? She didn't know how much longer she could stand the suspense.

They'd driven to Nick's house, straight into the garage. She heard the door close behind the car, isolating them from the world.

"Why were you at the hospital earlier?"

"How did you know I was there?"

He shut off the motor. "I saw your car."

She was trying to read between the lines. Was it possible he was more frightened about her cancer coming back than he'd let on? Had he been putting on a brave front for Jessica, when all this time he was worried sick?

Before she made too many assumptions that could be wrong, she got out of the car before he could come around and walked through the kitchen to the living room.

While she waited for him to say more, she took off

her coat and placed it over a chair. In the shadowy light of one of the lamps he'd turned on, his features looked gaunt, his eyes bleak and pain-filled. He stood in the center of the room with his strong legs slightly apart, as if bracing himself.

"I'm waiting for an answer."

Tell him the way it is, Samantha. The way it's always going to be until the end.

"A recovering cancer patient has to be checked and rechecked on a constant basis. You know that."

He folded his arms. "Not on the day she pulled off a coup that will benefit the park for a score of years to come. What changed after your plane landed at the airport in Jackson? Don't insult my intelligence by telling me you had a standing appointment at St. John's for five o'clock in the afternoon on today of all days."

She averted her eyes. "I'd just walked in the door when I received a call from my doctor in Coeur D'Alene. It seems the results of my last blood test never arrived at his office from the lab. The nurse who told me everything was normal had mistakenly read the first set of results. So he set things up here for me to have another test."

"But the first one indicated you were well, right?"

Her heart came into her throat. "Yes."

"So the results of this test will reveal the same thing."

"Yes. I'm positive they will," she said, wanting to assure him because the lines in his rugged face had grown more pronounced.

"You wouldn't lie to me. You haven't been sick and didn't tell anyone?"

She shook her head. "I've never felt better."

There was a whiteness around his lips.

Oh, Nick—

"When will you know the results?" His words were terse, anxious.

"They said it would take a few hours, then they'd inform the doctor. Because it's so late in the day, I won't hear before tomorrow."

His gray eyes glistened with tears. She moved toward him. Her whole body was trembling. "Don't be afraid for me."

"How can I not be?"

With one question, he'd bared his heart and soul to her.

"Because this is going to be the state of my life from here on out. Blood tests and the wait for results. I'm convinced I was given a stay of execution long enough to get to know my daughter and assure her she had a mother who loved her and never wanted to give her up. I expect to live a long time."

"But some of the entries in your journal don't—" His hands had formed fists.

"What do you know about my journal?"

His eyes studied her features. "I know everything. The day the movers came, I emptied the last box they brought in. Your journal was on the bottom. I read it from cover to cover. Every word."

She gasped and looked away. No wonder he was frightened. She'd held nothing back in those entries.

"Don't be angry with me. You took thirteen years of my life from me, Sam. I had every right to find out why. At least that's what I told myself until I started reading about your pain. That's when I began the journey through mine…''

Her head swung back toward him. "What do you mean?" she asked in shock.

"Do you have any idea of my self-loathing for not coming after you years ago? For not understanding your grief? Your guilt? For not lifting a finger to help you because my damnable pride got in the way?

"In my rage I thought about finding you. For years I dreamed about walking into the library at Harvard where you were studying and dragging you out of there without giving a damn if I made a scene. I wanted you to pay for what you'd done to me.

"I'm not the saint you've made me out to be, Sam.'' He paced the floor, then stopped and threw his head back as if he were in the throes of agony.

"I've committed the greatest crime a father could commit against his daughter. From the beginning I shut out all the questions Jessica wanted to ask about you before she could dare put voice to them. I was going to show you I didn't need you, that Jessica didn't need you.

"It was easy. My anger over your rejection sustained me for the years I spent hiring one nanny after another. I must have gone through dozens of them.

"Several of the eligible nannies would have made great wives and mothers. They were vocal and willing. But I wasn't having any of that. Neither was Jessica, who was so jealous of every woman who came near, she made the perfect buffer.

"There were lots of women along the way, women I met at work or through friends. Naturally, they hoped we would end up planning a wedding. I scoffed at the idea. Your refusal to fight for Jessica and me because you couldn't trust me enough to love and care for you, had killed the desire for marriage on my part.''

Samantha hugged her arms to her waist while she listened to the pain that had been bottled up inside him all these years. Pain *she'd* caused.

''This summer when Jessica knew she'd be starting high school, she protested against me hiring another woman. The change in her had a lot to do with Leslie, the one female my daughter took to because she was Cory's nanny and posed no threat.

''Without making it official, Pierce's wife more or less filled the breach when there was an emergency and I couldn't be home on time, or not at all. We were limping along. Then I heard your voice on the phone....''

His emotions were so palpable, she bowed her head.

''The morning after Halloween, Jessica went to work with me. It took all day for me to find that place in my soul where I had started to forgive you for what you'd done to me.

''Jessica sensed something was wrong and asked me if I needed to talk. My little girl, the parent. She'd reversed the roles.

''I said, 'If you had a chance to meet your mother, how would you feel about that?'''

A hushed quiet followed while Samantha waited to hear the rest.

''You should have seen her eyes.... That's when pain and guilt scorched my soul like a red-hot poker. It was clear she wanted her mother. She'd always wanted her mother.''

His expression grew black. ''Later on, when you

told her you couldn't come for the mother-daughter party because of some work commitment, I swear I could have strangled you with my bare hands.''

''I'm so sorry.''

''Stop apologizing, Sam. Listen to what I'm saying.'' The cords stood out in his neck. ''It was my fault. All of it. I was so brutal to you on the phone and at the Elk Inn that you were terrified of my reaction, with good reason.''

She shook her head. ''Not terrified, never that. Only conscious of a blessing I'd been granted, and didn't dare ask for more. Don't do this to yourself, Nick,'' she begged. ''I've been down that path. Between the two of us, I think we've crucified ourselves long enough. We have to think of Jessica now.''

She heard his sharp intake of breath. ''You mean the Jessica who became an instant grown-up when she thought you'd rejected her? The one determined to take care of her good old dad?''

Samantha let out an incredulous cry. ''Old?''

He slowly nodded. ''Oh yes. She let me know she'd be there to watch over me in my old age. We didn't need anyone else. It had always been the two of us, and that was the way things were going to stay.''

''Oh Nick…'' Tears rolled down her cheeks.

''That's the kind of great father I turned out to be,'' he said in self-recrimination. ''My anger toward you has done psychological damage to our daughter.

''A parent is supposed to give his child the tools to grow up well-rounded and independent. You live in the hope that one day, at the right time, she'll find a great guy and go off happily into the sunset to start her own family.

"Not our Jessica. I'm the one responsible for stunting her growth. That became obvious when you told her you couldn't come to the party. She immediately informed me she was going to get straight As like you and become a biologist like me. Together we would live in the park doing the work we love side by side, and I would never be alone.

"Give a psychiatrist a crack at Jessica and you would discover a father who has done it all wrong from day one."

"But you haven't!" Samantha disagreed. "She's loving and forgiving. I've noticed how open she is to everything."

A solemn expression stole over his handsome features. "That's because you're in her life. It has changed everything." He took a step toward her. "It has changed me. Now I want to talk about *us*. I want you for my wife as soon as possible."

"You mean it?" she cried. "You're willing to risk marrying me knowing my history? Knowing that every month I go in for a test, you'll be worried about the results?"

His body went rigid.

"I'm not saying this for me, Nick. I'm saying it for you. Now that you've put your anger behind you and we've made our peace, are you certain you wouldn't rather find another woman to love who doesn't have my past problem?"

"There's a risk to loving anyone. You're worth that risk."

"Oh Nick! I want us to be happy. You need to be very sure about this before we make any plans or tell Jessica. At least sleep on it tonight and we'll talk more in the morning. Please take me home now. To be honest, I'm very tired. It's been a big day for so many reasons.''

SAM WASN'T LYING. She looked utterly exhausted and spent. It brought out an ethereal beauty. He didn't want to see her like this. It reminded him of all she'd gone through. Her journal entries still haunted him.

She was right about one thing. If he couldn't get past his fear for her, then a new nightmare would begin. If she was sick again, then so be it. They would fight it together. Tomorrow her parents were leaving. After she'd heard from the doctor, Nick would force her to marry him, even if it meant kidnapping her to do it. She would have no choice in the matter. Pierce would help him.

Not trusting himself to get within five feet of her, Nick left her to freshen up while he waited for her in the car.

En route to Jackson his cell phone went off.

"That's probably Jessica."

Nick checked the caller ID. "It's business." He clicked on. "Rex? What's up?"

"You know those guides camping in Garnet Canyon?"

"Yes?"

"From the stories filtering in, there was a sudden earth tremor. I'll be damned if they weren't caught in an avalanche. I need you on the mountain to help with the rescue. Are you home?"

"I'm on my way to Jackson."

"Then I'll tell one of the rangers to bring some extra gear for you."

"Fine. I'll be at the rendezvous point as soon as I can."

"What's wrong?" Sam asked the question the second he'd hung up.

"There's been an avalanche. It has trapped some guides and professional skiers doing winter maneuvers. They've been working toward their mountaineering certification with the American Avalanche Institute. If they come out of this alive, they'll have experienced one lesson that couldn't have been gained any other way."

The thought of being buried under a mountain of snow was too horrible to contemplate. What if more fell while Nick and the others were out there?

"Where are you meeting everyone?"

"The airport. I'll fly in with one of the rescue helicopters."

"I thought you were a biologist!"

"I am, but I also trained under Pierce to learn mountaineering skills for emergencies like this. He's probably there now. This park is his baby."

"You two are very close, aren't you."

"Yes. In some ways he reminds me of Joey."

"Jessica told me he was killed on his motorcycle right before graduation. I'm so sorry. He was a wonderful friend to us. If I'd known—"

"Don't go there, Sam."

She flashed him a brave smile. "I won't. Since the airport is on the way to town, I'll drop you off, then go on home. When you want me and Jessica to come for you, we will."

"It could be an all-night operation. We'll have to wait and see. If so, Pierce will give me a ride to the house after we get back. I'll phone you tomorrow to bring my car home.''

''No matter how long it takes, Jessica's going to be anxious until she hears from you.''

Too soon they reached the airport. It was hell having to be separated right now. While he was taking the house key off the ring, he could feel Sam's anxiety.

Without conscious thought he caught her face between his hands and kissed her long and hard.

''I'll see you in the morning.''

As he strode away, Sam climbed into the driver's seat and started the car, but she was still trembling from his passion. Like the tremor that had caused the avalanche, Nick had unleashed such a powerful force inside of her, all she could do was ride it while it swept her along at heart-stopping speed.

When she finally landed in her driveway in Jackson, she rested her head against the steering wheel, willing her equilibrium to come back.

''Mom?''

At the sound of Jessica's voice, she recoiled and opened the door. Her daughter's face was a study in fright. ''Where's Dad? What's wrong?''

She needed a minute before answering any questions. Nick had disoriented her, and Sam was afraid it was permanent.

''Your father had to help rescue some people trapped by an avalanche. While I was pulling the keys out of the ignition, they slipped from my hand.''

''No they didn't, Mom,'' Jessica said with that

forthright honesty of hers. "Are you still feeling sick?"

Samantha got out of the car and shut the door. "What do you mean *still*, darling?"

"When Dad and I were driving home from Shiver's earlier, I saw your car pulling away from the hospital."

"Why didn't you ask Grandma and Grandpa? They would have told you I went in for a routine blood test."

"Promise?"

"Promise. I'll be getting periodic blood tests from now on. They take about five minutes and don't hurt."

"I bet you're scared, huh."

Always the truth, Samantha. "Yes."

"If your cancer comes back, will you have to get more chemo?"

"Yes."

"I hope you're okay."

She grabbed her daughter and hugged her tightly. "I hope so, too. But if I'm not, I'll do whatever I have to do to get better again."

"My history teacher's husband has cancer. I told her about you, that yours might come back. She said it's not really so terrible because everyone has to die sometime. And since she knows her husband doesn't have a long time to live, it has helped their family to enjoy every day they have with him. She said it could be a blessing."

"Oh darling." Samantha held her tighter.

She was going to have to meet this teacher of Jessica's and thank her for the priceless gift she'd given her.

"You don't have to worry about anything, Mom. I'll go to all your doctor's appointments with you. I'll take care of you. You'll never have to be alone."

My precious, precious girl.

The words reminded Samantha of the conversation she'd just had with Nick at his house.

Clearly, Jessica was able to deal with the cancer threat much better than Samantha or Nick had ever dreamed. It was the situation between her parents that was tearing her daughter apart. There was only one way to solve that problem.

Tonight Nick had bared his soul to her. He'd asked her to be his wife. He'd called on her heart, body and soul, all of which had always belonged to him.

Later, when she went to pick him up, she would tell him she wanted to get married no matter what. Nothing was more important than being together. But right this minute, it was time to help their daughter.

"Come on, darling. Let's go in the house. It's freezing out here."

Her parents met them at the door. *Two more people Samantha needed to help.* Two loving, marvelous human beings riddled with guilt and pain, who'd never been able to forgive themselves for what they imagined they'd done to ruin her life.

Tonight all the pain and the guilt and the self-flagellation were about to end.

They went into the living room. Her father relieved both of them of their coats. "Where's Nick?"

"Dad's out with the rangers helping some guys caught in an avalanche," Jessica explained in a matter-of-fact tone. She'd grown up with a father whose life was dedicated to the rescue of animals and humans.

Samantha had a lot to learn from their daughter, since right now part of her was terrified something could happen to Nick, either on the mountain or in the helicopter.

"Did you have a nice time at the Gallaghers'?" her mother asked.

With that question Samantha's heart picked up speed. "Why don't you all sit down and I'll tell you."

Something in her tone must have alerted them it was no casual directive. They did her bidding, but three pairs of anxious eyes remained fastened on her.

Filled with a restless energy, Samantha stood behind a chair and held on to it.

"There was no party. Nick only said that because he wanted to be alone with me. We went to the house and had a long talk about everything. It was one that should have taken place years ago, but that's irrelevant now. What's important is Nick and I are going to be married."

A collective cry of relief rang throughout the living room. Jessica's young, smooth face radiated joy. She jumped up to hug Samantha and almost knocked her over.

Through the profusion of red-gold curls, Samantha smiled at her parents and watched the lines of sorrow vanish from their faces. All that remained were the etchings of life experiences, both the good and the bad, that had formed their character over the years.

Their eyes sent her an implicit message. They rejoiced in her decision to grab her happiness with both hands and not let the amount of time she had left on this earth matter.

While she rocked her daughter in her arms, they heard her cell phone go off.

"Maybe they didn't need your father, after all, and he wants us to come and get him!"

She let go of Jessica long enough to pull it out of her purse. To her disappointment the caller ID said Out of Area. It could be Marilyn, or even Reed, her former boss.

"Hello?"

"Samantha Bretton?" She recognized that voice.

"Dr. Blake?" His call had the effect of knocking the wind out of her. Sudden tension filled the living room once more. "I didn't expect to hear from you until tomorrow."

"Good news deserves to be delivered as soon as possible."

She gripped the phone tighter. "I'm still normal?"

"You are. As I told your parents, the loss of a lab test result is something that rarely happens. I'm sorry you had to go through the ordeal of waiting and worrying unnecessarily."

She gave her family a thumbs-up, but could hardly see because of her tears. "I'm not. I'm convinced it happened to help me make the most important decision of my life. I've moved to Jackson, Wyoming, and I'm getting married."

"Now you've made *my* day. When you get a new doctor where you're living, I'll have the records sent. To be safe, you should plan on having another test in a month. Have you experienced more flulike symptoms associated with the Interferon?"

"Once in a while I get a chill, but nothing else to speak of."

"Terrific. Phone me anytime, Samantha."

"I will. You have no idea how much this call has meant to me."

"I think I do. Good night."

"Good night, Dr. Blake, and thank you."

As she hung up, the floor suddenly moved beneath her feet. She grabbed hold of the end of the couch to keep from falling. It was a heavy sofa, yet it seemed to be moving of its own accord.

Everyone looked at each other as a few books fell to the floor. The brass candlestick on the hearth toppled over. Jessica's eyes grew round while they waited to see if anything else would happen. When it didn't she cried, "We've just had an earthquake!"

"Will you look at that dining room chandelier?" Sam's father exclaimed.

Sure enough, it was swinging back and forth like a pendulum.

"Do you get these often?" Samantha's mother asked Jessica.

"No. Dad says there are tremors all the time throughout the Yellowstone-Teton corridor, but we don't usually feel them."

"I remember there was a major quake in the fifties near here. It broke the Hebgen Lake dam in Montana and created a lake."

"Quake Lake! We studied about it at school."

Samantha's thoughts flew to Nick and Pierce. "Jessica, honey? Call Cory on your cell and find out if he and Leslie are all right."

"Okay. Poor Lucy," her daughter moaned. "I bet it frightened her to death. Dad says earthquakes terrify animals."

"And people," Samantha's mother murmured.

"Mom? Are you okay?"

"Yes." She smiled. "Just startled."

"How about you, Dad?"

"I'm fine. Come on, my love. Let's walk around and see if there has been any structural damage to the house."

He helped his wife to her feet. They set the things up that had fallen, then disappeared into the other room.

Samantha kept an arm around Jessica while she talked to Cory. "Just a minute…" The girl lifted her head. "Mom? Cory told me they didn't feel anything, but Leslie wants to talk to you. I'm going to turn on the TV!"

"Thanks, honey." She took the phone from her before Jessica dashed off. "Leslie?"

"Hi. Are you all right?"

"We're fine."

"Cory said your chandelier was swaying."

"You should have seen it!"

"I don't know, Samantha. I'm kind of glad I didn't. Cameron's mother called me while Jessica was talking to Cory. She's the first person designated to relay information on our phone tree. Her husband just got word that the epicenter was in Idaho."

"I thought it came from Yellowstone."

"I assumed the same thing. From what I've gathered, no one in Moose was affected. Sometimes it happens that way."

Beads of perspiration dotted Sam's hairline. "Leslie—"

"I know what you're going to ask," her friend interrupted gently. "I haven't heard from Pierce. The minute I do, I'll call you. So far no park rangers have reported any problems to dispatch except for the avalanche."

"Thank heaven."

"Yes indeed," Leslie commiserated. "Cory says they're talking about it on the cable network."

"I'm going to go look right now. If I hear from Nick, I'll call you."

"Good."

After they hung up she rushed through the house to the family room, where Jessica had turned on the TV.

"…but the early reports indicate no fatalities yet. The epicenter of the 6.9 earthquake near Borah's Peak in central Idaho sent out tremors that have been felt in parts of Montana, Nevada, Oregon, Utah, Washington, Wyoming, and the provinces of Alberta, British Columbia and Saskatchewan, Canada."

By now Samantha's parents had joined them. "Nothing's broken, honey. No cracks in walls or ceilings that we could see. We were lucky."

"That's a relief. Thanks, Dad. Jessica, honey? Will you turn to another station and see if they've got any local information?"

"…tuning in, some Jackson residents got a surprise tonight when the Idaho quake knocked glasses and cans off shelves and caused some vending machines in a few local businesses to topple over. Fortunately, no injuries have been reported yet.

"The biggest story tonight focuses on a rescue attempt being carried out in Grand Teton National Park. Seismologists say an earlier tremor foreshadowing the major quake dislodged a wall of snow off the Grand

Teton, burying some avalanche experts who've been camped at the base for several days, carrying out a training session.

"Rangers and other rescue workers are doing everything possible to free the victims. The public is being asked to stay away. We'll keep the following Jackson number on the screen for those people inquiring about the victims through the sheriff's office. Please do not call unless you're a relative."

While the announcer was still talking, Jessica turned to Samantha. "Dad gets so mad when people show up to watch. They just get in the way."

"It's human nature, Jessie." Samantha's father turned off the TV. "I've got a great idea. While we're waiting to hear from your dad, let's get in the car and go out for a steak dinner. I'd like to celebrate your mother's new job." *And her good news from the doctor,* his expression said.

"It's a terrific idea, Dad." If Samantha had to stay here and think about all the things that could happen to Nick, she would go mad.

Two HOURS LATER Samantha pulled into the driveway of her house. They'd been at dinner all that time. There was still no word from Nick.

Her parents looked tired. Once they entered the house, she urged them to go to bed. Jessica wanted to watch more cable news coverage of the earthquake, but by midnight her eyelids were drooping, and no wonder. It had been a long, emotional day.

Samantha turned off the TV. "Come on, honey. Time to go upstairs." Jessica didn't protest.

Tucking her daughter into bed was a joy that Samantha cherished. "Thank you for letting me treat you like a little girl sometimes."

Jessica was almost asleep. "I like it," she whispered.

"Honey? Since your grandparents are here, I'm going to drive to the house and wait for your father."

"That's good. It'll make him so happy to find you there, Mom."

"If by any chance he calls you, pretend I'm here asleep. I want to surprise him."

"Don't worry. I won't give you away."

"I can always count on you. Is your house key in your purse?"

"Yes. It's in the living room."

"I'll find it. Talk to you in the morning." She leaned over to kiss her forehead. A contented smile on her daughter's face was the last thing Samantha saw before she turned out the light.

Not the least bit tired herself, she hurried downstairs to wash her hair and shower. After donning jeans and a cable knit sweater, she left the bedroom with her journal. After retrieving her jacket and the key, she was ready to go.

Once she'd left the town behind, the grand image of the jagged Tetons shooting up from Jackson Hole in the middle of the winter night startled her. Tonight she understood why they were heralded as America's most famous mountain vista. To think this was Nick's backyard. Now it was hers, too....

All was quiet in the park. As she drove into Moose, she felt above the visor for the remote control device. Once the house came in sight, she raised the garage door. With the aid of Jessica's key, she let herself into the kitchen.

After removing her jacket, she sat down at the table to write in her journal. Until Nick walked in the front door, she would bring her entries up to date.

Jackson, Wyoming
January 3

It's quarter to three in the morning. I'm in Nick's kitchen, waiting for Pierce to drop him off. They've been out on a dangerous rescue operation.

As soon as Nick gets here, I'm going to tell him I want to get married as soon as possible.

Seven hours ago I made that decision. It seems fitting that as soon as I did, there was an earthquake. It shook the earth and a huge part of the continent.

Tonight at dinner my adorable daughter asked me and my parents why we thought the quake had happened when it did.

Dad said no one knew the answer. Pressure had been building under the earth's crust for years and for some reason it finally found release today. He gave her a perfectly sound, logical explanation, but I have my own theory.

I'm convinced there has been a special force at work in the cosmos. Today I got the job I wanted. Tonight I received another clean bill of health from the doctor.

All the stars and planets have lined up in a

particular way to open my eyes. I can see clearly now. I see what Nick saw so many years ago.

We belong together!

I've come to my senses at last.

Is it any wonder an earthquake followed?

I'm reminded of a game my friends and I used to play in elementary school. Red Light, Green Light. When it was red, you couldn't cross the line.

Today it's green, green, green.

CHAPTER FIFTEEN

THE MAN STRAPPED IN the toboggan drifted in and out of consciousness. He muttered something. Nick crouched down next to him. "What are you trying to say?" He put his ear to the man's bluish lips to listen.

"L—Leo..." His voice faded before he blacked out again.

Nick signaled the others to get the man to the snow machine, and from there to the chopper.

After putting his skis back on, Nick used his poles to push off toward the last group of rangers. They were huddled around one of the injured guides, who was suffering from a dislocated hip.

"Pierce?"

His friend turned around.

"Has everyone been accounted for from the master list?"

"Yes. This man's the last one."

"Was there a member of the group named Leo? The guy we just shipped out on the toboggan kept muttering that name."

Pierce frowned. "It doesn't sound familiar. I'll ask."

While Nick waited, he lifted his head to study the couloir where the avalanche had buried eight men in a sea of ice and snow. They'd survived because of their expertise and the quick response of the rescue teams. Still, it was a miracle their lives had been spared.

But the greatest miracle of all was Sam. She was a survivor. Nick couldn't wait to get back to her so their life could begin. They were going to have a life together. A long one.

"Leo's the guy's brother." Pierce said a minute later. "We told him we'd get word to him. We know eight men camped here, and eight have been shipped out to the hospital."

"That's good enough for me. Let's go home." Nick waited for him to put on his skis, then they shushed down the mountain to the snow machines waiting for them below.

When they arrived, one of the rangers approached. "Chief? Big news. There's been a whopper 6.9 earthquake in Idaho near Borah Peak. It was felt over most of the west and into Canada. The tremor that triggered this avalanche must have been a precursor. So far there's no report of injuries or damage in the park."

Pierce shot Nick a look before he said, "What about Jackson?"

"I heard of two fatalities, but most likely there won't be a detailed assessment before tomorrow."

With his heart banging in his chest. Nick whipped out his cell phone.

Pick up, Jessica. Wherever his daughter was, that's where he would find her mother.

"Hi, Dad. Where are you?"

She didn't sound alarmed, she sounded as if she'd been asleep.

"I'm on my way home."

"It's almost six in the morning. I bet you're tired."

Actually, he'd never felt more wide awake. "Honey—I just heard about the earthquake."

"It was amazing. Mom was standing up when it happened. If she hadn't grabbed hold of the end of the couch in time, she would have been thrown to the floor."

"Is she all right?"

"Yes. Everyone's fine and sound asleep."

His eyes closed tightly in relief. "That's good. Tell you what. I'll have Pierce run me home from the airport. When you and your mother wake up in the morning, she can bring you over. Okay?"

That's when he'd kidnap Sam and drive her to the church, where they were would get married. Pierce had already made the arrangements with the pastor.

"Okay. Dad? Did anyone…die tonight?"

"No."

"I'm glad. I love you."

"I love you, too."

The guys were waiting. After hanging up, Nick took off his skis and got on the snow machine. The trip to the chopper seemed to take forever, but once they'd climbed on board, it wasn't long before they reached the airport.

While in the air, the pilot told them about the fatalities in Jackson. They learned that the quake had caused a car with two teenagers to veer off the road. It overturned on the shoulder. They'd sustained head injuries, and wouldn't have died if they'd been wearing seat belts.

Tragic as it was, Nick couldn't help but be thankful it hadn't been Sam or Jessica.

Pierce had to be thinking the same thing about his own wife and son.

His wife.

Nick had always thought of Sam as his wife. He couldn't remember a time when he didn't feel married to her. It explained why he could never build a lasting relationship with another woman.

Our time has finally come, sweetheart.

Ten minutes later Pierce dropped him off in front of his house. Nick had discussed his strategy for the kidnapping with him. "I'll be waiting for your call," his friend said with a grin.

"Thanks, Pierce."

After waving him off, he hurried to the porch and let himself in the front door. Before hitting the sack, he needed a ton of food, a shower and shave, in that order.

On his way to the fridge, he froze. A woman with red-gold hair was sitting at his kitchen table. Actually, she was slumped over it with her head resting on her arms, sound asleep.

The sight of Sam gave his heart the workout of its life. He tiptoed toward her. She'd been writing in her journal. Unable to resist, he read a few words.

Talk about shaking the earth! There wouldn't have to be a kidnapping, after all.

She loves you, Kincaid. She wanted him in sickness and in health. They were, finally, going to be a family.

SAMANTHA STIRRED, thinking she could hear water running, but suddenly the noise stopped. She lifted her head from the table, shocked to realize she'd fallen asleep while she'd been writing in her journal.

Her watch said ten after seven. She couldn't believe that she'd been exhausted enough to sleep in the chair. But now that she was wide awake, she sensed she wasn't alone.

Had Nick come home?

She flew from the kitchen and through the house. Her feet barely touched the ground. As she turned down the hall toward his bedroom, she noticed him coming out the door dressed in a pair of sweats.

"Nick—"

"I know, darling—"

Samantha ran to him and Nick swung her around, both of them intoxicated by the knowledge they'd never be alone again.

He cried her name in a voice of intense yearning before his mouth covered hers. The world wheeled away. Only their love for each other remained as they tried to show each other the depth of their long suppressed feelings.

She quaked in response to the familiar feel of his lips, hands and body. Being back in his arms again, she could almost believe there had never been the painful thirteen-year separation.

Overwhelmed to find release like this, she smothered him with the love pouring out of her. When they eventually reached the bed and she looked into his eyes, she discovered his were wet, too.

He lifted trembling fingers to her face, tracing the bones and hollows the way he used to do. "I thought you were beautiful before…" He swallowed. "Sweetheart—"

His lips made a relentless sweep of her face and throat, finding the path they'd taken so many times in the past. He ended up burying them in her hair, crying out his need of her. "I love you, Sam. I've always loved you."

She crushed him closer. "I've always loved you, too," she said in a shaking voice. "I've missed you so terribly, Nick. I swear it was the memory of the love we shared that held me together during my darkest hours."

"We're back where we belong now. From here on out, we'll share everything, because this is forever," he vowed.

The realization that they were together at last, really together, that nothing would ever keep them apart again, still hadn't sunk in. Samantha couldn't get close enough. No kiss lasted long enough.

When the phone rang, they both let out a groan. She knew that because he was a ranger, he would always be on call. In case this was an emergency, he had to respond, but she could hardly bear to let him go long enough to answer it.

He pulled her with him as he reached for the phone on the bedside table.

"It's our daughter," he whispered against Samantha's lips, made swollen and tender by his.

She smiled. That was different. "You have to talk to her. Before I drove over here, I told her *and* Mom and Dad we were planning to get married."

At that revelation his eyes gleamed.

"Naturally, she's dying to know if you're home yet, let alone if we're together," Sam added.

"Nothing's sacred in our house," he teased, kissing her mouth long and hard.

"You mean the one in Jackson? I bought it for us."

"That's the one I intend on living in with you. I love it."

"I love you."

Their mouths clung feverishly. The phone was still ringing.

"Quick, darling. She won't be satisfied until one of us answers."

Nick clicked the phone on. "Good morning, honey."

"Dad?"

He grinned to hear the shock in her voice. "Yes?"

"You don't sound like yourself."

"I don't? What do I sound like?"

"Different, and younger, and *so* happy!"

You've got that right, daughter of mine. With my wife-to-be nestled in my arms, her gorgeous blue eyes trained on my face, life is almost perfect. "I'm going to be even happier in about four hours."

"How come?"

"Because there's going to be a wedding at the church."

"What?" Sam sat straight up, with an ecstatic expression. He put his hand around the back of her head and pulled her close so he could kiss her again.

"You're kidding!" Jessica's squeal of joy came over the phone line. "For real? Today?"

"I would never kid about the most important day of my life. If you guys think I'm going to wait a second longer than absolutely necessary before marrying this beautiful woman, then you have another thing coming.

"Pierce is arranging everything as we speak, so put

on that pretty dress you wore to his wedding, and tell your grandparents to get ready.''

''How soon are you coming home?''

''As soon as we pick up the license at the county clerk's office in Jackson. Your mom's making all kinds of noises that she needs more time to prepare, but since she couldn't be more beautiful than she is right now, I'm not going to worry about it. See you in a little while, honey.'' He hung up.

Sam had broken down, sobbing for joy.

He could relate. He, too, felt such relief that they would finally be joined. After kissing her again he said, ''Ever since you drove from the airport with me, I've had a dream of marrying you in the Tetons' rustic log Chapel of the Transfiguration.

''It's near the southern entrance of the park. There's a large window behind the altar framing the magnificent mountains. I can visualize us standing in front of it a few hours from now while we make our official vows to each other, before our daughter, our parents and our closest friends.''

''I can't believe this is happening.''

''Believe it, sweetheart. The time for the Kincaid family to rejoice is finally here.''

''But how can we get married so fast?''

''Very easily. There's no waiting period in Wyoming, no blood test. All we need is the license. Pierce has contacted the pastor and is arranging a private ceremony for us.''

''What about your work?''

''My work can wait. My love for you can't.'' He kissed the palms of her hands. ''I need you in my bed before the day is out, but I don't want you to suffer guilt because we once again anticipated our wedding vows.

"This time we're going to do it right, sweetheart. Today is a shiny new beginning for both of us. I won't allow anything to tarnish it. We'll drive to the church and claim each other in front of everyone before we enjoy our honeymoon."

He heard her breath catch. "That's going to be hard on Jessica. She's never been separated from both of us before."

He kissed the heart-shaped mouth he craved. "Our daughter can stay at the house with your parents for a few days while we hang out here. Knowing we're close by will help her."

"You're right. You're always right."

He could tell something else was bothering her. "What's wrong, sweetheart? Why does the mention of a honeymoon make you nervous?"

She averted her eyes. "If you must know, I'm frightened."

He put a hand under her chin and lifted it, forcing her to look at him. "Of what?"

Her eyes filled. "I—I'm not the seventeen-year-old you once made love to."

Nick smiled. "I'm not the twenty-year-old."

"You're more gorgeous than ever."

"So are you," he said in a husky voice.

"No." She shook her head. "My body has aged."

"So has mine."

"But mine has been sick. My hair's not the same. I'm thinner."

"You're more womanly."

"Don't try to make me feel better, Nick."

"Are we having our first fight?"

"Don't tease me, darling. I want to be the girl you remember, and I'm not!"

"No. You're not. You've grown up. I loved the girl you were, but I love the woman more. You're wonderful and remarkable, and I need to be your husband before the day is out. Do you hear what I'm saying?"

"Yes." Her voice trembled. "But what if I disappoint you?"

"In what way?"

Her face went red. "You know. I—it's been a long time."

"Did cancer rob your memory of the nights we made love in the dark on your father's boat so he wouldn't know we were out there?"

She hid her face in his neck. "You know it didn't!" she admitted in a shaky voice.

Nick laughed before pulling her closer. "Do you have any idea how happy it makes me to know you've never been intimate with another man?"

"But that's the problem." She lifted her head. "I know you've been with other women, and I'm scared that I won't compare."

"You've got that wrong, Sam. There were a few women in the past, but none of them could compare to you. Why do you think I stayed single all these years? As Pierce said, I never fell out of love with you."

Nick studied her lovely features. "I want to get you pregnant again so you can raise our next child. You were deprived of that joy with Jessica."

"I don't think it's possible now," she cried softly.

He smoothed some red-gold curls off her forehead. "Are you sterile?"

"I don't know. Now that we're about to be married, I have a lot of questions."

"Then let's call your doctor and get answers."

"You mean right now?"

"Why not? This ought to be the perfect time to reach him."

"My cell phone's in the kitchen. I have his number programmed."

"Then look it up and call on the house phone. If he's there, I'll pick up on this extension."

"All right."

"First I want something to help sustain me while you're gone."

"Oh, Nick."

They kissed hungrily before reluctantly he let her go.

Once she left the bedroom, he took advantage of the time to dress in his formal blue suit. While he was adjusting his tie, he heard Sam call out that the doctor was on the line. Relieved they'd caught him either at home or on rounds, Nick hurried over to the bedside table and picked up the receiver.

"I'm here, Sam. Good morning, Dr. Blake."

"Mr. Kincaid? I hear congratulations are in order."

"Yes. Now that we're going to be married in a few hours, we have some questions for you. In light of Sam's medical history, we need to know what to expect. I'll let Sam talk now, and I'll listen to the answers."

"Very good. Go ahead, Samantha."

"As you know, I never thought I'd be getting married, so the issues having to do with pregnancy never entered my head. Now everything has changed, and long before this morning our daughter let me know she has always wanted to have a little brother or sister.''

That didn't surprise Nick. Jessica was crazy about Cory. She would go nuts over a baby in the house.

''Naturally, we'd love to be able to make that dream come true. I can't imagine how wonderful it would be to have another baby with the knowledge that Nick and I could nurture and love it together.

''But considering my recent illness, I'm wondering if I'm sterile, and if I'm not, would getting pregnant give our baby cancer?''

''I doubt very much you're sterile. Give it a year. If you haven't conceived by that time, then make an appointment with a fertility specialist to find out why.

''To answer your question, most women who've been treated for cancer in the past and are currently disease-free like you can plan on a pregnancy with the greatest of confidence.''

''Honestly?''

The excitement in her voice brought more tears to Nick's eyes. He knew something would always be missing in her life if she weren't given the opportunity to mother a newborn. The doctor's words had just offered them hope.

''I'm very sure. You came through your treatment beautifully, with no long-term effects from the chemo or medication. Are you still having regular periods?''

''Yes.''

''Then that's an excellent sign.''

"It's the best," Nick interjected. The news was getting better and better. He felt euphoric.

"Let me reassure you that cancer only affects about one in a thousand pregnancies."

"I had no idea," Samantha murmured.

"It's too bad there are so many misconceptions out there. You may have heard that pregnancy can allow cancer to develop and grow more easily, but the statistics don't seem to support this.

"If you should get pregnant and your cancer does recur at the same time, your challenge will be to diagnose it early."

"We'll make sure Sam is tested regularly," Nick interjected.

"That's good," the doctor answered. "Once she's pregnant, it will be vital, because at some point you'll have a difficult decision to make about whether you want to start treatments that could place the fetus at risk.

"Then, of course, you may have to consider terminating your pregnancy in favor of pursuing the most aggressive therapies available. But that's a decision to be contemplated much further down the road between the two of you, should such an eventuality occur.

"My opinion, for what it's worth, is to 'go for it,' as my grandson says. We only get one stab at this life, so why not take all the risks you can to make your dreams come true?"

"My sentiments exactly," Nick replied. "That's why I'm making Sam my wife today. Thank you for talking to us."

Nick could hear Sam clearing her throat. "I want

to thank you too, Dr. Blake. We're going to take your advice. Bless you for being such a wonderful doctor.''

While she was still on the phone, Nick hung up the receiver and raced through the house to the kitchen. Sam took one look at him and flung herself into his arms. They clung to each other while she wept for happiness.

"MOM? Are you ready?"

"Almost."

Samantha emerged from her closet. She'd just put on the top of her cream-colored suit and was fastening the buttons. It happened to be the only outfit in her wardrobe appropriate to wear to her own wedding. Jessica looked adorable as usual in a dressy two-piece knit.

"That shade of blue is heavenly on you."

"Thanks. Leslie helped me pick it out before her wedding." Her eyes studied Samantha. "You always look beautiful in everything!"

"How come I'm so lucky to have a wonderful daughter like you?" She hugged her. "This outfit wasn't my first choice, but I'm afraid your father didn't give me a chance to buy a wedding dress."

"Do you care?" she asked with the faintest tinge of concern in her voice.

"No, darling." Samantha smiled. "I've dreamed about this moment for years. Nothing else matters."

Relieved once more, Jessica said, "Dad's so excited, he's been walking around the house whistling. I've never heard him do that before."

"Sometimes he used to whistle while he was waiting to surprise me with something special. It was a dead giveaway."

"I didn't know that. You and Dad really loved each other."

Samantha nodded. "We really did. My greatest regret is not marrying him when he first asked me. But that's all in the past now. I've closed the door on that chapter and am never going to think of it again. Today we're starting our new life together."

"I have a gift for you. It's something borrowed."

"What is it?"

"I'll lend you my locket because it has Dad's picture in it." She took it off her neck and put it around Samantha's.

Nothing could have touched Sam more. She felt its shiny smoothness with her fingers. "Do you have any idea how much I love you, Jessica?" She put her arms around her once more.

"I love you, too. Mom?"

"Yes?"

"Dad says you're going to honeymoon at our other house. How come you're not going away some place exciting?"

She eyed her daughter covertly. "You wouldn't mind?"

"Of course not!"

Her dear little liar. "To tell the truth, I think Grand Teton National Park is the most exciting place I can think of."

"Well, it is, but since you're always going to live here, you should go some place fabulous like Hawaii!"

"I've been there with your grandparents and it *is*

fabulous. I've been thinking our family and Cory's ought to vacation on Maui over your spring vacation.''

Her eyes lit up. "That would be so cool!''

"It would. As for a honeymoon, I'd rather be with your father in the home he made for the two of you. I just need to be with him in the place where he's most comfortable and familiar. We have a lot of catching up to do. I can't think of a better spot.''

Jessica looked totally relieved. "It's kind of like when you and Dad took me around Fort Collins, huh.''

"Yes. It's exactly like that. I want him to show me around his life, let me see it through his eyes. We have years and years to take other trips and create new memories. Right now it's important to savor what we have right here.''

"Mom?'' Something serious was on her daughter's mind. "Do you think you would ever want another baby?''

"Yes. It's something I've always longed for.''

"*Could* you have another one? I mean—'' She stopped midsentence. Samantha could tell she was uncomfortable, yet the hope in her eyes was blinding in its intensity.

"It's all right, darling. You can say whatever is on your mind about my illness, ask me anything you like. The answer to your question is yes.''

"Honest?''

"Yes. Your father and I talked to Dr. Blake this morning. If we're meant to have another child, he says it's fine.''

"Oh Mom!''

While they held on to each other, Samantha could hear Nick calling to them.

"Dad's in a hurry."

"So am I, but I have one more phone call to make before we leave for the church."

"I bet I know who it is."

"I'm sure you do."

"Okay. I'll tell Dad you'll be right out."

"Thanks, darling."

As soon as she was alone, she phoned Marilyn. "Guess what's happening to me in about forty-five minutes?" she said when her friend came on the line.

"Something tells me you're getting married."

"Yes! Our wedding will be at the church in the park. I'm so sorry you won't be here."

"It doesn't matter. What's important is that we're both going to live. Let me be the first to congratulate you, *Mrs. Kincaid.*"

"Can you believe it?"

"After our miraculous recoveries, I can believe anything!"

Tears sprang to her eyes. "Marilyn? How can I thank you for all you've done for me? If it weren't for you, I—" She couldn't talk. Too much emotion made it impossible.

"I know what you're trying to say. I feel the same way about you. How would you like a houseguest for a weekend next month?"

"Do you even have to ask?"

"Yes, I think I do. By then Nick might just be willing to share you."

"He and Jessica are going to love you as much as I do. I'll call you in a few days and we'll have one of our long talks."

"I guess you don't feel you can take a lengthy honeymoon knowing your daughter would miss you too much.''

"You understand everything."

"Maybe not everything, but I *do* know your husband-to-be won't appreciate your staying on the phone any longer. Your future's waiting for you."

Samantha could hear Nick calling to her from the hallway. "You're right. I'll talk to you soon." She hung up, then rushed out of the bedroom, straight into his arms.

He flashed her that old heart-stopping smile before his head lowered and he drew a deep kiss from her.

"Hey, you two." Her dad had made an appearance at the end of the hall. "We're ready to drive you to the church. Much more of that and you'll be late for your own wedding."

"We're coming," Nick assured him after tearing his lips from hers. They were both out of breath. Samantha felt like a teenager who'd been caught on the front porch making out with her boyfriend.

Thank heaven she wasn't that teenager any longer. She was the woman Nick had always wanted to marry. He was the man she'd always worshipped. They'd found their way back to each other.

His thoughts echoed hers when half an hour later they stood before the pastor and Nick whispered, "We've come full circle, my love."

Samantha felt him slide a ring on the third finger of her left hand. When she looked down, she discovered it was the same ring with the etching he'd couriered to her in Denver on Valentine's Day over thirteen years earlier.

She lifted tremulous eyes to meet his adoring gaze.

The pastor cleared his throat. "By the authority invested in me, I now pronounce you, Samantha Frost Bretton, and you, Nicholas Pratt Kincaid, husband and wife from this day forth. You may kiss your bride."

EPILOGUE

Jackson, Wyoming
June 3

It's ten at night and I've decided to catch up on some writing. Nick is out taking care of a pair of black bears causing trouble at the Signal Mountain Campground. The house is quiet.

Our darling, brown-haired, two-year-old Tyler, named after his grandfather Kincaid, is finally asleep. Jessica, who graduated with top honors from Jackson High School three days ago, left today on a bus trip with all the seniors for a chaperoned vacation to Disneyland.

We're very proud of her. She's been offered a four-year academic scholarship to either UCLA, Stanford or the University of Utah. My parents are overjoyed to think she might attend their alma mater, but I have a hunch Jessica will stay closer to home and choose to attend college in Salt Lake. She's her daddy's girl and always will be.

I just got off the phone with Marilyn. She and her husband, Rich, will be coming to the Tetons for the Fourth of July. He's a pharmacist she met at her job in Phoenix. They fell in love right away and had a fabulous wedding Nick and I attended with the children. They're expecting their first baby in October.

Motherhood must be contagious, because Leslie is expecting baby number two any day now. Cory loves his little sister, Diana, but he's hoping for a brother this time. Pierce and Leslie decided they would wait to see what they had and be surprised.

Of course, Cory has announced to everyone they're going to call the new baby Max. According to Leslie, that's what Cory wanted to call his dog until he found out it was a girl, then he had to change the name to Lucy.

Now that summer's here, Nick's cousins will be coming down from Gillette next weekend with their horses. We're all going to take a two-day pack trip into the high country. Mom and Dad will stay here to baby-sit Tyler for us.

Since my grandparents have passed away, my parents visit us every three weeks. They're crazy about the children, but they're also crazy about Nick. I knew they would be if they ever got to know him.

I love my job, my friends, my family. I love my children. I love my husband. He's my lover, my friend, my rock, my idol. He's the reason I stay well.

The miracle is still in effect and life is glorious.

A Family Christmas
by Carrie Alexander

(Harlequin Superromance #1239)

All Rose Robbin ever wanted was a family
Christmas—just like the ones she'd seen on TV—but
being a Robbin (one of those Robbins) pretty much
guaranteed she'd never get one. Especially after
circumstances had her living "down" to
everyone else's expectations.

After a long absence, Rose is back in Alouette,
primarily to help out her impossible-to-please mother,
but also to keep tabs on the child she wasn't allowed
to keep. Working hard, helping her mother and trying
to steal glimpses of her child seem to be all that's in
Wild Rose's future—until the day single father
Evan Grant catches her in the act.

Alouette, Michigan.
Located high on the Upper
Peninsula—home to strong
men, stalwart women and
lots and lots of trees.

NORTH COUNTRY
Stories

Available in November 2004 *wherever Harlequin books are sold*

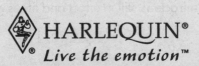

HARLEQUIN®
Live the emotion™

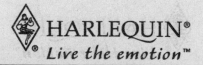

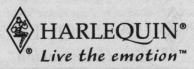

If you enjoyed what you just read,
then we've got an offer you can't resist!

Take 2 bestselling
love stories FREE!
Plus get a FREE surprise gift!

Clip this page and mail it to Harlequin Reader Service®

IN U.S.A.
3010 Walden Ave.
P.O. Box 1867
Buffalo, N.Y. 14240-1867

IN CANADA
P.O. Box 609
Fort Erie, Ontario
L2A 5X3

YES! Please send me 2 free Harlequin Superromance® novels and my free surprise gift. After receiving them, if I don't wish to receive anymore, I can return the shipping statement marked cancel. If I don't cancel, I will receive 6 brand-new novels every month, before they're available in stores. In the U.S.A., bill me at the bargain price of $4.69 plus 25¢ shipping and handling per book and applicable sales tax, if any*. In Canada, bill me at the bargain price of $5.24 plus 25¢ shipping and handling per book and applicable taxes**. That's the complete price, and a savings of at least 10% off the cover prices—what a great deal! I understand that accepting the 2 free books and gift places me under no obligation ever to buy any books. I can always return a shipment and cancel at any time. Even if I never buy another book from Harlequin, the 2 free books and gift are mine to keep forever.

135 HDN DZ7W
336 HDN DZ7X

Name	(PLEASE PRINT)	
Address	Apt.#	
City	State/Prov.	Zip/Postal Code

Not valid to current Harlequin Superromance® subscribers.

Want to try two free books from another series?
Call 1-800-873-8635 or visit www.morefreebooks.com.

* Terms and prices subject to change without notice. Sales tax applicable in N.Y.
** Canadian residents will be charged applicable provincial taxes and GST.
   All orders subject to approval. Offer limited to one per household.
   ® are registered trademarks owned and used by the trademark owner and or its licensee.

SUP04R   ©2004 Harlequin Enterprises Limited

Do you like stories that get *up close* and *personal*?
Do you long to be loved *truly, madly, deeply…*?

If you're looking for emotionally intense, tantalizingly
tender love stories, stop searching and start reading

Harlequin Romance®

You'll find authors who'll leave you breathless, including:

Liz Fielding
Winner of the 2001 RITA Award for
Best Traditional Romance
(*The Best Man and the Bridesmaid*)

Day Leclaire
USA Today bestselling author

Leigh Michaels
Bestselling author with 30 million
copies of her books sold worldwide

Renee Roszel
USA Today bestselling author

Margaret Way
Australian star with 80 novels to her credit

Sophie Weston
A fresh British voice and a hot talent!

Don't miss their latest novels, coming soon!

HARLEQUIN®
Makes any time special®

Christmas comes to

HARLEQUIN ROMANCE®

In November 2004, don't miss:

CHRISTMAS EVE MARRIAGE
(#3820)

by Jessica Hart

In this seasonal romance, the only thing Thea is
looking for on her long-awaited holiday is a little
R and R—she certainly doesn't expect to find herself
roped into being Rhys Kingsford's pretend fiancée!

A SURPRISE
CHRISTMAS PROPOSAL
(#3821)

by Liz Fielding

A much-needed job brings sassy Sophie Harrington up
close and personal with rugged bachelor Gabriel York
in this festive story. But how long before he realizes
that Sophie isn't just for Christmas—but for life…?

Available wherever Harlequin books are sold.

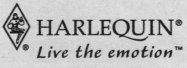

HARLEQUIN®
Live the emotion™

www.eHarlequin.com

HRCTJHLF

Seattle after Midnight
by C.J. Carmichael
(Superromance #1240)
On sale November 2004

"Hello, Seattle. Welcome to 'Georgia after Midnight,' the show for lonely hearts and lovers...."

P.I. Pierce Harding can't resist listening to Georgia Lamont's late-night radio show. Something about her sultry voice calls to him. But Georgia has also attracted an unwanted listener, one who crosses the line between fan and fanatic. When the danger escalates, Pierce knows that he will do anything to keep Georgia safe. Even risk his heart...

Available wherever Harlequin books are sold

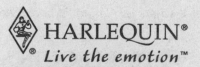

HARLEQUIN®
Live the emotion™

www.eHarlequin.com